STARRY EYED

GALAXIA SERIES
BOOK 1

R.A. SANDS

Copyright © 2026 by Raquelle Sands
All rights reserved.

No part of this book may be reproduced, stored in a retrieval system, or transmitted
in any form or by any means—electronic, mechanical, photocopying, recording, or
otherwise—without prior written permission of the publisher, except for brief
quotations used in reviews.

This is a work of fiction. Names, characters, places, organizations, and events are
either the product of the author's imagination or are used fictitiously. Any
resemblance to actual persons, living or dead, or to actual events is purely
coincidental.

First edition

ISBN (paperback): 979-8-9944497-0-7
ISBN (ebook): 979-8-9944497-1-4

LCCN: 2026904881

Published by Stories by Sands
San Diego, CA, USA

Cover design and interior formatting by R. A. Sands
Edited by Caerwyn Hawksmoor

Printed in the United States of America

STARRY EYED

For those who learned to feel at home,
standing watch beneath unfamiliar stars.

R. A. SANDS

PERSEUS CONSTELLATION

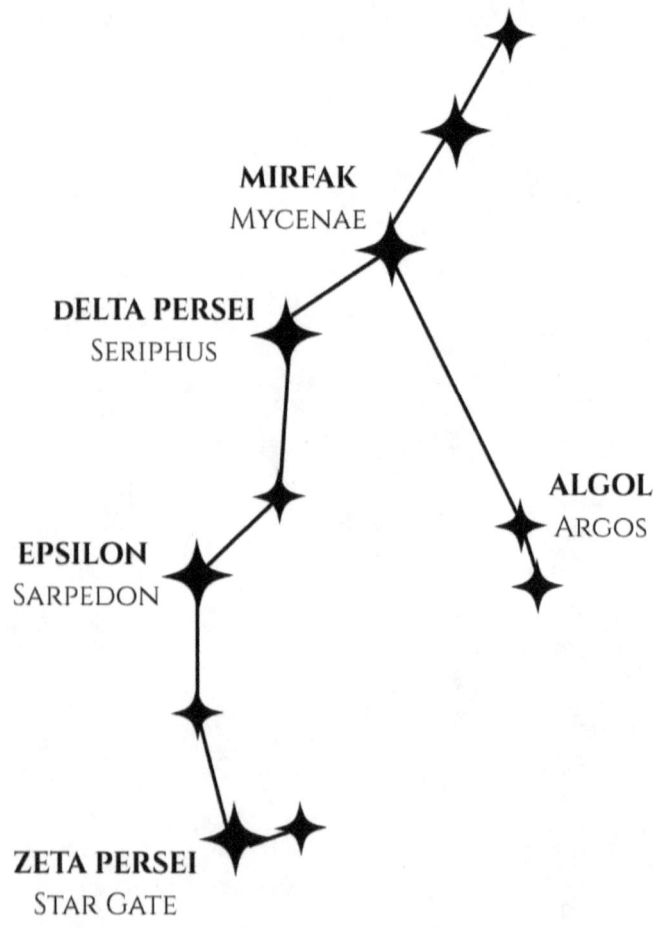

STARRY EYED
TABLE OF CONTENTS

Table of Contents v
PART 1 vii
CHAPTER 1 1
CHAPTER 2 11
CHAPTER 3 21
CHAPTER 4 31
CHAPTER 5 41
CHAPTER 6 53
CHAPTER 7 59
CHAPTER 8 71
CHAPTER 9 81
CHAPTER 10 99
PART 2 111
CHAPTER 11 113
CHAPTER 12 121
CHAPTER 13 129
CHAPTER 14 137
CHAPTER 15 147
CHAPTER 16 155
CHAPTER 17 165
CHAPTER 18 173
CHAPTER 19 183
CHAPTER 20 191
CHAPTER 21 209

CHAPTER 22	213
PART 3	219
CHAPTER 23	221
CHAPTER 24	237
CHAPTER 25	241
CHAPTER 26	249
CHAPTER 27	259
CHAPTER 28	265
CHAPTER 29	275
CHAPTER 30	279
CHAPTER 31	287
CHAPTER 32	291
CHAPTER 33	299
CHAPTER 34	303
CHAPTER 35	305
CHAPTER 36	309
CHAPTER 37	313
CHAPTER 38	323
Acknowledgments	325
About the Author	327

STARRY EYED

PART 1

R. A. SANDS

CHAPTER 1

Running through a Spanish garden is whimsical, unless you are running for your life.

I would do anything to be in those gardens again. Amongst the lush green vegetation and vibrant fuchsia flowers, the sweet smell of honeysuckle or sharp lemon verbena, and to run my fingers along the patterns of the smooth ceramic tiles. Yet I am far from Spain now as I stare out the window at the starry sky. As far as my eyes can see, tiny speckles of light, white, blue, orange, red, stare back at me from light-years away. Yet it is not the stars that hold my attention; it is the space between them.

Blank. Empty. Nothing.

I feel nothing.

I feel alone.

Tears streak down my face, but no noise escapes my lips.

Space is nothing but a void, no light, no air, no sound, no life.

I wake with a start, my heart pounding to the rapid beat of my alarm. I press my hand to my chest and try my best to slow my heart rate, unnerved by the frantic energy already coursing through my body. With a puff of air, I push off my covers and press my bare feet to my bedroom floor to practice my morning Aikido routine.

As my limbs move in circles, my breathing steadies. The aches in my joints begin to loosen, and my mind empties. While the fighting discipline is not exactly a form of meditation, and I am certainly no master, it has served me well over the past three years as a near-daily practice. It is the only time my brain doesn't race ahead of my body.

When I finish my quick routine, it's dark in my room, well before sunrise. My flight to Spain is early, which means I need to beat the sun to the airport. I shower and dress in a matching set of black linen pants and a flowy shirt. I apply a light layer of makeup, enough to brighten the contrast of my pale skin and paler blonde hair.

A small smile graces my lips as I round the corner to see my parents nestling together over cups of coffee. My father's blue eyes flash towards mine, his own smile deepening his ever-present wrinkles. My mom moves towards me, barely reaching my shoulder as she hugs me.

"I can't believe you're leaving us again already."

My father stands and grabs his car keys. "Hana, it's okay. Our little world traveler must translate for all those wealthy businessmen to make even more money."

"I couldn't have done it without all your training, wise old professor." I exaggerate with a flare of my hands.

My mom gives me one last squeeze before letting me go. "No matter where you go, Aurora, you'll always have a place back home."

I kiss her cheek before following my father to the door. Despite being twenty-six, when I am in the United States, I live with my adopted parents. I travel too much for it to make sense to pay rent. With my parents' advancing age, I want to spend as much time with them as I can when I'm here.

My father loads my luggage into the car while I slide into the passenger seat. "We are proud of you, you know that, right?"

"Of course. How could I have expected to live a boring life when you always taught me to dare to do."

He reaches over the center console and squeezes my knee. "Dare to you, and you will reach the stars."

As we drive towards the airport, I run my fingers over the dashboard. "Did you ever find out what was wrong with mom's car?"

My father shrugs. "The mechanic said the battery was completely drained. Probably because it's electric and was plugged in during the power outage."

I hum in response. It helps ease some of my guilt about thinking I had damaged her car when I tried to start it last night. In my defense, I have always been cursed with bad luck with cars. The hospital is pretty sure I was pulled from a car accident when I was surrendered as a baby.

"I just hope the power outage doesn't affect traffic at the airport today."

"In the 1360s, the palace was rebuilt, combining style elements from its Catholic and Islamic influences." I quietly explain to my current employers, translating Spanish to French and English.

Both men stand before me, taking in the Real Alcázar de Sevilla's mosaic walls as the tour guide narrates to our small group. My mind works quickly, translating the tour guide's explanations into French for the well-dressed businessman to my left and into English for the more laid-back entrepreneur to my right. My brain is working overtime, the summer heat battling against the shawl I wear over my shoulders for modesty. Sweat drips down every plane of my body, and I am making too much money to complain about it. This tour is billable, though I would gladly spend my own money to ensure I didn't miss the historic royal palace in Seville.

Another hour in the squelching heat, and the tour is over. I call the private chauffeur service so both of my clients can retire to their hotel rooms for a siesta. Relieved they will not need my services until dinner, I twist my hair up and off my neck so I can continue my own adventure. Tiny beads of sweat line my spine, threatening to stain the lightweight fabric of my sundress. There is a reason everyone takes a siesta in the hottest part of the day; it does not help that Spain is experiencing a record-setting summer heat wave. Grumbling aside, I know that the pooling sweat is worth it, a fact I am reminded of as I head back inside the palace.

This is my favorite part of my job. A dream job. A dream life. I get to talk to people from around the world in numerous beautiful languages before exploring the places those languages came from. Like this, Alcàzar is a perfect artistic expression of the human condition.

It is exquisite.

Thousands of years of cultures fighting to be displayed through complex geometry and artful craftsmanship.

My chin lifts as I enter my favorite section from the tour, a rectangular chamber with pillars and arches that hold up the balconies above me. A long pool stretches the length of the room, guarded by plants. Above, the sky opens wide to the scorching mid-afternoon sun, baking the earth below and casting stark shadows beneath the balconies.

"It's breathtaking."

I jump at the closeness of the deep, melodic voice. A quarter turn to my left reveals the muscular source. The man is handsome, with deep, golden-tanned skin that hints at Mediterranean origins. He's definitely past college-aged, but can't be much older than I am. His wavy brown hair and hard-edged features frame ashen green eyes. Eyes that have been taking their own tour of my appearance to meet my gaze with a charming smile.

I push my platinum blonde hair over my shoulder coyly. "This is one of my favorite parts of the palace. It feels otherworldly." A wondrous glint remains in my eyes as they flick back towards the man.

"Yes, I suppose it does," he agrees.

I watch his mouth form each word. He elongates each syllable as if he is focusing on his English pronunciation. His tongue flicks across his lips, and I return my gaze to see him taking his own appraisal. I bite my lip to hide my smirk as he averts his eyes, taking in the chamber as a faint blush rises on his tanned cheeks.

"I heard you speaking English earlier. It is always nice to hear a familiar language."

My eyebrow quirks upwards. From the way he speaks, English seems like a foreign language to him as well. I consider asking him which other languages he speaks to see if my proficiency extends to his native tongue. Before my curiosity wins, sympathy seeps into my chest as the loneliness in his voice registers.

Since I was little, I have had a strong desire to forge new friendships and create my own definition of family. Perhaps it is a side effect of never knowing my biological parents. While my incredible adoptive parents filled my life with love, cracks of loneliness permanently mar my heart.

I offer him a compassionate smile. "The unknown can be frightening for the faint of heart. Although I have to wonder, where is the fun in an adventure that doesn't raise your heart rate?"

I think back to the first few trips I took after graduating. Without a tour group or hostels to stay in, it had been lonely. My saving grace had been finding the experienced nomads, who always offered companionship and guidance to novice travelers. I want to be like them, offering a friendly smile in an unknown world.

"The best activities should always increase one's heart rate." The innuendo hides in his smile. "What raises your heart rate?"

My treacherous heart immediately responds to his flirtation. I narrow my eyes mischievously while I respond with feigned indifference. "Perhaps the gardens will fulfill my desires."

"I would be surprised to find a more beautiful sight, but if you would allow me, I'd like to join you in the gardens." His voice is as smooth as honey as he holds out his large hand. "I'm Andrin."

"I would love the company, Andrin." I take his hand.

"Aurora."

My own name comes out in a gasp as a little zap, like static electricity, jolts across my skin when our hands touch. Shocked, I instinctively try to take my hand back, but he gently holds it. I swear his green eyes sparkle as his smile widens. I feel my face heating as he finally releases my hand, and I spin towards the entrance of the gardens.

Desperate to distract myself from the flutter in my chest, I blurt out a question. "Do you speak any Spanish?"

I know I am more fortunate than most travelers. I have yet

to find a person with whom I do not share a common language. Learning new languages has always come easily to me, perhaps because my adoptive father is an etymology professor at Harvard. Through my own studies, I have mastered six languages so far. This mastery landed me a dream job as an international translator since my college graduation four years ago.

He chuckles, a deep, throaty sound. The sweet scents of lemon verbena and honeysuckle fragrant the air as soon as we step down the cobblestone pathways into the gardens. The gardens are a lush oasis amid the desert-like heat.

Andrin's words flow in a slow cadence that is foreign to me, "Very little, I'm here on family business. Where are you from?"

An amused snort slips out before I can stop it. I hold dual citizenship in the United States and Germany through my adoptive father, but my original country of origin remains unknown. My fingers dance over the velvety petals of my favorite flowers, the bougainvillea and wisteria providing vibrant pops of fuchsia and lavender amid the emerald-green foliage. As we turn down a pathway of dense evergreen trees, the shade brings a refreshing wave of coolness.

"I technically live in the United States, but I work as a translator. It's the most amazing job. It lets me be from anywhere and everywhere." I smile, looking up to the treetops where sunlight fractures like broken glass.

The heel of my shoe slips in a crevice of stones, making me stumble. Smoothly, Andrin's arms slide around my waist to keep me upright. Heat rises on my pale cheeks from my embarrassment as his hands linger on my waist.

"Good catch." I laugh, bashful but oddly content to be in his arms. A gigantic bird passes overhead, pulling my focus as it casts a large but fleeting shadow. "Whoa, did you see that?"

Andrin does not look up; his intense stare remains locked on my face. "There's so much you don't understand." The serious tone of his voice sends a flood of dread through my system.

I look around the garden path, realizing how far we have walked from the populated area. There are only two directions, both narrow and questionably viable options for leaving. The gardens are nearly empty, save for the midday siesta. Would anyone hear me if I scream? I can run fast. Can I outrun him?

"I should be heading back to my hotel. My clients will need me soon." I try to take a step out of his grasp, but his arms only tighten.

Andrin sighs, as if resigned to something beyond what he believes I could comprehend, and looks up at the sky. "You're in danger, Aurora. It's not safe here."

Run. Run. Run.

Right now, I really wish I had learned a more violent form of martial arts. Aikido is about ending conflict, not escalating it. I learned it to keep myself from getting attacked. Except I literally walked myself right into the arms of a man much larger than myself, and I don't think it will help me much now. I need to get away, now, my instincts scream inside my head.

I slam my heel into the arch of Andrin's foot. With a grunt, his arms loosen. I dip my shoulder and pivot off my foot, following the shift of Andrin's weight. Once free of his grasp, I bolt. The uneven earth beneath my feet threatens to break my ankles as I force them to move faster. Andrin quickly recovers and chases me.

He is fast. I won't make it to the end of the tree-lined path before he reaches me. I cut to my right and push through the thicket of trees. Branches tangle in my dress and hair, another force threatening to snatch me. I continue my trample through the gardens, a myrtle shrub falling victim as I search for help. My frantic search for another person or a way out is fruitless. I am lost. I am trapped in an empty garden maze, a large man chasing me.

A flash of red off to my left distracts me.

Help.

I turn towards the figure, but slide as the pathway shifts to pebbles. The small stones dig into the flesh of my palms and knees. Before I can push myself up, a hand grips a chunk of my hair and pulls. A squeal slips out of my mouth at the sudden pain. The ache of my scalp is nothing compared to the slashes that cut into my bare shoulder. Warm blood drips down my arm as I fight to rip it and my hair free. The searing pain overpowers my ability to flip over.

My motions turn frantic. Red fills my field of vision. Except it isn't blood, it's feathers. Long, red feathers fluttering to the ground. Footsteps rattle the pebbles of the path. Someone is coming.

"Help me!" I cry out, "Help!"

The grip on my hair and flesh suddenly releases. I lift my head to see my savior, but confusion washes over me. It's Andrin. He runs towards me from the end of the evergreen path. I hear a rustle behind me before I'm pushed back to the ground.

Andrin crushes me from behind as he lifts me by my shoulders. I howl as his fingers dig into my torn flesh. He spins me around, and I spit in his face. He rears back long enough for me to push him off and escape again. He recovers quickly, his arms wrapping tightly around my waist.

"Why are you doing this?" I barely croak out from my oxygen-deprived lungs, my pathetic squeak sounds almost foreign to me.

His voice is close to my ear as he grunts, "I promise it will make sense soon. And—I'm sorry."

Except I'm not listening to his words anymore. My eyes are fixed on the sky as a monstrous, seven-foot-tall woman covered in red feathers rockets into the sky.

A jolt hits my body, then searing pain. Everything in my vision blinks white. Then all I see is black.

CHAPTER 2

It is cold. Freezing. My body feels achy, and I fight to open my eyes. Light and darkness battle for dominance in the room, like an illuminated skyline in a bustling city at night. I squint my heavy eyelids and blink until I can open them fully. I force my brain to focus. Where am I?

As I fight to focus my blurry vision and stretch my aching limbs, I ascertain I'm on a bed with threadbare white linens. I lift my head despite the nauseating throb it elicits. The floor is dull, dark steel, which matches the cabinets that seem to almost meld into the walls. I blink through my migraine, and I do not recognize my surroundings.

I absentmindedly pat the bedding around me in search of my phone. My fingers fail to find it. Did I lose it? Was it pickpocketed? A foggy memory pushes itself to the forefront of my mind. I was already at the Real Alcázar. A chill raises the hairs on my arms, forcing an involuntary shiver through my body. I don't think it was just my phone that was taken; I think I was, too.

I push myself up, so I am sitting with my legs dangling over the side of the bed. The bed, if you could call it that, is more like a suspended platform, made of metal, like what I saw while touring the USS Yorktown in Charleston. These prison-like furnishings are a far cry from my usual five-star accommodations.

Then I see it. The view from the floor-to-ceiling window is neither a skyline nor a sweeping countryside. No, it's darkness. Vast darkness. With bright light speckles. Stars. My stomach churns. A large globe of blue with smears of white and green suspended in the darkness. Earth.

My stomach reacts faster than my brain. With a horrible burn, I heave and choke out the bile. I do not have time to catch it as it spills out of my mouth, down my shirt, and onto the floor. Earth. That floating mass is Earth. The next wave of nausea is quickly replaced by dizziness. This time, as my eyes close, I welcome the comfort of the darkness.

My eyes feel bruised as I blink them open. A throb on the side of my head echoes my heartbeat. I squeeze my eyes shut to keep the light out. I shake my head, trying to shake off strange dreams. This jet lag is really taking a toll. I groan as I roll over. The sun is way too bright.

A shot of adrenaline shoots through my system. I am late for the Alcázar tour. Where is my phone? Why did my alarm not go off? What a horrible, strange dream. I shoot up and force my eyes to open against the bright light.

Except it's not the lights that make my blood run cold. It's the dark, polished metal. Perhaps it wasn't just a dream. I don't get up from my cot. I move my tongue around my mouth. I can taste the metallic remnants of bile. Bringing my hand to my head, I feel the small lump that has grown on the back of my skull. Looking down at my body, I am surprised not see any stains. My stomach sinks as I remember what I had seen.

I am afraid to turn my head. Scared to find the window I saw in my nightmare, terrified that it may not have actually been a nightmare. One breath. Then a second. I have to see; I have to know the truth. Slowly, I turn my head. There it is. I stand.

Chills run through me as I approach the glass.

Black sky. No, black space.

With the only place I have ever been in my life floating beyond. A glorious blue sphere, now with a spear of bright white light cresting beyond.

The Earth. The Moon. The Sun.

It must be a picture. A gigantic television that takes up the entire wall. I cannot really be looking at my home planet.

"Aurora."

I spin at the sound of the grave voice. It is soft, almost pensive. Hot anger surges in my body. Clenching my fists and jaw, I stalk over to the source of the voice. It is coming from a circular window in the metal door. Golden light illuminates a face I would very much like to claw to shreds.

"What have you done?" I growl, spitting each syllable.

"Aurora, there is so much to explain," Andrin says condescendingly.

"Where are we?" I demand, pushing against the door, no handle in sight. Fury overtakes fear as the realization hits. "You trapped me in here!"

"You need to slow your breathing. An elevated heart rate can cause you to lose consciousness again. The oxygen levels up here are higher than you are used to on Earth." His voice is aggravatingly calm despite the ludicrous things he is saying.

My blood boils, and my voice rises several octaves. "Slow my breathing and heart rate? Are you seriously trying to explain to me how to calm down? After you kidnapped me? You are a severely deranged individual!" A string of expletives leaves my mouth as I lose the ability to put together coherent sentences.

I bang my fists against the metal door as I abandon swearing entirely and start to scream. I am trapped. I have no idea where I am, but I am trapped. A word he said slices through my consciousness: Earth.

I spin around, looking at the window again. It is not some gigantic television screen. It is real, which means I am no longer on Earth, which doesn't make any sense. I look down at my clothes and shudder as yet another horrifying realization strikes me. He changed my clothes. The feeling of violation momentarily supersedes my fury.

"We are in an Orbital Station still within the Sun's gravitational pull."

My piercing glare meets a pair of pale green eyes. He flinches. I startle as I notice the golden light in the window is actually his skin. The olive-toned tan that Andrin had in the palace has been replaced by metallic gold.

"What did you drug me with? Your skin looks– Where are we? Why did you bring me here? How long did you keep me unconscious for?" I slam both of my hands against the door.

Andrin responds with the same irritating calmness. "It has been a week. I also didn't drug you. You have been unconscious because your body didn't handle the trip up here well. I will have someone bring you food."

My heart skips a beat—a week. Quickly, I wiggle my toes and fingers. No tingling pain in my skin or stiffness in my joints. All the symptoms I should have if I had missed an entire week's worth of my daily immunosuppression medication.

I let go of the anger in my tone and try another approach. "You need to let me go. I have an autoimmune disorder and will start seizing if I don't take my medication." I leave out my confusion at how I have already survived this long without it.

Andrin looks conflicted, pausing before he finally responds. "You don't actually have an autoimmune disorder. Your body was not meant to process Earth's atmosphere. The nitrogen levels were too high for you. That's what caused your illness. You will not need medication anymore."

"How—how could you possibly know that?" I want to deny his accusation, but my body agrees. "Why am I here? What do you want from me? What are you?"

My questions bleed together in rapid succession. My head pounds as my confusion and frustration mix.

"To you, I am an alien, Aurora. My kind are called Persei," He responds calmly. "The rest will have to wait."

I see pain flash across his face and hear sadness in his tone, but my rage consumes any hint of curiosity at this observation. I slam my fists against the door again, continuing to scream profanities at him. This time, in all six languages that I speak. He only places his palm against the window before turning away from me. I am still screaming as I watch him walk down a corridor of unending metal. While his form recedes, my anger does not.

I pound my fists against the door until it feels like my hands will break. I need to find a way to break out of here to escape. Seething, I spin back towards my sterile room. I throw open the drawers and closets that are built into the walls. White linens and small tablets resembling candy fly through the air as I toss them from their storage place. Nothing sharp or sturdy enough to break through glass or fight off Andrin once I am outside of this room. Useless.

I cannot break my way out of this room. I have no phone to call for help. Even if I did, would it work? Who would I call?

My parents. My mom and dad. They must be so worried about me. I have missed our weekly calls. Will I ever get to speak to them again? I could die here. Never hear their voices again.

I have to leave this room.

I have to get home.

I stare at the impenetrable metal door blocking my escape. Brute force will not get me out of here. I will have to find another way.

Panting, I slide down the length of the door until my knees hit my chest. I watch the Sun crest over Earth. My first outer space sunrise, I suppose. I feel the salty sting of tears in my eyes, but they refuse to spill, as if even my tears are trapped.

I have cleaned up the room. Really, I stuffed everything I discarded back into two closets, so my destruction is not evident. I smoothed my hair down the best I could to fix my appearance. In the Alcàzar, Andrin seemed attracted to me. I hope to use that against him now to let me out of the room.

Two solid knocks echo against the metal door before it hisses open. Andrin's golden head pops through first, assessing the safety of the room. He steps inside cautiously, one eyebrow lifted when he sees my docile state.

"How are you feeling?"

I shrug and give him a closed-mouth smile. I am afraid that if I reveal my teeth, my faux smile will turn into a snarl.

"Slightly discombobulated, but much better. I'm ready to leave the room now," I say with picture-perfect composure.

He speaks slowly, "I am glad you are feeling better. However, I think you should remain here for a little longer to adjust. We are going to start travelling further from Earth, and the transit might make you feel sick."

I school my features to keep my face light and unaffected, even as I scream inside. My sense of urgency to escape, before I am too far from Earth, skyrockets. I stand abruptly. Andrin takes a defensive step back. I reach out my hands and hold the muscles of his biceps. I'll have to turn up my charm tenfold to expedite my release.

"I really appreciate your concern," my voice drips saccharine sweet. "It was honorable of you to save me back on Earth. If you drop me back off at my hotel in Spain, I am sure there is a way I can show you just how gracious I am."

His eyes narrow, but he doesn't budge. I slide my fingers up his arms, around his shoulders, and trail them down his chest. At least if I have to make good on my flirtations, he has a nice human torso.

Andrin's Adam's apple bobs as he swallows. "I cannot leave you on Earth. It is not safe for you there."

"You kept me safe." I move in close, tilt my head up slightly, and pull out my best puppy-dog eyes. "I am so lucky to have met such a strong, protective, and intelligent man. I can't possibly understand all of this advanced alien technology, but you have saved me once, and I know you will save me again."

Andrin grabs my hands, lifting them off his body. He places a waxy package in my hand as he steps away.

"You are safer up here. I just came here to check on you and give you some food."

Hesitantly, Andrin steps back while I advance. I can't let him leave me here again. He said we will start transiting soon. To where? Nowhere I want to go, that's for sure. Panic rises in me again as I feel my opportunity to escape slipping through my fingers.

"Andrin–" I plead. "Please! Let me go!"

I desperately grip his arms, his clothing, but he continues to brush me off as he moves towards the door. He holds his arm out to keep me back before quickly slipping through the door and locking it shut once more. I have to grind my teeth to hold in an exaggerated scream. The cushiony substance wrapped in wax paper absorbs the anger of my fisted hand.

I stalk up and down the small room like a caged animal waiting for him to return. After only a few minutes, I groan and drop onto the stiff bed, accepting the uselessness of my actions. As I inspect the items Andrin had given me, my stomach gurgles.

I rip open the waxy wrapper to find a block of squishy brown material and a pouch with a small nozzle filled with a transparent blue liquid. Skepticism and hunger mix in my stomach as I sniff the substance. It doesn't smell like anything, but it is packaged like food. I stare at the items long enough for my stomach to twist again in desperate longing. My eyes survey the sterile metal room again, and I acknowledge that this may be my only chance to eat.

Taking a tentative bite of the squishy block, I grimace. It might as well be a sponge with its lack of flavor and strange texture. I close my eyes and pretend I am in my favorite bustling restaurant in Beijing, eating Mapo tofu instead of this bland impostor. The drink, on the other hand, has a strong herbal flavor. It reminds me of a non-alcoholic version of the numerous Xeque Mate cocktails I had while at Carnival two years ago. The juxtaposition of flavorful drinks and flavorless food almost balances them out, making both palatable.

Almost.

My eyes fall to the expanse outside the window between swallows. I curse my pitiful, failed attempts to escape. I will have to use brute effort, a mad dash, a charge. I mentally steel myself for my next opportunity to get through that door.

I wish I could go back in time. Perhaps if aliens are real, time travel is possible too. I shouldn't have stayed in the palace. I should have gone back to my hotel for my own siesta. Instead, I followed the golden-skinned alien into the gardens, and now I fear that if I do not get out of this room soon, I may never return home.

CHAPTER 3

Time passes, maybe minutes or hours, as I wait for another opportunity to get out of this room. There is no clock, and the movement of the sun does nothing to estimate time from my position in space. I am dangerously close to approaching insanity.

A click of the lock followed by a hiss of air indicates it is finally time. The door is about to open. I jump up and rush towards the sliver of an opening. Just as I reach the door, what looks like a thicket of spindly sticks wraps around the doorframe as it swings open. A tangle of orange-brown wood lands on the floor, followed by another. I stand frozen as the remainder of the creature steps into the room. Unnaturally vibrant green moss covers what appears to be the back of the hand and the thin arm.

The creature is short, reaching roughly the height of my ribcage. Most of its body is skinny. Bipedal, almost human in stature, but that is where the similarities end. Its head is large and hairless with pale lavender flesh and eyes the size of baseballs. Other spindles sprout from their shoulders and head, reaching up with small green shoots of tree foliage and tiny pink flowers. Its small mouth is a pit of black. I look down from its mouth and round eyes to its hands, which hold another waxy package.

We both stand, riveted in place, gawking at one another. Almost as if it is as shocked to see me by the door as I am to see that it exists.

I inhale a sharp breath, but the exhale blows out as a scream. The creature lets out a shrill wail in response. It drops the package. We both stand, high-pitched sounds belting.

My scream turns into a battle cry as I swallow my horror and force myself forward again. I will get past this thing and out that door, even if I have to fight it.

The creature jumps a foot in the air, petals and leaves tumbling to the floor. In three quick steps, I am nearly upon the alien. Its branch-like limbs move in a fast fury, the bulbous head shaking back and forth. In a strange skeletal movement of joints, it rambles out of the room.

The door begins to swing closed quickly, and I reach a hand forward, desperate to stop it. Except the floor is slick. The balls of my feet slip on the fallen petals that litter the wet metal floor. The stench of ammonia fills my nostrils as my nose meets the ground. My neck cranes upward at an awkward angle as I watch the air-pressurized door hiss closed.

Rolling onto my back, I rub my hands against my sore face. Tiny leaves and vibrant flower petals stick to my damp palms. The floor has been recently cleaned, most likely after I emptied my stomach all over it.

Groaning, I sit up. A new food packet lies near my feet, and I kick it away in protest. They are feeding me, which is a good sign. I think. It means they want to keep me alive. It should mean they will open the door again. I will be ready to escape the next time it does, whenever that may be, hopefully, not by that strange creature. Andrin looks human enough, despite his strange, gilded skin, but that thing—that thing is otherworldly.

While I wait for the door to open again, I plan. I will get out of this room no matter what is on the other side. I will get out of here and get back to Earth. I must keep my head this time. No temper, no shock. I try to think of Aikido, the calm discipline I struggle so hard to achieve under normal conditions, let alone survival. I will need it now more than ever. I need my logical brain to stay in control if I want to succeed. I decide to take to the floor and practice my strength and balance movements. It always soothes my mind, and I might need the warm-up to be prepared to fight.

This cold, unfamiliar room feels like the counterpoint to the sun-warmed dojo I first stumbled into three years ago. Shinhan Hikaru spoke little, which didn't bother me since Japanese is one of the few major languages I don't speak. Yet while he didn't communicate verbally, the forms his body made spoke volumes.

While I found the dojo by accident, it was as if the Universe meant for me to be there. An earthy scent of oud and green tea lured me towards a foliage-covered arch. The hand-painted sign was tucked between rows of shuttered shops in a bustling market street. Yet as I pressed through the gate doors, the garden absorbed the noise. One of the screen walls had been opened, revealing a mat-covered floor and art-covered walls. The art and architecture of the building drew my attention first, but the curl of the Shinhan's hand welcomed me in.

On bare feet, I stumbled through the movements with a well-practiced class. Yet no one seemed to mind. As the Shinhan demonstrated, it didn't look like fighting. It looked like yielding. Each movement flows. The attacks folded in on themselves as the small group of bodies moved, rising and falling like a tide.

By the end of the session, my body burned, but not from pain. As if I had never truly moved it before. My mind felt calm, as I had only aspired to understand from those who spoke of meditation.

I had been controlled. Not because I was forcing myself to be, but because the dojo demanded it.

I came back the next day, and the one after that. At the end of the week, Shinhan Hikaru offered me tea, and another student translated our conversation. It was when I officially decided to become an international travelling interpreter rather than a corporate interpreter. I wanted more opportunities like that one, to experience more life.

When I left the city weeks later, I promised myself I would continue practicing Aikido. A practice of harmony and control. It was a promise to myself, something I had yet to fully learn but wanted to keep.

My mind is calm by the time I notice a glint of gold in the window.

When the hiss begins, I am already sprinting, my bare feet pounding against the cold metal floor as I propel myself through the small space between Andrin's arm and the door. The hallway is narrow, with more dark metal on all sides. Red light provides the only illumination. I pass one closed door before arms wrap around my waist. I launch my elbow backwards, and it hits something solid before I swing my foot around and clip the back of his knee. Andrin's arm falls away with a grunt.

I don't look back. Every door I run past is closed. The long tunnel is empty, only the soft hum of ventilation and the pounding of Andrin's feet in quick chase behind me give me any clues about my surroundings. Light shines down from an opening in the ceiling to my left. A bare ladder stretches up into the opening of the next floor. Launching myself forward, I latch onto the side rails and jump onto the second rung. The toes of my left foot reach the third rung when Andrin's hand clamps around my ankle.

With a quick tug, he pulls me down. My short drop is halted as Andrin wraps his arms around my torso. I flail, kick, scream, bite. My legs scramble several feet above the ground while Andrin grunts against my struggle.

"Aurora, stop!" He orders.

I don't stop. I only fight Andrin's grip harder. I need to get away.

I plant my foot against the nearby wall and kick off. It sends Andrin backwards, his back slamming into the other side of the narrow hallway. His arms tighten. No longer firm, but suffocating.

"Stop fighting me!" He orders again.

My ribcage squeezes under the pressure. My breaths shorten to gasping rasps.

"No! You have to bring me back to Earth! Where are we going? Tell me why you brought me here!" I demand.

Exacerbated, he says, "I'll tell you! But you have to stop kicking me! And if you bite me one more time, you will find yourself with the knowledge of what Persei's teeth feel like on your own skin!"

I hiss. Under normal circumstances, it would have been a heated flirt, but now, the fear of a rabid alien bite fills me. I breathe deeply. I am not calm, but I can pretend. I need to clear my head. Satisfied, Andrin lets me go, and I quickly step away, creating space between us.

"This Orbital Station is an inter-constellation spacecraft. We are in Northern Quadrant 1. The Copernican System is 1.64×10^9 Astronomical Units from the center of Galaxia. I had to bring you here because you are in danger," Andrin explains.

"Funny, I didn't feel like I was in danger until I met you." I cross my arms over my chest as my voice fills with venom. "Then all of a sudden I have a bird lady and a golden idiot attacking me!"

He takes one step towards me, and I take one step back. "That bird lady who attacked you in the palace? She is a Harpyiai, and she was hunting you."

"Why should I believe you? Maybe she was trying to save me from you. You are the one who abducted me and is keeping me prisoner." My voice is filled with venom as I say, "You are the one I need to be kept safe from."

Offended, Andrin motions wildly around us. "Look around, Aurora. You're in space. Things are more advanced than you can conceptualize with your limited knowledge from living on a single planet your whole life."

I narrow my eyes at his patronizing words. "I will be the judge of what I can and cannot comprehend. Bring me to your control room and prove to me that what you are saying is true."

"You are not a prisoner here. I needed you to stay in your room to avoid motion sickness and to avoid doing anything destructive to the station. Since that avenue was not successful, we can try it your way. I will bring you to our Pilot House," Andrin concedes.

He motions down the hall behind me. I motion for him to lead the way, always keeping him within my line of sight. He huffs, but begins walking. As I follow, I mentally map out our path and attempt to recalibrate my impetuous escape plan. I have been so focused on getting out of that room that I haven't considered how I will get back to Earth.

"How did we get up here?" My dry voice is almost unrecognizable.

"We call it Aether Crossing. It is a form of energy conversion that utilizes high levels of power to transfer matter from one point in space to another."

I release a puff of air through my nose. Great, I only have to teleport myself back to Earth. There must be another way, one I am capable of using. They must have some type of escape shuttles, especially for a spacecraft this big. I will find one, use it to get back to Earth, and never think of space again. I huff out loud to myself.

Andrin turns to assess my outburst. Instead of dignifying his inquisitive look with a verbal response, I twist my face and point back in the direction he's walking. His mouth closes, and Adam's apple bobs before he turns around. The humanesque gesture would make me laugh if I didn't want to strangle him so much.

Besides his skin, he appears just as he had on Earth. Tall, but like a professional athlete, not a genetic oddity. He wears linen pants like mine, but his shirt is much tighter, cutting off at the shoulders to reveal the golden muscle of his arms. He wears gold vambraces, rigid tubular metal that covers both of his lower arms, and a matching thick metal band that rests in a point on his collar. The metal accessories nearly blend into his metallic skin.

A quick flash of shame cools my heating body. I feel ill at the realization that I'm still attracted to Andrin even after he revealed himself as an alien and abducted me.

I focus back on my surroundings, searching for every possible escape route. The hallways are long and narrow, lined with identical doors on both sides. At a glance, I do not recognize the symbols on the plaques by each door. Yet, when I concentrate, some of them start to make sense. Almost like my brain is trying to read something in a dream. The letters on the sign become understandable, much as they did each time I learned a new language. I feel the pressure of a headache forming just behind my eyes. My prefrontal cortex is working in overdrive. I squeeze my eyes together tightly in three consecutive blinks before I return my attention forward.

As I step over yet another raised door frame of the airlocks that segment the passageway, I recite the path we took in my head—left out of my room, past three airlocks, up a steep set of stairs, and a right turn. My toes curl in revulsion as I step from cold metal to grimy rubber flooring, clumps of dust sticking to the bottoms of my bare feet. Completely unaffected in his leather sandals, Andrin seems to glide effortlessly down the hallways. I regret not demanding shoes before this adventure.

Finally, we stop before a larger airlock set into the wall, like the one in my room. I squint my eyes, attempting to read the plaque posted beside the door. Slowly, the symbols reorganize in my brain to say *Pilot House*. This is it, the control center. Andrin opens the door and motions me to step in first. I swallow my hesitation, embrace my defiant pride, raise my chin, and step inside.

The control center room is expansive, but short. Six plush chairs are bolted to the floors, each facing a computer console with multiple button panels and screens. Beyond the consoles is a colossal sloping window, like the cockpit of a plane. Unlike the view from my cell, Earth is just one of many colorful circles.

Other planets in my solar system.

It is further away than it was moments ago, when I was in my room. I'm further away from home. Despite how far and long I've travelled on solo adventures before, I've never felt this alone.

CHAPTER 4

My teeth grind together from the metallic screech of one of the plush chairs as it rotates towards us. The occupant nods to Andrin, and Andrin returns the nod in silent communication. It is another type of alien: a thin, long-limbed bipedal creature that exudes masculine energy.

His facial features seem feline. Pale blue skin stretches over a large brow bone and sharp cheekbones with a small, triangular cat-like nose. Patches of topaz and orange decorate his skin with diamonds centered across his forehead, like the stripes of a housecat. His hair is braided into thick dreads adorned with wood and metal beads of many colors. His clothing is similar in style to Andrin's. Our eyes meet after finishing our silent inspections of each other. I force myself not to cringe at the strangeness of the glowing, pupil-less topaz eyes that stare back at me.

"This is my oldest friend and most trusted delegate and advisor, Syntag Izar Harma. As Syntag, he is in charge of this Orbital Station."

I give Izar a short nod. "If you're in charge of this UFO, then bring me back to Earth."

Izar stands and closes the distance between us with feline grace. I tense at the sudden movement, unprepared to defend at such close range. My panic quickly gives way to confusion as he kisses both my cheeks.

"By the stars," He says, analyzing my face as he pulls back. "I cannot. While I am in charge of this Orbital Station, I follow the orders of the Taxiarhos."

He gestures towards Andrin, the apparent Taxiarhos. Clearly, they are terms for a chain of command. Dictating Andrin to be superior to Izar.

Fantastic, my request will surely be denied.

My irritation halts as my brain finally catches up with Izar's words. Not his word choice, but the language he used. I have never heard the phonetics, yet I understood what was said. As he spoke, I could feel my brain working through the sounds, like pulling apart threads of a tapestry so I could see the colors of individual strands.

"I can understand you," I murmur.

Izar and Andrin exchange conspiratorial smiles. "Of course you can. He is speaking the Universal Language."

"What is the Universal Language?" I narrow my eyes at Andrin.

My glare does not scare the smirk off of Andrin's face. "It is the language from which all spoken words throughout Galaxia stem. You can understand it, because you possess a unique capability to understand universal languages from across all galaxies."

I find myself rolling my eyes and crossing my arms over my chest like a teenager. "I have mastered six languages and studied many others, but I have never heard of a Universal Language. Perhaps my wide range of knowledge is why I understand it."

Despite the steadiness of my voice, I am unsure if I believe the words myself. I do understand the language. The morphology and syntax remind me of multiple languages I already know. It is illogical, yet it makes my ease with languages more understandable.

My doubts and curiosity lead me to ask, "That doesn't fully explain my understanding. Why can *I* understand an alien language?"

They both pause, looking at each other. It is almost like they can communicate without speaking. I wonder if it is another component of the Universal Language, an alien telepathic connection, or because they have been friends for so long.

Andrin breaks their silent communication first, "You have spent your entire life on Earth, correct? You don't remember being anywhere else?"

The muscles in my shoulder tense. I do not like the implication of his words. It is almost as if he is suggesting—

My eyes flick between both men. "Yes, I am from Earth. That's where all humans are from. Also, the same place you just abducted me from."

"Well, you aren't really Human." Izar simply shrugs.

Andrin and I both swing our heads towards Izar. Andrin glares at the feline alien with as much malice as I have sent his way. My mouth is agape. Shock, disbelief, confusion, and concern were flying through my brain.

Despite his serious features, I know it's not true. It can't be true. I won't let it be true. A hysterical laugh erupts from me.

"Alright, I believe I've discovered our dilemma." They look at me as my deranged laughter continues. "A mistake has been made. You are searching for someone else. We can all pretend none of this has happened, as long as you tractor beam me back to Earth."

As they continue to stare, my laughter dies out. Please laugh, please admit it is a silly misunderstanding. Yet neither of them budges.

The silent communication fight between Andrin and Izar resumes until Andrin takes a step towards me. Once again, I step back and reestablish our separation. Izar moves around us both to the center of the room. He steps on a floor panel, and a thick beam of blue light creates a floor-to-ceiling column.

I move towards the column when Andrin speaks, "We did not make a mistake. You were in danger on Earth. And Izar is right; you are not Human."

Not human.

Alien.

I am human. I was born on Earth. I was surrendered to a hospital as a baby. My birth parents died in a car accident. Nothing has made sense since I left those Spanish gardens, but I do know one thing. I know who I am. These aliens cannot take that away from me. My name is Aurora, and I am a human from Earth!

My fists clench at my sides. Anger pulsing hot through my veins like a live wire despite the freezing room temperature. I seethe as I enter Andrin's personal space and push my finger against his chest.

"Listen to my words. I am a human. Always have been, always will be. It's okay to admit that you are wrong, just put me back on Earth." My words come out in choppy bites.

Andrin takes another step closer, making my finger bend. "You yourself admitted that your ability to understand languages is unusual. You have always been capable of more than others, but here, we can give you the nutrients you need to access your full capabilities."

I pause. I can feel the truth in his words. I felt it in my body when he asked if I had always been on Earth. Moreover, with embarrassment, I must admit, I have always felt *Other*.

Since childhood, I have stood out amongst my peers for my physical agility, mental acuity, and medical fragility. I remember winning top marks in honors classes or medals for running, just to end up in the hospital hours later. Despite extensive medical testing in an attempt to determine the cause of my immune dysregulation, doctors could never pinpoint the etiology of my skin and joint sensitivities. Luckily, they eventually found a combination of pills that kept my immune system in check.

Yet, if I have alien biology, could Earth's atmosphere really have been the cause of my idiopathic immune dysregulation? Andrin's claim that I would no longer require medication since the Nitrogen levels on Earth made me ill seems to hold. My rational brain knows that Nitrogen in the air is not toxic, but it can cause decompression sickness. As if I had been scuba diving at extreme depths for extended periods of time. Which was always the best hypothesis doctors had, despite my lack of exposure to activities that might have caused it. However, lately, rationality and reality have been diverging.

"Have you heard of the Andromeda Galaxy?" Izar asks.

I have to physically blink out of my thoughts to comprehend Izar's words. The blue light beams are no longer perfectly vertical; they have cast an image of swirling space, with multiple celestial objects drifting around one another.

"Yes. It is the closest galaxy to the Milky Way. Why?"

Andrin stands beside me and zooms in on the hologram. "We believe that you came from the Andromeda Galaxy. It was destroyed, and all known life within it perished. Yet, somehow, you were sent all the way to Earth. When we finally found you, your energy was like a beacon."

Perished. My heart squeezes painfully in my chest. Somehow, it feels more devastating to know I am an orphan on an intergalactic scale.

The hologram projector shifts from a spiraling galaxy to the solar system. My solar system, or at least the one in which Earth resides, is named Copernican. I poke my finger at the orb of Earth, only for it to shudder under the diffusion of light before returning to its original image. I cross my arms and turn back to Andrin.

"If I was sent there, why did you abduct me? Why not leave me on Earth?"

"A message was sent out to Galaxia, our galaxy. The leaders of the Galaxia Empire announced they had received indications that a surviving Mēdeian might be alive, along with an estimated position. They want you found."

"I lived for twenty-six years happy and healthy on Earth. Yet out of nowhere, two aliens show up. One attacks me, and the other abducts me. Why does anyone care about me now?"

Izar answers first, his eyes glowing the same color as the light beams. "There weren't any indications anyone had survived the Super Nova. The Empire didn't release what their sudden indications were, but you should know that dangerous species are after you now, beyond the Harpyiai you saw on Earth. The Harpyiai are from my home Constellation. My father is the Persei King's advisor and reported that one was searching for you as soon as he heard."

"The Persei have a deep-rooted history on Earth and feel somewhat territorial of what happens there," Andrin adds. "As for the amount of time you were on Earth, time is measured differently in other parts of the Universe. Your time is based on a theoretical Mean Sun passing over Earth. Planets use varied time measurements, which can alter how long a day is perceived. The gravitational orbit of celestial bodies can also greatly alter this perception. So, an hour, a day, or a year is different depending on where you are in the Universe. Like using the Metric versus Imperial system of units, they measure the same things, but don't quite equate."

My thoughts jump to my parents. They are already in their seventies. How much time have I missed with them? "How long have I been gone in Earth time?"

"From our current location, time is about the same as it is on Earth. You have been gone a week, including the time you spent unconscious when we first arrived," Izar states plainly.

How long will it be before I get back?

"Well, you found me. Now that the Harpyiai thinks I am no longer on Earth, put me back. I should be safe there. Let the Persei King know I'm safe and leave it at that."

They look at each other, speaking telepathically again, and I know I am not going to like whatever they say next.

"We cannot take that chance yet. There is no proof Earth will be safe for you," Andrin says.

My fingers clench at my sides. I want to point out that there is no proof that it is unsafe, either when the hologram flickers. The image before me shifts again, revealing a constellation of stars that is vaguely familiar.

Izar shifts to speak with Andrin. "Orders from the King came in just before your arrival. We have been ordered to stop at Argos."

"Perhaps I need to repeat myself. Take me back to Earth," I demand.

"The Harpyiai is not going to stop hunting you. If you go back now, it will track you down and harm anyone who gets in its way. It will not be the only alien after you, either. This is for your protection. We need time to neutralize the threats. You will come with us to Argos," Andrin orders.

My anger cools to a chilling fear.

I have been trying to get home to be with my family, but if I return now, I will only put them in danger. One alien is scary enough, but how many others will try to find me? Am I being selfish for wanting to return to Earth? Can I even trust what Andrin says? Besides my abduction, I have been relatively well provided for in a civilized manner. Could staying aboard this spacecraft for now be the safer option for my family and me?

Andrin directs his attention back to the projection. "We are closest to Orion Nebulous, so we should take the Betelgeuse Star Gate to get back to the Perseus Constellation."

I cross my arms and look incredulous. "Beetlejuice?" Izar snickers, and I turn my scowl towards him.

Andrin leans towards me, scratching the back of his neck as he whispers. "Betelgeuse. It's part of the Orion Constellation."

Andrin quickly moves on to save me from the embarrassment, which is already heating my cheeks. He points at the star within the familiar hunter constellation. I push my hair out of my face and over my shoulder. My fingers twitch as I fight to keep silent. Andrin scrolls his fingers over the map again. It rotates easily until the image displays a different set of shapes. Once it stills, he points to the bottom of an illuminated constellation.

"That is Zeta Persei. We will arrive through the Star Gate there and make our way up to Algol. Argos is a planet within the Algol star system. The journey should take about three weeks," Andrin tells me.

My brows furrow. "That means six weeks until I am back to Earth. My parents are going to think I am dead! They can't go a month and a half without hearing from me. I talk to them every Sunday. They are probably already worried that I've been kidnapped!" My own alarm has returned as I continue defending my case.

"Well—" Izar drawls, a devious smile revealing sharp teeth.

Realizing he's making fun of me, I bare my own teeth back at him in a snarl.

"Communication can be complicated. You will not be able to contact them." Andrin places his hand on my shoulder, but I rip out of his grasp.

"Don't touch me! I don't care about your galaxy or any of you. I have lived on Earth for twenty-six years happily as a human. If you're going to force me to stay on board until you are done with Argos, fine. Then, you will return me to Earth, and we can both forget each other exists, or I promise you, I will show you a dangerous alien."

My fear and frustration mask themselves as anger. When Andrin opens his mouth, I turn before he can respond. I may have been taken against my will, I may have no choice in their mission through space, but I will be returned to my true home. I storm to the door and pause, letting out a snarl.

"Someone open this door, now!"

Over my shoulder, I see Izar give Andrin a pointed look before coming to meet me at the door. I memorize how Izar presses the buttons before it slides open so that I can move through the ship independently. He leads me down the hallway, my bare feet almost as cold as the aching hole in my chest. Sooner than expected, he opens a new air lock. The open door reveals a large bay filled with gym equipment and sparring mats. Various alien species are already using it, some sparring with one another using a variety of weapons.

"I think this will help you more than sulking in your room," Izar says with a knowing smile.

"Do I get to hit you?"

Izar laughs, "You can try."

For the first time in a week, I let a smile grow on my face, but it is not a joyful one. "I hope you have doctors onboard."

CHAPTER 5

My muscles ache, and new purple and blue bruises are surfacing all over my body. I swing at Izar's unguarded face. In a swift parry, he blocks my fist with his forearm while ducking his head. My fist makes sloppy contact before he grabs it in his other hand and twists. A sharp shooting pain jolts up my shoulder, forcing me to follow the motion. His sly smirk mocks me further as I step back so he will release my arm.

"I thought you knew how to fight?" Izar snidely remarks.

I spin again as another strike comes my way, avoiding any further damage in our fight. "I do. Aikido taught me how to survive conflict."

While he is taller than I, his body is as thin as mine. I did not expect his sinewy muscles or feline grace to knock me on my back so easily. Despite my fatigue from only half an hour of fighting, my frustration has not yielded. With my last ounce of energy, I launch a kick to Izar's mid-thigh. He staggers a step before latching onto my ankle and yanking—the air puffs from my lungs at the impact of my back on the mat.

"How is that going for you so far?" Izar asks with a laugh.

I think back to the gardens, my first real fight I've ever had off the mats. I didn't have enough space to pivot or spin. Even now on the mat, few of my strikes land.

"You're hesitating too much," he says.

"I was taught to oppose force. To absorb, redirect, and neutralize it. I haven't done much hand-to-hand combat."

My hair sticks to the sides of my face and shoulders, forming a rat's nest during my struggle. Izar stands over me, dangling a small towel before letting it fall on my face. I snatch it and quickly wipe the sweat from my brow. My anger has simmered to a low boil, but the rest of my body feels too weak to put up a fight anymore. Izar offers me a hand, and I allow him to help me up.

"With some work, I think we could make you a decent fighter," Izar says through his sharp-toothed smile. "You really weren't that bad."

I send every remaining ounce of mental energy into the arrogant alien's mind, trying to send a telepathic curse. "I'm lucky my organs are still inside my body."

Izar's lack of reaction tells me I cannot use any alien mind-communication abilities.

Izar shrugs. "You did better than I expected. Much better than a Human by far. If you train hard, there's a chance you could beat me one day."

"Would you mind refraining from casually discussing my lack of humanity?" I bristle, "On Earth, we have a phrase for that. It's called *too soon*."

Izar hands me a bottle, and I sniff it. "I think these are called electrolytes on Earth," he explains.

"Yeah, that is not very reassuring either," I retort. Izar only shrugs before I down the contents of the bottle. "Alright, at least not everything up here tastes like sawdust or pure sugar."

Izar snorts as he starts to head for the exit. Taking my sweaty towel and empty bottle, I follow him. Despite my frustration at being in the Orbital Station, I feel a slight bond with Izar growing. His acceptance of my frustration, rather than merely pacifying me, has created a safe outlet amid the strangeness. The outlet for my anger also brought me back to my logical brain.

While Izar might not be the highest-ranking person in the chain of command, he still wields considerable power. If I can use our common ground to help get me back to Earth, it will be much easier than finding my own way.

I slowly roll my joints as I say, "Since you're the Syntag, I would like to make a deal with you."

Izar closes the airlock behind us and leads me through the passageway. I try to take in the hallway as we walk, now filled with white lights instead of red.

"That sounds suspicious, but I am curious. What type of deal?"

"If I get good enough to beat you, despite what Andrin says, you take me back to Earth," I state.

Izar appraises my bruised and distressed form, brows furrowed. "I'll humor you and pretend that it is possible. Why would I benefit from that? A deal implies gain for both sides."

"If I can beat you and you don't take me back to Earth, I will make life very painful for you."

Izar chuckles. "Sure, I will take your deal. I will help get you home if you can beat me. Although combat fighting is only a portion of what training you will require if you want to be able to defend yourself. You should also develop your species-specific capabilities."

My joy in victory feels short-lived at the knowledge that I have more to learn. "Elaborate."

Izar shrugs, "It depends on what your DNA is capable of. Andrin would be better suited to help you with that. I excel with combat fighting."

This deal will be my backup plan if I cannot find my own way back to Earth. A good plan always includes a contingency, which is especially important since my primary plan does not yet exist.

"I have thought of my own request for this bargain." He pauses, his topaz eyes flaring in mischief. "You need to shower more regularly if you want to train together. You stink."

My face flushes, and I flip him off, to which he flashes his too-sharp feline grin.

I do need a shower. Between the exertion from my sparring match and the apparent week since I last used soap, I have accumulated a film of grime on my skin. Getting the shower in my room to work is a complicated task. I wonder why my alien understanding of the Universal Language does not extend to universal plumbing. It sits inside the cramped bathroom connected to my room. Next to the airplane-style toilet and sink is a metal stall only slightly wider than me.

I am still inspecting the small shower when there is a knock on my door. After a pause, air hisses, and Andrin enters. I'm thankful I'm still fully clothed.

"What do you want?" I ask lazily.

After my verbal altercation with Andrin earlier and burning off my anger with Izar in the training room, I have little fight left in me.

He holds up a stack of folded clothes. "I ran into Izar on his way back from the training bay. He said you were going to shower before breakfast. I figured you would want some fresh clothing."

I take the clothes and put them on the small sink. "Thanks." The polite phrase slips out despite my distrust and dislike of Andrin. We stare at each other. His face shows the kind of alertness one might have in a zoo enclosure with a feral animal. In his defense, he is not far off.

"Did you figure out how to work the shower?" Not an ounce of arrogance in his question.

I hate that I need to ask for his help. "Clearly no. Care to enlighten me?"

Andrin clears his throat and steps around me. "Press the button on the far left first, and water will come from the ceiling. The wall-mounted containers will dispense soap, shampoo, and conditioner tablets. From there, follow the prompts."

I push past him and close the bathroom door behind me. The shower buttons are also complicated. The cramped space is antithetical to the shower I used while in Bulgaria, where the water comes from a simple spout and drains into the open bathroom floor. A deranged giggle slips out at the familiar strangeness of trying to operate technology in a foreign country for the first time.

I searched through the pile of clothes Andrin had brought in for me for a towel, but there was none.

"Hey Andrin?" I call.

I barely hear shuffling on the other side of the bathroom door, "Everything okay?"

"Can you hand me a towel?"

I hear a chuckle against the door. "You don't need one. When you are done showering, press the button on the right with the spiral. Then close your eyes. Don't open them until you hear a set of three chimes."

"Okay—" My voice trails off in hesitancy.

He warns me again, "Seriously, don't open your eyes or they will be damaged. I will wait outside your room until you're ready."

When I hear the airlock hiss shut, I strip out of my clothes and step into the shower stall. I press the leftmost button. The water comes out in strange sprays; it beeps before a downpour of water covers me, then stops. I follow the electronic cue to take the clearly labeled tablets and apply them to my wet skin and hair. Once I am covered in bubbles, I press the button and rinse off in a torrential downpour.

Skeptically, I close my eyes and press the spiral button— one beep. A gust of wind fills the chamber, swirling around me. It is powerful enough to lift my hair above my head. I imagine this is what it feels like to stand under the dryer at the end of an automatic car wash.

Surprisingly, I feel the water droplets slipping from my skin and hair. When I feel fully dry, the miniature tornado stops, and my hair falls around my shoulders. I keep my eyes closed. I have only heard one beep so far. Two beeps sound, and I can see a flash of a bright light beyond my eyelids. I can only assume that is why I must keep my eyes closed. After a minute, darkness returns, followed by three beeps. I wait an extra minute before opening my eyes, just to be sure.

It is the strangest thing. When I open my eyes and step back into the bathroom to look in the mirror. My body is completely dry, and my hair looks great, like I had a blowout at a salon. I find a toothbrush and toothpaste clearly labeled in a drawer next to the sink. I scrub my teeth clean and inspect my makeup-less skin. I am grateful for my smooth complexion, but I would kill for some mascara and my signature berry-pink-tinted lip gloss.

I pull on the plain white under shorts and bandeau-style top first. The top is snug and constricts my chest. It is closer to a binding than a bra, but it will be sufficient for modesty purposes. Which is more than sufficient, given my small size to begin with. Then, I pull on the flowy linen pants and a basic short-sleeved boxy shirt, both made from the same off-white colored linen fabric. While the clothes are beautiful, the colors wash me out. They are far looser than my typical crop tops paired with jeans or tight skirts. They turn my willowy form into a boyish figure, but they fit and, most importantly, are clean.

    I open my bedroom airlock to see Andrin leaning on the opposite wall with his arms crossed. He looks up at me and breaks out his beaming smile. I falter.

    "Ready for breakfast?" He asks.

    I don't want to eat breakfast with him, nor even look at him. However, my stomach grumbles in response. "Fine, but I want shoes this time."

    Andrin nods to a pair of leather sandals by the door. I slide them on before following him back out of the airlock. The mental clarity that comes with my shower allows me to notice the cafeteria down the hall for the first time.

    Aliens in all shapes and sizes move with trays of food. As we step into the cafeteria, heads turn, and voices hush; so many heads, so many colors, foreign sounds, and unusual physiques. My empty stomach turns. I take three deep breaths. I thrive in new environments. Just because this isn't Earth doesn't mean I'm not myself. I blended in with humans for years; I can handle a cafeteria of aliens.

    Izar smoothly slides in front of us, cutting off my view and blocking theirs. "Welcome to the finest cafeteria on this side of Sagittarius."

Slowly, conversations fill the space again.

I let them lead the way to the wall, where others have gathered their trays. The food in front of me makes my elementary school cafeteria look like a Michelin-starred restaurant. I grab a metal tray and fill it with semi-solid cubes in various colors. I skip the ones that look like pet food kibble. Izar sets two juice-box containers on my tray before leading us to an empty table.

After watching both Izar and Andrin eat without utensils, I pick up an orange cube and take a small bite. I have to slam my hand over my mouth to keep my gag contained. Izar laughs while Andrin opens the juice container for me to drink.

Andrin gives me a strained smile. "Novice travelers always have the same reaction."

I try not to grimace as I pick up a blue cube. "For super advanced aliens capable of space travel, you should have spent more time developing flavorful food," I say, disdain poisoning my tone.

That earns a deep laugh from Andrin. "On Mycenae, the food tastes much better. During travel, efficiency is prioritized. Flavor is not vital to survival."

I flick one of the blobs with my fingernail as I grumble, "Maybe not for you."

After a few more bites of the grainy food, I analyze what Andrin said again.

"What is Mycenae?"

Andrin stiffens. "It is my home planet. The capital of the Perseus Constellation."

Izar pops a food pellet into his mouth and talks as he crunches it with his sharp teeth. "Each Constellation visible from Earth is a realm with its own rulers and governing bodies. My dear friend, Andrin, happens to be the heir of the Perseus Constellation."

I choke on my food again, this time not from the lack of flavor. I gulp down half of a juice box to stop my coughing.

"You? You're the heir of a Constellation? Like royalty?" My brain spins as I look around. "So, these aliens are your subjects?"

I continue my survey of the cafeteria. I make eye contact with the tree-like alien that brought food to my room. Its big eyes dart away as it conspiratorially chatters to an alien with multiple tentacles.

I nod my head in the direction of the personified Sakura Tree sprout. "That one came to my room to give me food. I might have screamed at it. At least I think it was that one."

"She is an Asprutan. Her name is Philomena. She works as a maid and servant of sorts on the station. You scared her, if it makes you feel any better." Izar flashes a toothy grin.

"Shockingly, it doesn't." Annoyed, I turn to Andrin. "Is that what everyone is here? Servants for you?"

Andrin does not seem to pick up on my quip. "A few are servants and cooks. Most of them are mechanics and engineers. They help keep the Orbital Station running."

I hum in response. I continue my observations in the cafeteria while trying not to taste the food I put in my mouth. The species vary greatly in shape and size. Most are bipedal. I see a handful more Asprutans, and three that have the same feline aesthetic as Izar sitting together, as well as several aliens with serpentine facial features and even some with scales. Some wear clothing, some don't.

"The Prince and I have to pilot the Orbital Station through the Star Gate. Can you find your way back to your room?"

I hadn't noticed both Andrin and Izar standing with empty trays in their hands. I pop another cube into my mouth and give them a thumbs up. They both give me a skeptical look, which makes me roll my eyes as I swallow. After the minor chaos I have caused since waking up, I can understand their hesitation.

"Yes, I'll be fine."

As I continue observing the other species filling the cafeteria, I am unsure whether it is a lie. How could I have assured my own safety in a spacecraft filled with aliens? They are strange in shape and size. Andrin and the few other golden Persei in the station are the closest beings to humans I have seen. Andrin and Izar told me I was the last of my kind from Andromeda, so perhaps, unless I see a human, I won't see another person like myself again. I have filled my life with a desire to meet new people and try new experiences. Have I finally found my limitation?

No, this feels closer to homesickness.

I will find a way home.

I repeat the phrase to myself over and over while I push the mushy food into my mouth. The chant becomes a panicked plea in my head. I struggle to breathe between bites, the air entering my lungs in short gasps. I stand abruptly, and the table rattles as my thighs hit the table top. A few aliens give me curious looks at my disruption before quickly averting their eyes. A gelatinous cube tumbles from my tray as my hands shake; it hits the floor with a wet splat. My cheeks heat as blood rushes to my face. I crouch to pick up the goo, but most of it is still stuck to the ground.

Philomena rushes to my side with a rag in hand. "I will clean it."

I can't find the words to protest or thank her, with my throat closing tightly. Our eyes meet, and she nods, releasing me to escape. I drop my tray in the same bin that I had seen Andrin and Izar do before rushing out of the cafeteria exit. My embarrassment continues as I nearly trip over the tentacles of someone entering.

I scramble down the passageway until I am far from anyone else. There is a large window in the hallway, exposing the darkness of space. There is nothing out there. The panic I felt in my room when I first awoke rises again. I have to get out of here. I can't go to Argos. I have to leave the Orbital Station before it travels through the Star Gate.

I gulp down air to calm my panting breaths, but it does little to calm my racing heart. When I no longer sound like an overheated animal, I clench my shaking fingers at my sides and stride further down the passageway. Passing one of the questionably sturdy staircases at the end of the wall, I climb it quickly. The metal fixtures rattle as my weight shifts along each step.

At the top of the stairs, I force myself to momentarily still. I cannot be stomping around the spacecraft if I want to escape without anyone raising an alarm. Once I calm down, I allow myself to start moving again. I curse as my pace is slowed further by the soft tap of my leather sandals against metal.

I pass by numerous closed doors. There are no windows in these halls, no way to tell how far from Earth we are beyond my previous view of blank space.

I freeze when I hear Andrin and Izar's voices around the corner. The hallway behind me is empty, and I can turn and avoid their notice.

"She—"

I pause. Are they talking about me? I hold my breath and listen.

"Why can't he know—"

Eavesdropping is probably not a good idea, but I must know what they are saying about me. I flatten myself against the wall and lean closer.

"The Commodore sent that message to everyone in Galaxia. My father ordered the station to cut all nonessential external communications so it doesn't get out that she is on board. She survived a Super Nova, who knows—" Andrin's voice drops conspiratorially.

Izar's aggravated whisper is even harder to hear. "Is that—the King—interested—"

If I can get just a little closer, I can hear them better.

"What are you doing?"

CHAPTER 6

My heart jumps out of my body, and my stomach drops. Spinning away from the wall to create distance from Andrin and Izar, I muster an air of nonchalance. Philomena stands on the far end of the hall, tilting her bulbous head in confusion. Her proportions are so strange, I wonder how her little form can support her head.

"I'm just a little lost. Could you help me find my way back to my room?" I ask quietly, hoping that Andrin and Izar do not have supersonic hearing among their alien capabilities.

Her huge eyes blink, once, twice. "Of course, Princess. Please, follow me."

My face twists at the title. "My name is Aurora. I'm not a princess."

As she leads me down the hall and stairwell, she tilts her head at me again. I wonder how she can possibly speak English. If all species can understand English through the Universal Language, or if she was specifically picked to help me because of her proficiency. Her musical voice floats effortlessly through my ears, like a breeze through treetops, whispering words to my brain. The tiny pink flowers that sprout from the miniature branches on her head remind me of her own crown.

"I know who you are. I'm your doera," she states with pride.

Far enough from Andrin and Izar that I feel safe enough to speak at a normal volume, I ask, "My what?"

"I am to serve you in any capacity you require. Attend to your clothing, cleaning, and any other needs that you have," she explains.

Aliens have abducted me. I have been escorted around the ship by an alien prince and his advisor. Then, to top it off, I have a lady's maid. It is, in all fairness, a far more pleasant outcome than I initially expected.

I search my empty brain for a reasonable response and come up blank. "Oh. Well, thank you, I guess."

We have arrived at my room's door. She nods and walks away. This one appears to open differently than the regular passageway airlock and the door to the Pilot House.

"Wait, Philomena!" She pauses and turns around. "Can you show me how to open these doors?"

"There is a keypad access on all doors that open to rooms that share an exterior boundary. The airlocks will automatically shut if there is any significant pressure drop, so to access it afterwards would require an emergency code."

I watch as she types in the code. The characters look close to Greek. The pattern she types sweeps down like a hook.

"Will this work for all doors?" I ask.

Her bulbous eyes lock with mine. "It will work for any door you have access to."

Is she being sassy? It is hard to tell, but I swear her toothless mouth smirks, if that is even possible. She definitely knows I was eavesdropping earlier. I give her a sheepish smile, and she scurries off.

I've decided that I like her.

I enter my room and slowly count to one hundred, giving time for Philomena to get out of sight before reaching for my door.

"All hands stand by for Star Gate passage." A computerized female voice blares from a speaker high on the wall.

A sudden jerk shakes the Orbital Station and sends me sprawling across the floor—my heart and breathing race like two instruments battling in a stretto. As the shuddering of the Station settles, I push myself to my knees. I'm thankful for the cool air now as I battle a wave of motion sickness. I haven't felt this seasick since a client of mine took a poorly timed charter boat in the Caribbean.

My breath halts in my throat as I look out the window. Like a science-fiction movie or an immersive amusement-park ride, millions of streaks of light line the blackness. This is what the inside of a Star Gate looks like. I am getting further from Earth by the second. I let myself get distracted by Andrin and Izar's conversation. I might have missed my only opportunity to find an escape route. I need to find a way back now before it is too late.

Checking the hallway first, I sneak out of my room. I go in the opposite direction this time and find a stairwell going down. It is darker down here and appears empty. A large door waits with a keypad at the end of the hall.

Exterior boundary.

It seems promising. After entering the code, a chime sounds, followed by several clicks. Air hisses as the door splits open horizontally. That's—cool.

The bay is wide open. A rough, asphalt-like substance covers the floor, and the walls show their bare metal beams.

Gear and equipment are secured to the walls. A metal track inlaid in the ground runs down the center of the room to an enormous, garage-style door. Next to it, there is another airlock with a tiny circular window. The soles of my leather sandals slap the ground as I hurry across.

Another keypad. I press my nose against the glass as I peer through the small window. The room is no bigger than a closet, and the far wall is composed almost entirely of windows. Outside of that window, I can see the smears of light against darkness.

This has to be an escape pod. My way back home. My fingers press the code into the keypad.

A hand clamps around my wrist.

I jump, but the blue hand doesn't release me. I try to yank it away, but the alien only pulls on my wrist harder. I freeze for just a moment before swinging my opposite arm up, ready for a counter defense, but they move too quickly. They twist my arm until it is pinned behind my back and shove me against the still-sealed door. I was so close. I just needed to press Enter, and I could have escaped. I try to wriggle free, but I am pushed harder against the glass.

"Are you trying to kill everyone? Or just yourself?"

Izar? With one last shove, he releases me and steps back, seething. His topaz eyes glow with fury. I shake my hand out.

"That hurt!" I squeal.

He scowls. "Good. Maybe you'll learn not be so reckless. Do you even know what you were about to do? You could have killed everyone aboard! What were you thinking?"

I find a spot on the asphalt to stare at while I roll out my sore shoulder. "I thought it was an escape pod. I want to go home!"

"Is everyone on Earth this catastrophically selfish, or do you feel a sense of entitlement now that you found out you're not Human?" Izar snarls through his sharp teeth. "The keypad closer to the bulkhead is for the Charging Pod. You almost opened the bay door that would have sucked everything inside the station into time and space! Not to mention we're in the middle of a Star Gate tunnel!"

"I didn't know! It is all of your faults that I am here in the first place! I wouldn't need to find a way back if I had been left on Earth!" My neck is craned upwards as we scream face-to-face.

"I just made a deal to help you this morning! Now we are too far; we're no longer in your solar system. Even if you figured out how to use the Charging Pod, it wouldn't get you back to Earth. The only way to return now would be to Aether Cross from a Pod, and only the most powerful beings are capable of Aether Crossing beyond a few miles at a time."

I stamp my foot like a toddler. "I want to go home. You don't understand what it's like to be taken from your home."

"Actually, Princess," He hisses, the moniker dripping in condensation. "I do."

I scowl at him while Izar puffs himself up for a lecture. He enjoys lecturing me as if I were a naive child. It grates my nerves.

"My kind, the Harmakhis, are from Scorpius. We have been battling the rule of Sagittarius for a millennium. My family left as refugees when I was little and swore our loyalty to the Persei Royal family. I might be Andrin's advisor because we are friends, but I am subservient to the wishes of the King. I don't get to go home either," He scolds.

I am silent. Shame shrouds my temper. Nothing that I could say would be enough. An apology is not the proper response to how I feel. I am not sorry. It is not right that Izar can't go back to his home Constellation, but that is not my fault. An awkward stretch of time passes, and I no longer feel it would be appropriate to say anything. I also don't want to ruin what might be my only option for getting off this ship.

I offer a sheepish grin. "Would it make you feel better if you hit me?"

Izar steps back, looking offended. "No!"

"Relax, I meant combat training. I'll even let you land a few punches this time."

I beam at the annoyed expression on Izar's face. After a silent moment, he ruffles my hair before stalking away. He only makes it a few paces away before he pauses and dramatically turns back towards me.

Izar huffs, giving in. "Fine, but you are running laps first."

I am too busy fixing my tousled hair to comprehend immediately.

"Wait, I said training. Not running." I start to jog after his retreating figure. "How did you know I was even here in the first place?"

"I know everything that happens around here. I am Syntag after all. Now, hurry up and change. I already had Philomena drop off your exercise clothing in your room. You owe me three miles before training as punishment for almost killing everyone onboard. I will add a lap for every minute you make me wait."

CHAPTER 7

Four miles. I run four miles around the circular track that surrounds the training mats. For the last mile, Izar stands gloating over the mats where I will surely be beaten to a pulp later. Once I finally finish running, Izar hands me a protein bar and an electrolyte drink. Unwrapping the waxy coating of the bar, I take a bite and grimace. Somehow, it is reassuring that the space protein bar tastes just as bad as most do on Earth.

"While you are training, you should take a break to eat and drink every hour. Our food has superior nutrition for your biological makeup. We can work on your speed and strength. I will teach you hand-to-hand combat techniques, and we will discover any extraterrestrial capabilities you may have."

The spark returns to my eyes. "Do you think I will be able to Aether Cross?"

Izar shrugs. "Maybe. It depends on how much Aether you can control. It is something beyond and between space. Andrin will help you with that. It's beyond my capabilities. For now, get on the mat."

I groan at the thought of being face-to-face with the mat and with Andrin.

Izar starts his teaching with defensive maneuvers, which I pick up quickly. My circular footwork is superior for avoiding his linear charges. I turn and step forward, shifting my weight back and forth instead of blocking. It helps me for the first hour, but he quickly analyzes my technique.

"I have respect for your previous discipline, but simply redirection, absorbing, and attempting to avoid damage won't keep you alive against another alien that wants to harm you. You must learn to block a strike and make one as well."

I nod as I pant, my head barely lifted as I brace my hands against my knees.

"Alright. Tomorrow we can work on strikes. I don't think I can take any more today. I've already had three of those protein bars, and I still feel ready to pass out."

Izar shakes his head as he steps closer. "You think the Harpyiai will give you a water break if she comes after you again?"

His hand darts out, and I shift my weight away. Except his foot kicks out on my weight-bearing side. With my center of gravity off kilter, I'm sent to my back, my limbs in the air like a dead cockroach.

Andrin appears over me, his golden skin shining with his own sweat. I add it to the list of things that annoy me about him. One, he abducted me. Two, he is always pleasant, even when I scream at him. Three, he looks like a Greek God statue after working out, while I am flushed like a tomato.

"Do you need help getting up?" He offers.

I scowl at him. "No." I try to push myself up but slip on the slick surface.

"I heard you're interested in developing your Aether manipulation capabilities."

His hand is outstretched in front of me. Sighing, I accept the help. A spark jumps between our skin, but he does not let go. He lifts me on my feet like I am a rag doll, even though my limbs feel as heavy as lead.

"Do you ever feel a spark when we touch?" I cringe; that sounded like a pickup line.

My stomach twists, a flush spreading across my cheeks. I hate that I find him attractive when I want to push him into open space.

Andrin's eyes look bright and hopeful. "Yes, I do."

I take a step back, realizing I am using him to support my weight still. "I meant like a static shock. I feel it every time you touch me."

The excitement does not fade from Andrin's eyes. "Yes, that's the energy flowing through you. It is the Aether. It must be seeking out mine."

Leaving me slightly wobbly, Andrin retreats to the other side of the training mat. After rummaging through a bag, he pulls out something shiny and metallic. I watch as he secures the golden necklace and bracelet set onto himself before returning. He reaches for my wrist, but I pull it back, staring at the metal cuffs skeptically.

"These," he says, patiently waiting for me to take his offering, "are vambraces to channel your energy. We will use them to start working on your Aether manipulation."

My curiosity beats out my skepticism as I snatch them from his hand and clamp them on each of my forearms. "Okay, what now?"

"First, we should try to assess how much power you have right now. Hold your hands together and try to feel your Aether."

I hold my hands an inch apart and stare at the space between them. If this is some alien practical joke, I am going to kill both Andrin and Izar. A quick spark jolts from one hand to the other.

I gasp, my eyes flying up to Andrin's beaming face. "Was that it?"

"I think so. Try again, whatever you are feeling, focus on that. Emotions can be some of the most powerful catalysts for Aether."

I hold my hands apart again, this time, nervous excitement building inside of me. "Nothing is happening."

"Shh, be patient."

My eyebrows shoot up. "Did you just shush me?" A spark jolts between my fingers again, but holds.

A smile breaks across my face in awe. The tiny beam dims quickly to my changing emotions. I need to focus.

"You irritating me seemed to do the trick," I grumble.

"I have noticed your quick temper. It is most likely a side effect of your pent-up energy," He continues to smirk at me despite my growing scowl. "Energy and Aether can be almost interchangeable for those with the ability to manipulate them. It is a good thing I'll be around to rile you up and help you release it."

Andrin's comment sends a flush of heat through me. Several types of frustration battle for dominance inside my brain and body. A tingle of energy dances from my sternum to my fingertips. I focus on the electrical current. Andrin remains close to me, his brows furrowed in concentration. I cannot believe I am trying to create an electrical current between my fingers, like at a hands-on science museum, because the guy who brought me here in the first place wants to see a cool party trick. The beam intensifies. It jumps from my right pointer finger to the metal at my wrist.

"Aurora, you're doing it!" Andrin exclaims.

His hand clasps my left wrist over the vambrace. The beam sparks. My wrist burns hot. Suddenly, I feel exhausted. It has been a while since I slept. I should probably—

Andrin's arms catch me as I tumble into darkness.

I wake to a knock on the door: a dull metal thunk, three times. After the third, there is a pause, followed by the click and hiss of the door. I am sitting up in bed by the time Andrin opens the door and leans his head in. Andrin pauses at the airlock. Once he assesses it is safe to enter, he steps further into my room.

"How are you feeling today?"

I shrug, "Crippled by existential dread and fathomless desolation. I'm trapped in a space station, who knows how far from the only place I have ever known, the one I had assumed I would inhabit for all eternity. So, you know, not bad considering that."

Andrin's jaw is open, confusion clear on his face.

"I'm fine," I sigh and close my eyes before his words register. "What do you mean by today? The last thing I remember was trying to channel energy."

Andrin steps farther into my room, leaning against the wall across from my bed. I sit up, feeling strangely good. I find some comfort in the fact that I am still dressed in my gross, now-dried, sweaty clothes. My head doesn't ache. My muscles aren't sore. Dread starts to seep into my stomach.

"How long was I out for?" I ask.

"Don't worry, you only slept for the night. You had a long morning, so you probably just overloaded yourself. Aether has to come from somewhere; it needs a source to draw off of. Energy must always be converted."

"Newton's second law," I mumble.

"Who's law?" The wave of confusion on Andrin's face is enough to lighten my mood.

"Forget I said anything. It is an Earth thing. Something that I'm sure would only amuse those of us who possess limited intergalactic knowledge." I sigh when my jest seems to fall flat, again. "So, when do I get to practice again?"

Andrin chuckles, clearly more amused at my tenacity than at my jokes. "Izar has requested the privilege of morning practice after you eat breakfast. We will practice in my office after lunch."

"Great. Then I'll see you after lunch." I remember my grimy state and cringe. "Now I need to shower and change."

Andrin leaves with a wave, and I hurry to get ready. I let my dirty clothes drop to the floor, but something on my arm catches my eye. Just above where the top of the vambraces I wore yesterday ends, near my elbow, is a smear of dried blood and blue goo. I rub both substances away and see clear skin beneath. Not a scratch in sight. I let myself revel in my small victory. I must have gotten a good hit against Izar after all.

Excitement is already building in me. When I get into the cafeteria, Andrin and Izar are nowhere in sight. I fill up my tray and look around the room. I feel like I am the new kid at lunch. I spot two Asprutans, one that I think I recognize as Philomena, at a mostly open table. She looks up as I approach and makes space for me.

I muster as much cheer as I can while I greet them. "Good morning!"

"Good morning, Princess. This is Oki, he is my inosculation."

I smile at Oki; he looks similar to Philomena, but his branch appendages appear redder in color than orange, and his flowers are white instead of pink. I make a mental note to ask later whether the color difference is due to gender, like in animals, or to geographic origin, like in plants. Asprutans seem to fit into both categories.

"It's an honor, Princess." While Philomena's voice is like a breeze through the treetops, his voice sounds like the thumping of branches against one another.

"Please call me Aurora." I force myself not to grimace. "Why are you calling me princess?"

Oki opens his mouth first, but Philomena cuts him off. "We were told you are a very important member of the Andromeda Galaxy. We use the title of 'Princess' as one of honor."

How many crew members know who I am? I suppose they all must. I cannot imagine a mission to retrieve a lost alien from a fallen galaxy can be kept out of the gossip ring for very long. The assumption that I am important just because I survived places a great deal of pressure on me to be special. After I struggle to produce Aether, I think most on board will be very disappointed by the limited entertainment I can provide.

"I appreciate it, but truly, I prefer just Aurora."

They both nod before they resume eating. I cram my own food into my mouth and swallow as quickly as possible to avoid tasting it. While the three of us sit in silence, I notice the tiny flowers and leaves growing from each of their bulbous heads, dancing together like a playful caress of wind through a garden. They seem very familiar with each other. More in a romantic sense than familial. Inosculation. It sounds like the Latin *insoculatio*, meaning to unite.

"Pardon my ignorance of Asprutan customs. Is inosculation similar to being married?" I ask.

"There is nothing to pardon. I am only knowledgeable about Earthly customs from my study of the Orion Nebula while attending the Imperial University. Which is why I received the honor of being assigned to you." Philomena smiles. "It means to be one. When we approach our end of life, we will pick a spot on our home planet, and merge so we may forever rest intertwined."

"That's beautiful." A smile breaks across my face as they lean their heads together, the tiny foliage interacting as if sensing the other.

It is fascinating to watch natural phenomena that are entirely foreign to me. The sweetness of the moment is almost enough to distract me from her words. She earned a degree in learning about a culture outside her own, just as I have. The kinship makes my heart warm. Perhaps since she attended the Imperial University, she will know more about the Imperial Commodore.

"I do have a question for both of you."

They lean apart, and Philomena straightens. "I'm at your service for anything you require."

"Yesterday, I overheard someone talking about a Commodore. Do you know anything about them? They sounded—important." I keep my voice casual and slow, like I'm not tingling with anticipation.

Philomena shoots me a conspiratorial look while Oki answers. "The Commodore is the leader of the Imperial Fleet. He is also the heir of Galaxia, so one day he will become our Emperor."

What does the Imperial Commodore and future Emperor want with me? Why send out a message to find me in the first place? I open my mouth to ask another question, but I see Izar appear in the doorway of the cafeteria. I shove the rest of my breakfast into my mouth before saying goodbye to Philomena and Oki.

I quickly realize how right Izar is when he talks about food as fuel, literally. I don't feel tired, despite the long hours of physical training. My body feels neither sore nor weak. My muscles feel fluid. My blood feels electric as it pulses through my body. Izar demands more work. I demand my body to push further, harder, faster. After a single day of training and rest, the movements have become natural to my body.

"You did well today." Izar hands me a towel. "Did you ever feel different than the Humans around you?"

I shrug and try to think back to my childhood, the childhood I can remember after being surrendered at a hospital. I have always been thin but strong, just like my mom. She had always been lean, despite the abundance of food she ate at her Filipino restaurant. While she was not my birth mom, it was my norm. I had never thought my strength or speed was unnatural. Her love of triathlons was what got me into running in the first place.

"I was better than other kids my age at a lot of things, but I thought that was because of how I was raised."

Izar's sharp teeth settle into a self-satisfied smirk. "I'm sure it helped a bit. You are biologically very different."

My mind jumps to my immune system and the Universal Language. I have been able to understand every alien I have come across on the station so far. My body has been healthier here than I ever felt on Earth, even without medicine. I am desperate to get back to my family and my life on Earth, but it is getting harder to ignore the fact that my body was not made to live there.

"You have told me that the Persei care about me, but not why. I understand that I am an alien, but so are all of you. What about me has piqued the Commodore's interest enough to send out a message to find me? Why did the King order his own son to retrieve me?"

Izar coughs. He delays his response by fixing the knot of braids atop his head. "How do you know who the Commodore is?"

I keep my face stern, unwilling to get distracted. "Thin walls and alien hearing. Why me?"

His eyes glance around the nearly empty training room as he closes the distance between us. "The Andromeda Galaxy collapsed when the main star at the center of the galaxy went Super Nova. It was unexpected. The star should have had hundreds of thousands to millions of years left of life. Yet it burnt itself out suddenly, triggering a massive black hole. Somehow, you survived it when no one else did."

"I doubt everyone is looking for me because they want an interview. How did I allegedly survive this Super Nova?" I wring the towel between my hands.

His catlike nose twitches. "There are two main theories, but no one knows for sure. The first is that someone knew it was about to collapse and sent you away. The second is that they knew you could survive the collapse because you possess Aether levels we have never experienced in Galaxia.

"Since the Commodore has taken an interest, some will want to use you to improve their standing within the Empire. Either way, many believe that as the lone survivor of a lost galaxy, you are important and are key to ensuring their advancement within the galaxy."

Of course, the other life forms within Galaxia are not searching for me for my benefit. They don't want to help me. They want to use me to gain notoriety or power. Suddenly, I feel more at home. Greed, apparently, is what rules humans and aliens alike. I inhale deeply to steel my nerves.

"They want energy? Aether? Power? They can keep searching the rest of Galaxia. They aren't getting it from me."

I storm out of the training bay and straight to find Andrin.

CHAPTER 8

Storming through the spaceship, I get lost twice before I find the right door: the title, Taxiarhos, on a placard confirming my victory. I slam my fist against the door until Andrin opens it. His smile at my appearance drops when he takes in my seething form.

"The entire galaxy is after me to use Aether that I don't even have. You just fetched me for your dad to do the same!"

Andrin exhales. "Of course not. My father told me the risk you might be at. Aurora, I don't want anything bad to happen to you. That's why I volunteered to get you." He moves from the door, as if to invite me inside.

My eyes narrow, and I hold my stance in the doorway. "Why did you volunteer? Why would you come? You don't know me. You don't need my Aether. I can barely make a spark."

He grabs my shoulders and our skin sparks, as if in agreement with me. "No, not to use you. The Persei history and prophecies are rooted in heroic actions, all the way back to our origins with our Golden Elders. My Constellation deserves a leader who is willing to do the same, to keep those in need safe."

I want to call him on his dramatics, but the intensity of his face and grip makes me think he actually believes what he is saying. His hands slide down my arms, waiting for my response. The hairs on my arms rise as his touch trails.

I shift my weight to my back leg to gain a few extra inches of distance from him. "That's it? You travelled across the galaxy because you want to be a hero? I think the self-serving desire defeats the purpose of a heroic action."

His Adam's apple bobs in his throat, a habit I have observed when he seems unsure or nervous. "Not because I want to be a hero. I volunteered because it is righteous to assist those in need. That is the kind of leader I want to be."

The words grate at my pride, instantly freezing the heat that had begun building under my skin. I stare at him, waiting for his mask to crack. It does not.

"I'm not some damsel in distress who needs a prince to save her," I bite.

Andrin only laughs at the sass in my tone. The warm honey sound softens my ire.

"I could see that from the moment you woke up on the ship."

His light-hearted tone halts any agitated remark I can muster. I let my eyes wander around Andrin's office. The familiar saffron scent lingers like a warm hug in the air. The walls and floors are made up of the same dark, polished metal. The area rug, couch, chairs, and decor remind me more of my dad's faculty office at Harvard than the rest of the sterile spacecraft. I stand in the center while he rifles through a cabinet. He returns and hands me a solid golden sphere, small enough to fit in one hand yet heavy enough to feel considerable. A few seconds of silence pass before I raise my eyebrows at him.

"A golden ball? What am I supposed to do with it? Throw it?"

His eyebrows raise in response. "Please do not throw it. Think of it like the vambraces. Channel your Aether through it."

I blink at him, waiting for further explanation. When none comes, I confess, "I don't know how to do that."

He rolls his head from side to side, trying to find a way to translate the sentiment behind his words to my Earth-bound level of understanding. "This orb is a conduit, like the vambraces. It cannot hold an energy charge, only provide a pathway for your Aether to easily travel."

"Is this pure gold?"

"Yes."

I release a low whistle. "Princey has money."

"Perseus Constellation has numerous planets rich in mineral deposits, especially gold." Andrin shrugs. "Still, don't throw it. Use it like the vambraces, focus your emotions on it."

I tried to get frustrated like yesterday. Nothing happens. My natural frustration as I stare at the ball for minutes yields no results. Boredom begins to override my frustration, and my eyes wander around the room again.

"Your room is nice. I suppose being a prince has perks." I bait.

"Thank you. These quarters come standard across this class of Orbital Station and are left empty unless the Taxiarho embarks. My bedroom is through that door."

He jabs his thumb over his shoulder with the blandest expression I have ever seen. I stare at him, waiting to see if he is being serious. After a moment of silence, we both blink at each other.

He finally asks, "What have I done this time?"

I break out laughing so hard that a small snort escapes. It makes Andrin chuckle, too, albeit a bit awkwardly. Yes, he is serious.

"You know, for someone who knows so much about the Universe and everything in it, it is obvious you only learned English academically. What you just said could have been interpreted as an invitation for sex back on Earth."

I take joy in seeing the red tint of Andrin's gold face. Smugness brews inside of me, knowing I have made him uncomfortable in his own space. The gold orb warms in my hands, a slight glow emitting from the metal.

"Look! I'm doing it!" I exclaim.

"That's great!" He pauses, appraising me with a contemplative focus, before his excitement takes over. "We could start trying to practice Aether Crossing."

"Aether Crossing? Really? I thought it takes a lot more energy."

He shrugs. "It does, but I am curious to see what you are capable of."

Andrin takes the orb from me and moves me to the center of the room, so I have space around me.

He moves his hands around as he explains, "There are energy fields all around us. It is how we can manipulate Aether in the first place. The key to Aether Crossing is to find the gaps between Space. Aether exists beyond light and gravity; it exists in the absence of matter in the Universe. You have to focus on a particular point in the Aether, and your matter will be transported through it."

I wait for more explanation, but he stares expectantly at me. "I don't know how to find Aether, let alone a gap in it. That's not part of *Aliens Are Real 101* back on Earth."

Andrin's face twists in confusion, making me sigh. I let the sarcasm dry on my tongue.

"You wouldn't know it, but back on Earth, I'm kind of funny."

"Oh, my apologies. You know how to summon Aether, so we can start there. Almost like creating a wormhole. Send a pulse of Aether into a tiny, concentrated point."

I fight the urge to roll my eyes. I have to start somewhere, and my sarcasm isn't helping me move forward. The sooner I can learn to Aether Cross, the sooner I can return to Earth. Whether through my deal with Izar or from a Charging Pod.

"How can I focus on a specific point in space if we are moving through space on the Orbital Station? How can I ensure I make the wormhole in the right spot?"

Andrin walks to his own window and presses a few buttons on the wall-mounted control panel. A sheet of light flickers around us. The light shines in a soft yellow hue along the walls, ceiling, and floor. It's some type of barrier. Andrin waits a moment before pressing the buttons again, making the lights dissipate.

"This barrier will keep our matter and Aether within this room. Most of the Orbital Station has a similar barrier, like most places within Galaxia. It is as much to keep us in as it is to keep others out."

I give him a pensive nod, my eyes continuing to drift, searching for any hint of the now invisible barriers. At least I will not have to worry about launching myself into the cosmos.

There is only one place in Galaxia I really want to travel to. Learning how to Aether Cross will bring me one step closer to returning home. Rolling my shoulders back, I focus my eyes on a single spot in the room. Nothing happens—no spark, no glow, nothing. With a huff, I try to hand the orb back to Andrin.

"This is futile."

Andrin shakes his head and refuses to accept my answer. "Try again. You're learning a new skill, and it is going to take time."

I grumble internally, then realize this is the first skill I have had to work to learn. Most things came effortlessly to me. The unexpected wound to my pride doesn't motivate me to try again. Andrin watches me patiently, his own arms crossed over his chest. I let out an exaggerated groan and halfheartedly attempt to refocus.

I stare at an intersection of metal welds on the floor. I force my eyes to focus long enough, and the world around me blurs. My fingers tingle, the hair on my arms stands on end. With a spark, I force the Aether through my bloodstream and out the tip of my finger. It crackles with a blue-white that vanishes in a blink. With that single spark released, I feel the absence of Aether beneath my skin.

"It's not working. I don't have enough Aether for it," I release a huff. "Maybe I'm not the kind of alien that is capable of really using Aether."

"Yes, you are. You're special. You can do this."

My fingers clench at my sides, frustration, anger, and a more bottomless pit of fear all bubbling to the surface. I need to succeed to get home. The Commodore, hell, the galaxy, is looking for me to use Aether that I don't even have. I grew up on Earth, and I was a normal Human for twenty-six years. I'm not special. Izar said not all aliens can manipulate Aether.

Maybe I'm just regular, which is fine. It is the first time I've felt regular in my life, but perhaps that's a good thing.

It doesn't sit right. The sour seed of frustration that has been in my stomach since I arrived on the Orbital Station flares, then surges.

"I need a—"

Heat flares across my skin as I frantically search for a trash can. I cover my mouth at the impending acid burning my throat. Realization flares in Andrin's eyes, and he grabs me by my shoulders. A wave of dizziness hits me like a wall as he rushes me through the rooms and in front of a toilet. The surge is violent.

When it is over, I slump on the floor. A cool, damp rag cradles the back of my neck. My body shivers with relief. Chilled water droplets trail down my spine under my shirt. When the world stops spinning, I lean back. There is no wall, but Andrin braces my back.

"One of the theories of how you got to Earth is that you Aether Crossed yourself as a baby using the energy released during the Andromeda Galaxy Super Nova," Andrin says.

My brows crinkle. "Somehow, that is one of the most ridiculous things that I've heard since learning aliens are real. My parents died in a car accident."

I pause; my parents didn't die in a car accident. They were from the Andromeda Galaxy; we just always assumed it was a car accident.

"Or, that's the account they were told when they had adopted me as a baby after I had been surrendered to a hospital. An unknown woman had dropped me off looking ragged. She said there was a crash. Everyone had assumed she had been intoxicated, and my mother. Before they could get her information, she had disappeared."

Andrin brushes my hair back from my face, his fingers lingering on my jaw, inspecting my face. He waits patiently for me to finish my story, but it's all I know about the time before my adoption. I feel vulnerable under his gaze, especially while discussing something so personal. His touch is also quite distracting.

"Why are we going to Argos?" I ask to shift his attention.

"My father sent me a direct order. My number one priority, as the future King, is to protect the Persei. Our people and our planets. My father wants me to understand that responsibility, a responsibility that has been passed down to me since the Golden Elders."

"Golden Elders?" I ask, my eye flicking over to his gilded skin.

"They are some of the oldest documented Persei. They were the first Persei capable of manipulating Aether, and it gave them extraordinary capabilities. They were the generation that first explored the planets beyond their solar system and colonized every habitable planet within the Perseus Constellation. They are the legacy of what it means to be a Persei. I have to protect my Constellation."

"Why is Argos in danger?"

Andrin sighs, sitting back against the wall. I let the space between us grow, welcoming the distance.

"Argos is a planet that orbits the star Algol—the fresh water resources there are imperative for the survival of others nearby. An invasive alien clan is attempting to seize control of the water source there. To make the planet habitable for them, they introduce ammonia to the water. By doing so, it poisons the water for my citizens. Having a clean, reliable water source is imperative for future colonization plans. The invasive species' presence threatens Persei's interests and citizens."

I cannot determine whether it is ironic or inevitable that every civilization resorts to conflict over resources.

"What are you going to do to stop them?"

Andrin straightens, pride filling his chest. "Izar and I are going as backup for the last Persei Guard there. He needs help finishing the water neutralization mission. We have to restore safety to the water supplies."

"After that, you will bring me back to Earth? You said after Argos you would take me back."

"I will get you home safely. Don't worry." I watch Andrin's expression for sincerity. I see no shifts of emotion. "Do you trust me?"

I don't know. My instincts tell me I shouldn't. My endocrine system is still firing on all cylinders in survival mode. Yet the wanderlust in my blood pulses stronger than ever. My need to explore and travel has always been overwhelming. It's why I picked an international profession. The longer I am onboard this Orbital Station, the harder it is for me to distinguish between the reality I have always known and what is awaiting me. In a few days, my entire world has shifted.

"I guess I have to."

R. A. SANDS

CHAPTER 9

Two and a half weeks of training, sweating, and bleeding on the sparring mats, burning my skin on the golden orb, and vomiting trying to Aether Cross have strengthened my body and mind. My naturally tall and lithe body has become lean and powerful.

Izar has us free spar today. No direction. He attacks, I defend. I see an opening, I attack. We move faster today. My limbs feel firm, my core strong. It is nearly time to stop when Izar calls for a pause.

"Do you feel tired?"

It is a trick question. If I say yes, he will make me drill more until I cannot move. Tell me I need to push myself harder to get better. I move my limbs around, testing them. I still feel fluid and ready to move.

"I'm ready for another round."

Izar appraises me before asking, "Are you ready to advance beyond hand-to-hand combat?"

My eyebrows quirk. "What is beyond sparring?"

"We have many weapons, ones that should seem familiar to you, albeit with technological advancements." Izar heads toward the wall where a stand of training weapons stands. "Like your Earth Grecians, the Persei prefer spears, javelins, and occasionally swords. You will learn how to wield a spear because it has a longer range of accessibility and will require less strength."

"No guns? You must have access to cutting-edge, laser-shooting, plasma-blasting alien guns."

Izar pauses, the beads in his hair clinking against each other as his head tilts in a humanesque gesture. "No guns. The disastrous consequences of the possibility of damaging a spacecraft and killing everyone onboard outweigh the possible benefits of guns."

The muscles on the back of my neck tighten. This is the second time Izar has revealed the Orbital Station's fragility. In a universe full of otherworldly technology and genetically abnormal beings, the alien universe's vulnerabilities are jarring.

He strides back towards me with two poles in his hands. With a flick, he tosses one my way. It is only in the air for a second before my fingers wrap around the long pole. A quick flash of light breaks across the room, then dims to a soft blue-white glow. Izar's own blue eyes glow with satisfaction.

"That is the real deal." He tosses me another pole, this one without a spearhead. "This is what you will practice with."

He motions for the glowing spear, so I toss it back to him. Effortlessly, he grabs it out of the air and puts it in its stand, holding his own training spear. My eyes veer back to the case of poles, wondering what makes them glow. It feels powerful. A sharp line of pain appears at my side, an ache spreading quickly. My eyes dart back towards Izar, and my mouth drops open like a fish.

His feline grin flashes as he spins the pole in his hands. "The number one way to die is to get distracted."

Izar swings his spear towards me again, and I drop to the floor. My wooden pole rolls away from my prone form on the mat. With a laugh, Izar brings his pole down towards me. I barrel roll away until there is enough space between us that I can jump back up into a crouch.

"You can't just attack me like that and expect me to fight back!" I pant.

Izar shrugs impishly. "You said you've done jo staff training before. I thought I would see if you have any more surprises up your sleeve. It is entertaining to watch you struggle sometimes."

"You enjoy being antagonistic far too much," I complain.

"True, but it is to make you better. You hold back too much on your strikes. I'm hoping the spear will force you to claim the space. Now, take a fighting stand with your hands one-third of the way in from each end of the pole. Keep your left palm down and your right palm facing up."

He teaches me how to rotate the pole as I push and pull it towards my body. My shoulders and lat muscles begin to ache after only a few minutes of the kayaking-like movement. While the positioning differs slightly from what I know, the movements come easily after a little practice. The spear mimics the art of Aikido, even the practice without a jo staff. The staff becomes an extension of the blade that is my arms, but my balance still centers at the hilt.

Once I have the basic movements down, he demonstrates how to block and hit with the pole at its full length. That's where the familiarity ends. To make contact feels strange. The strikes are linear, much like the training he's been teaching me. Yet the crack of the spears together sends a jolt through my body with each contact. Despite my hesitation, we move quickly through drills, learning to use it as a blunt weapon, a projectile, or a conduit for my Aether. I can understand why a spear is the weapon of choice for the Persei.

While chugging a bottle of electrolytes, a blur of movement flies across my periphery. Dropping the bottle, I grab my staff and spin around. I slam my pole down perpendicular to Izar's, forcing it to stop with a loud crack. He winds back for another hit, but I sweep my pole across his ankles. His knees bend in surprise, and I move around him until I face his back. Another sweep to the back of his right knee, and he drops to a lunge. I prepare to strike again, but he moves faster, sending the butt end of his pole into my shoulder. Pain shoots down my arm at the force, loosening the grip of my left hand. Another cracking hit against my pole sends it flying across the room.

"Finally," Izar straightens, looking almost as tired as I feel but arrogant in his victory. "I think I found the secret to stopping your hesitation. Now rest. That's enough for the day."

"No. More." I purse my lips, knowing I sound like a child.

Izar stands and appraises me. He angles his head towards my pole so I can retrieve it, and we re-engage, round after round. The drills these past days have prepared me for this. For the fluid movement of the pole. I have little force behind my blows, but they hit true. Until my underhand grip slips. Izar's strike snaps the pole with a thunderous crack. The lower end of the pole slides down my loose grip, embedding splinters into my palm as I struggle to grasp it.

Izar and I both release a stream of profanities as we take in the damage.

"It's time to stop," Andrin commands as he approaches from behind me.

The usual spark announces the large hand on my shoulder as Andrin's. He moves around me until his other hand can gently grip my wrist to inspect my injured hand. Instead of releasing me, he instructs me to follow him. Izar grabs the splintered wood from me, and I allow Andrin to lead me by the arm out of the training bay. He brings us to his room and punches in the keypad code. I cannot help myself as I watch, memorizing the pattern.

He motions towards his living room. "Sit on the couch, I'll be right back."

"I'm covered in sweat. I don't want to stain the fabric of your couch," I protest.

He tilts his head and raises a single eyebrow at me. "Then stand. You should be more worried about the blood on your hand."

I look down to see a small pool of crimson cupped in my palm, oozing from the punctures where splinters are embedded into my skin. It is worse than I thought. Instead of arguing further, I sit and wait.

Andrin returns from the side room quickly and kneels before me, placing medical supplies on the coffee table. An ache begins in my chest, desperate to appreciate the sweetness of his gentle actions as I force the thoughts from my brain. With a wet towel in hand, he opens my fingers so my palm is flat. He pats away the excess blood. I jolt when he sprays my skin, my palm tingling and numb. I cannot feel a thing as he uses tweezers to place the wooden shards.

While the spray is intriguing, his next medical device is astonishing. He squeezes a black, glittery gel from what looks like a toothpaste tube. Using the wet towel, he smears the paste over my entire palm. I watch his face, the hard set of his defined jaw, and a slight crease between his brows, as his concentration remains on my hand. After a few seconds, he wipes away the paste, and I glance down. My jaw drops before my gaze flicks between my skin and his eyes. I flex my palm, move my hand back and forth, and finally run a finger over my now blemish-free palm.

"How?" I ask.

"The gel is filled with nano technology that stitches your missing skin together with duplicate cells. It can find any wound and heal it. Yours were small, so it was quick and easy, but it will also work on larger wounds with time."

"Incredible." My voice is breathy as it leaves my lips.

I am still gawking at my hand when Andrin answers a knock on his door. Philomena stands in the doorway, a tray of food in hand. I give her a small wave before she bows, and the door closes. Andrin sets the tray on the coffee table in front of me before sitting on the couch.

"You should eat," He orders. "You did a lot today."

"Are we going to practice Aether Crossing again tonight? I'd rather not eat before that." The thought alone makes my stomach turn.

Andrin shakes his head. "No, using the spears was enough of a drain on your Aether for today. We don't want you to burn out. Now eat."

Despite knowing it will not be appetizing, I no longer resist. I am starving. I eat the usual gelatin and tofu cubes, accepting the blandness after so many meals. Last on the tray is a small foil package I haven't seen before. I pick it up and inspect the suspicious new item on the tray. A gasp slips out when I rip open the packaging. I look at Andrin to express my surprise, but he is already smiling, as if he's been awaiting my discovery.

My voice comes out higher than usual as I ask, "Is this mochi?"

His smile widens at my childlike tone. "Mochi ice cream. Apparently, there was a crate stored in our deep freezer. One of the cooks found it."

My heart warms slightly as I wonder if Oki is the cook who found it and thought of me.

I bring it to my lips but freeze. "Wait, have you had it before? It wouldn't be fair for me to take it if you've never tried it before."

I want it for myself, but after his help, I feel like the offer is the least I can do in thanks. Plus, after receiving training for my Aether almost every day since I woke up, I've grown to warm to him. Slightly. It still makes me angry if I think about why I'm here in the first place. Yet the more time I spend with him, the more I trust his genuine desire to help me. It's hard to be an angsty brat to someone who has doted on me and offered help at every turn.

"There's plenty more. I want you to have these." His beaming smile is infectious.

I don't need any more insistence, as I bite the sphere in half. My front teeth burn at the ice cream's freezing temperature, yet I salivate. Vanilla. Such a simple flavor, yet so sweet, velvety, and decadent. A moan rises in my throat. My eyes shoot open, my cheeks flushing. I hadn't even realized my eyes closed.

Andrin's lips are parted, his eyes sharp like a lion. Fierce. Alert. Hungry.

I swallow, urging the heat to leave my face. "It tastes excellent. Are you sure you don't want a taste?"

I want to bash my head against the wall. My brain is failing in its one job of filtering words before they come out of my mouth. A small smile creeps up the corner of his lips again.

"Perhaps later. I'm quite satisfied watching you enjoy it."

My body warms further at his words. Before I can say anything more embarrassing, I shove the other half of the mochi ice cream into my mouth. I pray it will cool me down. I stand up quickly, and Andrin follows. I need to leave. I refuse any attempt to process whatever that reaction was.

"Well, thanks for fixing my hand. And the food. And the mochi ice cream."

My words come out in breathy gasps. This is embarrassing. However, I can see the muscles of Andrin's chest rise and fall almost as rapidly as I breathe. I cuss as my shin knocks into the coffee table in my scrambled attempt to keep space between us.

"Of course. I'll make sure to get you more." Andrin's eyes remain locked on mine.

He still stands between me and the door, like a giant golden wall.

A computerized female voice blares across the room. "Make preparations for Star Gate passage. Orbital Station Rho will exit Star Gate Zeta Persei in one hour."

The announcement makes me jolt again, but Andrin only sighs in frustration.

"I have to go to the Pilot House for the transit. We'll only have another full day of travel before we arrive on Argos," Andrin explains.

I wipe my now blood-free, but sweaty hands against my bare thighs. "That's good. Soon we'll be on our way back to Earth."

I launch myself out of the room like it's on fire. I'm excited to be going home, but the butterflies in my stomach are unwelcome guests. I force myself to ignore the visceral reaction I had in Andrin's room. I feel entirely out of control.

It's embarrassing. I need to get some sleep. I need a cold shower.

I use the back of my hand to wipe the vomit from the corner of my mouth. I prefer a punch to the stomach over the roller coaster my internal organs are on. I have felt like crap since the Orbital Station took its rocky transit through the Star Gate last night. It was like being inside a washing machine rather than any vehicle. Trying to Aether Cross, however, feels infinitely worse.

Apparently, it's a side effect of forcing my atoms through a wormhole and reforming them on the other side. When Andrin had first explained Aether Crossing, it sounded unbelievable, yet simple. The brain-splitting migraine, which I am relatively certain actually causes my vomiting, is a side effect of creating the miniature wormhole. I have determined that Aether Crossing is neither believable nor simple.

"I want a break," I grumble.

My head is firmly planted between my knees as I sit on a training mat. I feel a presence sit down next to me, and a large hand begins to rub my back. Andrin's touch is firm but comforting. After a few moments, I feel well enough to lift my head. Izar drops a bucket and a heap of towels.

"This can be your break," Izar says.

I roll my eyes, but grab a towel to clean up my bile. "Next time, I'm aiming for you."

Izar snorts, leaving me to clean up my own vomit.

"It will get easier. It'll take practice and focus to channel your Aether." Andrin grabs a towel and starts helping me clean up.

I try to force a smile of gratitude as I say, "I feel like this is below what a Prince should be doing."

Andrin chuckles, "I'm sure most would be very shocked to see this. I don't mind if it's to help you."

A blush rises to my cheeks. I hope it restores color to my face instead of making me look like a tomato, as it usually does. We clean the floor quickly before standing in preparation. This time, Andrin takes my hand, and our matching vambraces clink together. My skin tingles at the contact.

I still haven't Aether Crossed. The best I have done is create the smallest wormhole, which felt more like insane heartburn. My body feels like the surface of a star. I am dripping so much sweat, I am not entirely convinced the bucket Izar brought over actually has water in it. The gallon of electrolytes I have drunk is the only reason I haven't passed out from dehydration.

Andrin's voice is soft as he instructs me. "Close your eyes. Take a deep breath and hold it. Don't let go of the air. Feel how your body reacts. Your heart rate should be increasing. You should start to feel the Aether inside your body building."

My heart is racing, and my lungs burn. I grit my teeth to keep from releasing any of the air. I feel like I am about to burst, and then—there, I feel—something like my blood is boiling just under the surface of my skin.

"Don't let go of the air! Now, imagine you're standing on the opposite corner of the mat. You must see it, feel it, believe it," Andrin insists.

The vambraces on my wrists burn like a hair curling iron—the corner. Need air.

Standing in the corner. Need air. Andrin drops my hand. Need air now.

"Exhale!" Andrin shouts.

A burst of air rushes out of my lungs, and pinpricks explode across my skin. I stumble, gasping for clean air. My eyes fly open as I grasp my knees with both hands.

"Aurora." Andrin's voice is soft, distant.

The searing pain of the vambraces burns ice cold. I look up towards Andrin's voice. He is on the other side of the mat. No.

With a joyous whoop, Andrin exclaims, "You did it!"

He smiles widely as his long legs quickly close the small distance between us. The distance I travelled.

I Aether Crossed.

"Bucket!" I gasp.

Izar rushes between Andrin and me just in time to shove the bucket into my hands. My head dives into the mostly empty bucket right as my knees buckle. Andrin's hands grip my shoulders to steady me as he slows my path to the ground. The second my knees hit, whatever remains in my stomach meets the bottom of the bucket.

A swat of a towel hits the back of my head, and I send Izar an obscene hand gesture in response. Andrin rubs my back again, just as he had done only minutes before. Thankfully, I have embarrassed myself enough with my early Aether Cross attempts that I no longer feel embarrassed about our weird encounter in his room last night. Well, mostly.

It takes me a few more minutes to realize my entire body is shaking. I'm shivering. I had been boiling before, but now I feel as if I have been wandering outside in the middle of winter, without any clothes on, for hours. An occasional muscle spasm sends a limb jolting in one direction or another. I sit back on my butt and let myself lean into Andrin's embrace, partially for warmth and partially because it's hard to keep myself up straight. I clean my face with the towel Izar so graciously got me, but I stay close to the ground.

"I can't believe I did that," I say to myself more than anyone else.

Andrin tucks some strands of loose hair away from my face. "You did great! I told you, you would get it."

"I didn't think you would develop this quickly. Let alone with that level of accuracy." Izar injects, his topaz eyes glow in narrow slants.

Between deep breaths, I ask, "How long did it take both of you to be able to do it without feeling like your body is going to rip itself apart?"

Andrin laughs, but Izar is the one who responds. "Years. It takes most aliens, even those capable of Aether manipulation, years to master. It took both of us months to do what you just did in a few short weeks."

"We were also very young when we started." Andrin adds. "Perhaps your body is more used to having an Aether reserve and expending it in small increments. That's how you're able to be so athletic and process information so quickly without much effort."

"I've never been able to do any of this before. Why can I now? Why do I feel so different here? Is it really just the food?" The skeptical tone of my voice sounds far more aggressive than I mean it to.

Izar pauses, as if also lost in thought. "The food helps. So does the air. We keep it highly ionized. Everything in the Orbital Station is designed to increase conductivity."

"So, Aether works like electricity?"

Izar rolls his head back and forth. "In some ways. It comes from the essence of the Universe, a time before Galaxia, when there were only the Gigas. Those with the closest bloodlines to the original species at the time of the Gigas are the most capable of manipulating Aether."

"What's a Gigas?" I ask.

"They are like the Titans of your Earth stories, but the bloodline theory is also a story," Andrin answers. "There's something else we use to amplify our Aether production. It's normally given to Perseus citizens throughout our childhoods, like a booster shot. We call it Astrobleme."

Curiosity makes me ask, "How? What's in it?"

"It has special metals with volatile ions that will mix with our blood. It helps DNA synchronize with Aether and manipulate electromagnetic fields with ease. That is, with time and regular doses." Andrin explains.

"And it's safe?"

Andrin nods. "When taken at regulated levels, yes. Like anything, too much is dangerous. All Persei had them growing up, so now it is part of our DNA; we only require an additional shot once a year."

"However, there are some pretty significant side effects if not administered appropriately." Izar injects with a bite.

Andrin and Izar exchange serious expressions. Both of their jaws set, eyes blazing. I watch their silent interaction with confusion and intrigue. Clearly, they have conflicting opinions on Astrobleme.

Andrin breaks the silence first. "You should get some dinner and go to sleep."

I nod, pushing myself up off the floor. The tremors of my body have finally ceased, but I feel completely depleted.

"And shower," Izar adds.

I stick my tongue out at him, to which he flashes his too-sharp feline grin.

Andrin calls out to me as I reach the airlock. "We will be finalizing the approach plan for Argos in the Pilot House if you need us. The approach will start early tomorrow morning if you'd like to watch."

I wave to both before closing the airlock door. Suspicion has replaced the nauseous feeling in my stomach. My body aches while I shower, but my mind is too distracted. The interaction between Andrin and Izar was strange.

After a week of training, I finally asked Izar how they communicated telepathically, and I instantly regretted it. In a howl of laughter, he informed me that telepathy is not a real skill. He assured me they have known each other for so long it is easy to communicate using only facial expressions. They are typically thick as thieves, but the topic of Astrobleme set Izar off.

We will arrive near Argos tomorrow. Then they will bring me back to Earth. Like most days, my thoughts return to my parents. This is the longest I have gone without contacting them. They must be worried since I deviated from my routine. I have surely been fired after abandoning my clients in Spain without any notice. Maybe I can get my job back if I tell them I was kidnapped. It's the truth.

I've been trying to find a way to make contact with those back on Earth, but all my attempts were futile. Yet Andrin received an order from his father, which means he has some way to contact the outside world. The only places I have not checked over the past few weeks that he frequents are the constantly manned Pilot House and Andrin's living spaces.

Since Andrin will be in the Pilot House with Izar, his office should be empty.

I dress quickly before sneaking down the hallway. It's after dinner time now, and the lights have turned red. No one else walks the halls. I quickly climb the ladder wells and find myself in front of Andrin's office door. I type the keypad code I watched him enter yesterday, and it slides open easily. A sting of shame shoots through me, knowing my trespass is a small form of betrayal in the fragile trust we have formed.

I push aside the shame as I push through the door. I rifle through his desk, and there are a few papers and notebooks, but nothing resembling a phone. I do not see any weird alien technology that could be a communication device, either, at least to my knowledge. With my hands on my hips, I stand in the middle of his office as if the answer will magically appear to me. Annoyed, I lean backwards, my hands bracing my weight on the desk. As my weight settles, I feel pressure release under my hand—a button. Quickly, I lift my hand, but a light flashes from the desk.

If this is some late alarm system, I am screwed. I have no good reason to be in here. I am clearly snooping. As the light flattens into a vertical sheet, I sigh in relief. I clutch my chest, attempting to steady my heart rate and breathe. It's just a regular hologram screen.

The screen displays a message, like an email view page. The message on the screen is boring, a set of numbers that reminds me of coordinates, under the name Argos. That is the planet we are supposed to arrive at tomorrow.

I move my fingers like a touch screen over the projection to make it scroll. The previous message in this chain appears. It is a casualty report. In the signature line, the title Lokhagos appears for a member of the Persei Guard. From the formatting, it reads more like a title than a name. Lokhagos must be a Persei military rank similar to Taxiarhos or Syntag, yet subordinate to the Persei Prince's position.

The casualty report recounts the death of their partner. My eyes fly over the blue text, the Aether in my blood tingles at the ends of my fingers. The Aether pulses as my eyes find a familiar word. Harpyiai. The Lokhagos reports that an unknown Harpyiai had arrived on Argos, argued with his partner in the middle of their mission, and then threw his partner into the water. The cause of death is stated as mauled to death by a herd of Scilla.

I pause. Scilla. That must be the invasive species harming Argos. Andrin had said he was going to Argos to finish the mission, but it might be dangerous. This message doesn't include what the guard and Harpyiai were arguing about. It doesn't say where the Harpyiai went. Could it still be on Argos? Does the guard know anything else? Is it possible that the Harpyiai I encountered and the one in this report are the same?

A name draws my attention from the display column of additional messages. I open a new message dialogue. My heart stops. My lungs seize.

> IMMEDIATE IMMEDIATE IMMEDIATE
> ATTN: ALL LIFEFORMS WITHIN GALAXIA
> FROM: IMPERIAL COMMODORE
> SUBJ: ANDROMEDA GALAXY HAS FALLEN
>
> REPORT ANY SIGHTINGS OF ROA MĒDEIA TO THE
>   IMPERIAL COMMODORE
> APPROXIMATE LOCATION: NQ1
> 1.64×10^9 AU FROM SAGITTARIUS A
> RIGHT ASCENSION: 14h 21m 20.64s
> DECLINATION: +78° 52' 08"
> TIME: UNKNOWN

I reread the projection, and again. They hang in the air like a mocking screen saver. This must be the message from the Commodore that made Andrin get me from Earth. He said I was from Andromeda, and Izar confirmed the Commodore sent the message. Except they also told me I was the last survivor of the entire galaxy.

Yet this message asks for Roa Mēdeia. My world shifts beneath my feet. The lost Mēdeian they are looking for is me, so that must be my real name. My name, my identity, none of it has been mine. I'm a stranger to myself. I cannot understand why Andrin hasn't told me who I am. What else could he be keeping from me?

A storm of emotions heats my skin, and a wave of dizziness almost overcomes me. Indefinable thoughts slip from my comprehension as I struggle to understand why I feel so distraught. The omission of my identity feels like a betrayal, while the revelation mimics a revealing of some withheld agency. I need time to process, to understand what this means for me.

Finally, my eyes fall from the now blurry lights, seeking the darkness of space outside the window. Tiny stars speckle my view; far enough away, they appear stagnant in the sky, despite our rapid transit through the cosmos. I let my mind drift to the worlds I have yet to discover. The galaxies I will never know.

I am not human.

I am an alien.

I am from a dead galaxy.

On Earth, I knew who I was. I knew what I wanted. Every second I spend in this Orbital Station threatens my increasingly fragile perception of reality. Yet every answer I discover leads me to more questions. Andrin and Izar have both been keeping secrets from me. They have seen this message and chose to keep the knowledge to themselves, knowledge about me. Why?

I'm from the Andromeda Galaxy.

I'm the last of my species, Roa Mēdeia, the lost Mēdeian.

I might not know much about my new world, but I will not let anyone stop me from finding the answers I'm seeking.

CHAPTER 10

A planet. More accurately, a planet and two stars, a bright blue star and a soft orange one. Argos is the stormy grey and black sphere that I will soon step foot on. A planet that is not my blue and green-smeared Earth. I expected to see a third star in the Algol system from the star charts I studied over the past few days, but I can't see it from our approach angle.

The daylight finally turns on hours after I have been awake, watching the planet approach. My nose is pressed to the window when the airlock opens behind me.

"That's Argos." Andrin steps close enough behind me that I can feel his breath on my ear. "Those two stars make up Algol as a binary star system. Algol A is the yellow star, and Algol B is the blue one."

I squint at the pale orange and the slightly smaller blue-white orbs of light. That completely contradicts what my studies had said. The blue star was supposed to be the primary, and the orange the secondary. Maybe the references were inaccurate. Surely the heir to the Constellation knows his system better than the database.

"Do you want to watch our approach?" Andrin offers.

I turn around to face him. He's close. I have to crank my head back all the way to see him. I remember that I'm only dressed in my baggy linen pajamas.

"I want to go." My voice comes out cracked, from its first use of the morning, and my nerves.

"Go?" His eyebrows rise as he looks back out the window. "To Argos?"

To Argos? Yes, that is what I meant. The email-like messages have been scrolling through my brain on a constant loop since I read them last night.

Andrin won't take me back to Earth yet. He says it's because I'm not safe while the Harpyiai is still searching for me. Andrin and Izar are about to go to Argos to see the living guard, the Lokhagos. The guard might be able to tell me more about the Harpyiai who was there.

I have to find a way back to Earth, and the first step is to figure out how to get rid of the bird-lady who is keeping me from my home. Andrin won't buy into my reasoning if it endangers me. Yet if he is going to keep secrets from me, I will do the same.

"Yes. I want to see it. Step foot on another planet. Before I go back to Earth, I want one last adventure. Please?"

I am shocked to hear the truth in my own words. I do want to see another planet. I became a travelling translator because I loved exploring new places. How could I miss this opportunity? My priority is getting answers from the Persei Guard already on Argos. Can't I want this for myself too?

Andrin's eyes meet mine again, his mouth pressed together in conflict. "Aurora, it could be dangerous. We're going there because someone was injured on the mission, and we need to make sure it's completed."

I cringe as he says my name. The name I may have told him. Yet out of everything he has revealed, he still keeps my actual name from me. Neither feels like my own now. I grind my teeth, forcing my tension through my molars as I think. He has revealed more information about Argos. He is not entirely lying to me. Perhaps he is trying to ease the number of shocking details I have to learn. He must have a reason to keep it from me, right? I push the tornado of thoughts to the back of my mind. I will have time to work through it all later, after I get down to Argos and talk to that guard.

"Please? I'll be careful. I've been training every day, and both you and Izar think I'm a protégée. Please? For me?" I make my voice sickly sweet.

I know I'm laying it on thick. My eyes widen as I plead with him. I see it; his resolve cracks as he sighs. He runs his hand through his dark brown curls and stares back out at the approaching stars.

"Okay," He agrees.

I squeal, surprising both of us when I throw my arms around his waist. It only lasts a second before I pull back. His eyes were wide, and his mouth parted again.

"Thank you." I cough out, now avoiding eye contact.

He nods and starts to walk towards my door. "I will have Philomena deliver a suit for you. Meet us in the Pilot House as soon as you can."

Philomena is quick to arrive. Her large eyes seem even wider with concern.

"Prince Andrin said you are going to Argos."

I send her a beaming smile as I gush, "Yes, isn't it great? I'm actually very excited."

She clasps my hands. The twig-like fingers curl around mine. She brings me close.

"You must be careful there. The galaxy is hazardous. Not all species will be happy to greet you." She warns.

I gently squeeze her fingers back. "It's okay. I'll be careful. I can't let this opportunity slip through my fingers."

She releases my hands but brushes the hair from my face. "So daring."

I smile at her as she steps back. There is something maternal about her. I do not know how old she is or how it relates to my age, but it is a preordained sense of comfort I get from her. The phrase she uses unknowingly helps conjure the memory of my own parents.

My father has always called me daring. His Daring Little Astronaut, when I was little, became his Daring World Traveler as I began exploring on my own. When I announced I wanted to be an astronaut, as a precocious eleven-year-old, he took me to an observatory. As we both gaze up at the stars, some projected and some through lenses, he began to quote Virgil.

"*Opta ardua pennis astra sequi.*" Of course, spoken in its original Latin.

I remember scrunching up my nose at the jumble of words. My dad often liked to quiz me, like he did his etymology students.

"The only word I recognize is stars," I whined.

He then chuckled, causing the wrinkles at the corners of his eyes to deepen. "It approximately translates to 'a desire to do the difficult-to-reach stars'. The colloquial expression 'reach for the stars' originates from that passage, *sic atur ad astra*, which means 'one's journey to the stars'."

I let out an exasperated sigh, "What's your point, Dad?"

I almost cringe at the memory of my pre-teenage attitude. Yet my father never took my angst too seriously. He had only slung his arm over my shoulder and brought me close to his chest. His finger poked my nose before pointing up to the fake sky.

"As long as you dare to do the difficult, you can achieve anything."

A smile grew across my lips, feeling determined I'd one day really see those stars. "Dare to do."

"*Opta ardua pennis astra sequi.*" My father's words echo through my memories.

"Dare to do," I mumble, the ghost of a smile still on my lips.

She tilts her head in confusion, but I shake my head and smile. By late high school, I had forgotten my desire to become an astronaut and had instead pursued my love of language. Somehow, little Aurora got to accomplish both her dreams, or maybe, the love for the stars was always the Roa part of me.

Philomena smiles back and pulls the airlock closed behind her. I inspect the white material she brought me. It seems like the same stretchy fabric as my workout clothes. I pull on the form-fitting, full-body suit and chunky mid-calf boots before I inspect myself in the mirror.

I resemble something between a tube of toothpaste and a morph suit. It is laughably stereotypical of what I would imagine an alien would wear. The skintight material hugs every curve of my body in a shocking way after wearing baggy clothing for the last few days. I notice the full, significant growth of my muscles for the first time; my thin runner's body has changed into a lean, sinewy build. My alien metabolism must really be working, as Izar had said.

After only a few more poses, I stop checking myself out in the mirror and finish getting ready. I finish splitting my hair and tying it into two French braids before I make my way to the Pilot House.

After typing in my own code, it opens, and I see Andrin and Izar standing side by side, staring at a holographic image of the solar system outside the sloped window. They are both dressed in similar morph suits, but the gold-plated football-style padding over their torsos and major muscle groups differs. They look like space travelers from a blockbuster movie.

"Do I get some cool body armor too?" They both turn to look at me, Andrin's eyes lingering.

Izar turns to speak first. "Why would you need—what are you wearing?"

Andrin steps forward then, his hands falling to my shoulders. "There are some on the table by the wall. There's also some food. We'll have to Aether Cross several times, and while we're connected, it will still take a draw from your Aether reserves."

Nerves prickle beneath my skin like the dance of both of our energies where his hands touch me. "Okay."

I keep my smile intact while I eavesdrop on the hushed argument behind me. I barely catch the sharp words between Izar and Andrin. I cannot tell precisely what they are saying, but Izar is clearly not happy that I will be joining them.

The argument ends quickly when Andrin joins my side and helps me strap the plates to my body. Despite their metal appearance, the plating is relatively light. My maneuverability is only partially restricted by the plates that cap off my joints. Andrin holds my hand, one at a time, as he secures a gold vambrace on each of my wrists again. We both keep our eyes firmly on the plating while he assists me. Once I am fully dressed, Andrin leads me back to the hologram.

"We can't bring the Orbital Station directly into the orbit of Algol stars. At best, it could cause the station to spin out of stabilization, and at worst, it could send us flying into the stars themselves. So, we have to Aether Cross from orbit on a Charging Pod to Argos and get back up here." Izar explains, his tone clipped.

"How long do we need to be down there for you two to do whatever it is you need to do again?" I ask.

"We need to deploy a water neutralization pod to make the water suitable again. We have a few locations to drop off, but it shouldn't take very long." Andrin explains.

I keep my tone light to hide the intention of my next question. "And the Persei Guard there will be helping you, too?"

I pretend not to see the look Izar shoots Andrin. "Yes, he should. Since you're coming, it would be helpful to bring your own pack with neutralization pods and food supplies. We can be more efficient that way."

I shrug. "Sure, of course, happy to help."

"You should grab a spear too," Izar says.

"Because of the Scillia?" His eyes flare, a combination of shock and anger on his face.

"Yes. Or if anything else tries to come after you. We've had years of experience training as warriors, but I'm sure you're more than capable of taking care of yourself, Princess." Izar snaps.

I rear back, shocked by Izar's aggression. He has never acted like this before. He's being cruel. With a sneer, he turns away from me. I shoot an exasperated look at Andrin, but he only gives me a sad excuse for a smile back. Clearly, Izar is not happy that I'm tagging along.

Andrin grabs my hand again, drawing my attention back towards him while Izar returns his attention to the hologram. "They want to keep the water toxic. If they see us trying to restore the water, I want you to be able to protect yourself."

Anxiety and anticipation fight for space in my stomach. "Exciting stuff."

"We have twenty minutes until we reach the optimal location to deploy a Charging Pod for Drop Off," Izar informs us as he moves his hands quickly around the rapidly changing image.

Andrin hands me a Nomex backpack while he and Izar grab their own. Then I am following them through the airlock, down the hallway, and down a ladder, depositing us in an open metal bay. The same bay I had almost opened before Izar caught me on my first day.

Various metal contraptions and containers line the cavernous walls. They continue to one of the walls and begin bringing supplies down from it. Andrin places items in front of me, and I pack the small backpack with everything there. It fills quickly, and by the time I pull it over my shoulders, it's surprisingly heavy. When Izar hands me a spear, it glows with a soft blue and white. He shows me how to collapse it so it can be strapped along the side of my bag.

"One last thing," Andrin says.

Andrin stands before me and places what appears to be a motorcycle helmet over my head. He checks the helmet's integrity by shifting it back and forth, forcing my head to turn with it. Once satisfied, his hands fall to my shoulders, and he grasps me firmly. His green eyes try their best to inspect my face through the helmet visor.

"You should be able to breathe down there, but it will help with the pressure difference. For your first trip, it's better to keep it on." He pauses, his eyes shifting slightly with concern. "Are you scared? You don't have to go if you've changed your mind."

My stomach has been flipping since I saw the brand-new planet this morning. A planet I did not even know existed until a few days before. My skin tingles, as if beta-alanine from pre-workout supplements is rushing through my bloodstream. Scared? Absolutely. The excitement crackling through me is overwhelming. Despite how deranged this entire experience has been, I cannot imagine doing anything differently now. I have to know more, see more, do more. I have to experience what else is out there. Gaining information about the Harpyiai was my original plan, but now, the idea of adventure is overwhelming.

I joke, "Fly me to the moon, Starman." My voice comes out slightly muffled inside the helmet.

Andrin blinks with his mouth slightly agape. "This isn't the Moon."

I roll my eyes. "Earth joke. Let's go to Argos."

Andrin flashes his smile and pulls on his own helmet. I feel like a superhero while I walk between the two of them to the end of the bay. We exit through the airlock I had tried to open when I first arrived. I purposely avoid eye contact with Izar. We find ourselves in a smaller airlock vestibule with only two tiny sets of windows and buttons along the walls. Izar presses buttons on the walls as the small room's lights begin to flash.

"Coordinates accepted. Pod 315 preparing for launch." The familiar computerized female voice from the announcement system fills the Pod around us.

A warning bell sounds before metal groans loudly. I feel a sudden tug at my feet. When I try to move them, I find my boots are stuck to the ground, like magnets holding me in place.

"Standby to launch in 3...2...1." The automated voice continues.

I look to Andrin in alarm, just as a sharp lurch sends me grasping for a wall. Instead, Andrin grabs my hand, steadying me as he stands straight up, completely unaffected.

"Launch successful. Time to Drop Point is two minutes and six seconds."

My brain empties of any intelligent thought. "Okay, one more time, how is this going to work?"

Andrin squeezes my hand, still held in his. "When we reach our Drop Off point, I will Aether Cross all of us to Argos. Just don't lock your knees and be careful to keep your tongue away from your teeth."

"My teeth?" I mumble, my tongue pressed against my front teeth.

"You don't want to bite your own tongue off if your teeth slam together." Izar's tone is taunting, like an older sibling. I will take a pestering sibling over his angry indifference any day.

Andrin ignores him. "It will feel like jumping off a single-floor building. When we land, your body will feel some impact. Keep your body loose, and it will absorb the impact just fine."

I run my tongue over my teeth again, my imagination filling my mouth with the coppery tang of blood. I shake off the feeling and turn back towards the small window of the door. A gasp slips from my lips.

The Orbital Station. It's as tall as a four-story building and just as long. Like a diamond, it is bulky in the center before thinning out on all sides. With a deranged laugh, I realize the shape reminds me of a kazoo. I am sure the large metal panels covering every surface except the windows used to be brilliant white, but the bottom and back of the Orbital Station are stained with scorch marks from the thrusters.

"Pod 315 has arrived at Drop Off point."

Another squeeze of my hand. "Ready?"

"You know, there's a famous quote on Earth about the first time a Human stepped foot on the moon. It goes, *One small step for man, one giant leap for mankind.*" I say more to myself than either of the men beside me.

I tense then relax every muscle in my body. My blood pumps through my body in an electric rhythm that thumps against my ears.

"I might not be included in mankind anymore, but this is closer to the stars than anyone from Earth has ever gone. I think this counts as stepping into the future."

PART 2

R. A. SANDS

CHAPTER 11

Blinding white light. Spinning. Every molecule in my body pulses and shakes. Hot, but so cold. It's like being split in two. Then, I am divided into an infinite number of smaller fractions of myself, and then collected. A tornado is weaving me back together—a second. A single moment, and it's all over.

A rush of air forces pressure against my chest, like a rollercoaster slamming to a halt. My eyes fly open, and I see slate-gray, rocky ground. Approaching. Fast. I release the tension in my taut muscles just in time for my feet to hit the ground. The pressure drives a rod of force through my bones, from the soles of my feet to my skull. My stomach surges, but I really do not want to throw up in this helmet.

I splay my fingers across the helmet until I can find a release button. Finally, I press a button, and the visor rises, letting a cool rush of air hit my face. I feel a pat on my hand, and I look over to see Andrin's hand tightly gripped in mine. Those pale green eyes search my face and body for any sign of injury.

"How do you feel? Are you okay?" Andrin asks.

The smooth control of his voice and gaze steadies my spinning world. I force myself to blink before tearing my gaze away to look around us. Izar is on my other side, already removing his pack. The ground is indeed slate-like. The geological makeup is unknown to me, an expanse of ridges and layers of lifeless rock. Steam rises from pools of gray-blue water at intervals. A few hundred yards away, a ridge juts into a span of water that extends to the visible horizon of Argos.

I'm on Argos.

A whole new planet.

I turn back to Andrin, a smile splitting across my face. "Never better."

Andrin flashes a smile back and takes off his own pack. Finally able to move my own body again, I follow suit. As we remove the packs, I see a tall, white-clad figure approaching us from the gray horizon. Andrin and Izar are busy pulling out forearm-sized tubes of water neutralization pods.

"Someone's coming," I say.

Andrin paused long enough to follow my line of sight. "That's the Lokhagos we are here to meet. A member of the Persei Guard."

Perfect. Exactly who I wanted to talk to.

Andrin stands and raises his arm. The guard jogs the rest of the distance on unbalanced legs. He bows his head to Andrin when he is a few feet away before hobbling the rest of the distance.

"By the Stars, Taxiarhos," the guard says to Andrin. "Thank you for coming to the aid of Argos."

Andrin steps in front of the guard so I can't see him while I pretend to remain busy reorganizing the neutralization pods between the bags with Izar. I try to crane my head beyond Andrin's large form to see what caused the guard to hobble. Is it the same guard who interacted with the Harpyiai?

I have to lean so far over that my fingers slip on the smooth surface of the cylindrical pod. It slides from my hand

and tumbles across the uneven surface with metallic clinks. With a few curses, Izar snatches it from the ground before I can, shooting me an exasperated look.

I shrink back at his ire, shrugging my shoulders. "Sorry."

Izar only shakes his head at me, scoffing. His frustration at me digs at something in my chest. While I have grown used to his grand emotional swings, his silent discontent hurts more.

Andrin returns, the guard in tow, redirecting my attention back to him and the mission.

"We have a lot of ground to cover in this region before we hit our next Drop Point. I'm going to hit the active zone with the Lokhagos, since he knows the area well. Izar, I want you stay within a hundred-meter radius of here so you can also keep an eye on Aurora."

I open my mouth to protest, but Izar speaks first.

"Have the Lokhagos show us on a map which pools are still active. Then have him stay behind to babysit Aurora. You and I can cover far more ground, much faster, considering the Lokhagos' current condition."

Heat flares across my face, and my Aether sparks beneath my skin. The Universal Language they both speak takes my brain a few seconds longer to translate, so I cannot respond as quickly. I clash my teeth together so hard I'm surprised I don't crack a molar. Izar could just come out and say he doesn't want to be around me. He doesn't have to say I need a babysitter.

"Syntag, thank you for your suggestion," Andrin says.

Yet his voice carries a deep resonance, conveying his true feelings. Izar stepped over the line. While they may be lifelong friends, Andrin is his superior. Izar not only disregarded a direct order in front of a subordinate, but he also tactlessly demanded a new plan.

Andrin turns to me, his voice calm and smooth as he asks, "Aurora, would you be comfortable staying with the Lokhagos? He is a good guard. He has done good work here on Argos. It's up to you."

The guard nods several times as he mumbles a thank-you in his native language, which my brain slowly unscrambles. I look back at Andrin and find his pale green eyes boring into mine. The steadiness of his gaze warms my skin and makes my heart race.

"Yes, I am okay with that," I say in the broken Universal Language I've foolishly neglected to study over the last few weeks.

Clearly, this is the language I will need to use when communicating with the guard. I wish I had practiced it more on the Orbital Station. I understand it better than I speak it, as has been the pattern in most of my cases of learning a new language. At least staying with the guard will help me gather more information about the Harpyiai. Although in the current moment, I want to get away from Izar's attitude and how Andrin is making me feel.

Andrin gives a firm nod before turning back to the Lokhagos. "Alright, tell me where the active zones are."

Before long, Andrin and Izar head off for the horizon with their packs full of neutralization pods. The Lokhagos picks up two long pods from the remaining pile and begins walking in the opposite direction. The Persei male favors his left leg; his right is clearly injured. This must be the one who interacted with the Harpyiai. I grab two of my own pods and jog after him. Only the scuffing sounds of our boots on uneven stone ground keep us company.

"What happened to your leg?" I ask.

An extra shuffle is added to the guard's step before he looks over at me. "I was stationed here with another guard. We were attacked."

"Attacked by the aliens here?" I try to recall the name of the invasive species. "The Scilla?"

Instead of answering, his boots halt before a pool of water. He opens the canister before letting it fall into the water. Steam rises from the pool, thick enough that I must kneel beside it to see in. The neutralization pod sinks to the bottom of the pool, no more than ten feet deep. A white cloud billows from the canister, then dissolves in the water. The longer I watch, the more I see.

Small, corkscrew-shaped silver worms begin to float to the surface. Soon, almost the entire surface is covered in metallic worms. I stand up to make sure I don't encounter any parasites.

"It wasn't the Scilla." His voice sounds more distant.

The Lokhagos moves on to the next pool before the white substance has entirely dissipated.

"I thought I read a report about a Persei Guard being attacked by a Scilla." I try to make it sound as if it is normal for me to be reading reports. "Was that the other guard?"

How many guards could really be stationed on this barren planet? Why would Andrin get ordered here to help if there is a whole group stationed here?

The Lokhagos nearly stumbles. As if the memories increase the pain of his hidden injury. His spine stiffens before he pulls himself up straight and turns to me this time.

"The Scilla did not attack him out of nowhere; a Harpyiai flung him into a herd of starving Scilla to be mauled to death. He did not have a fighting chance. He was torn apart." The horror drips from his voice.

"I'm—I'm so sorry. That's horrible," I stutter out.

His shoulder rises and falls. His chest puffed out as if preparing to fight again. I can't help but let my eyes drift down to his injured leg. He catches my stare, and his anger turns on me.

"This was a present from the Harpyiai. After she threw my friend into the sea, she dug her talons into my leg. Tore through muscles, ligaments, tendons, everything. All while squawking about some bright light."

The guard deposits another pod into the next pool. The swirling parasites rise in the water once more. Bright light? What does the Harpyiai want with a light? Was she talking about a star? Perhaps the Harpyiai the guards interacted with is different from the one that had found me. I guess it was silly to think there could only be one causing havoc within Galaxia.

I look away from the parasite-filled pool to see that the Lokhagos has already made it halfway to the next pool. Without any neutralization pods in his arms, he can move much faster. I have to jog to catch up with him.

"So, where and what was this light she was searching for?" I ask.

The guard huffs before he begins to pull the neutralization pods out of my arms.

"Look, I do not know. He did not know either. When the Harpyiai did not get the answers she wanted, she destroyed the rest of our neutralization pods and threw him into the water to be eaten."

He yanks the last canister out of my hand. Startled, I release it, unaware I have been clutching it so tightly. The sudden lack of resistance sends him stumbling backwards, and the canister on the top of the stack in his arms slides off. The metallic canister clunks as it repeatedly hits the stone floor. As it bounces into the air again, the pod's seal ruptures, white grains of a mysterious substance spilling out.

I stoop low to refill the canister when the guard shouts, "Do not touch it!"

Freezing in my crouched position, I look between the Lokhagos and the pile of granulated sugar. His face reveals his trepidation, so I put my hands up and rise.

"Sorry."

The guard continues to grumble under his breath, "Do you have any more questions about how I lost my best friend? I have answered enough questions. I did not realize they would send the prince's whore to interrogate me."

Anger flares through my body. White hot and searing. I have to clamp down on my teeth, so I don't snap right away. My Aether sizzles just beneath my skin, ready to fry.

"I am not the prince's whore. I'm sorry you lost your friend; I can't imagine your pain. You should, however, reconsider how you talk to others, because I can put you on the ground without any help from the prince."

My anger flares hot enough that I feel a pulse of Aether slip from my control. It is more than I have ever felt. I cannot contain it. It is not like the small static electric shocks between my fingers, but its release is still visible like a heatwave pulsing through the air in all directions around me. When it reaches the guard, he stumbles, as if he has been pushed. Fear flashes across his face.

"I—I apologize—I did not—" He stammers as he scrambles backwards.

I keep my voice stern and powerful. "Finish deploying the pods so we can get back to the intercept point."

He nods and hurries to finish his work. I force my spine to stay stiff. I cannot let him know I'm just as scared. I don't know what I did. I don't know how I did it.

Once he finishes deploying the pods, we quickly return to the intercept point, keeping plenty of space between us. After an awkward period of waiting, Izar and Andrin finally return. I force a pleasant smile back on my face when Andrin does his quick visual inspection of me.

"We can handle the second and third active regions of Argos you showed me on the map earlier. You should head back to your base camp, pack up, and prepare for extraction. Good work here, Lokhagos."

"Thank you, Taxiarhos. I apologize for any disrespect." The Lokhagos quickly nods before hobbling back in the direction he came from when we first arrived.

Slowly, I turn back to Izar and Andrin. Both of them inspect me with a mix of skepticism and suspicion. I was planning not to share any of that interaction with Andrin or Izar. A sheepish smile spreads across my face.

"I don't think we're going to be pen pals."

"You're a troublemaker." The mockery is thick in Izar's voice. "Put your mask back down."

With false bravado, I flash them both a mischievous smirk before slamming the visor back down. As they continue to analyze me, I throw up a mock salute. Finally satisfied, Andrin grabs my hand, the vambraces on both of our arms glowing. Izar places his hand on my shoulder, and they nod to each other. A flash of light, and we are spinning.

CHAPTER 12

The landing this time feels less harsh on my joints, though I feel more drained. Neither Andrin nor Izar seems as impacted by the Aether Cross as I am.

"This time, will you stay by the packs?" Andrin asks.

I nod. "Yeah, I need a breather anyway."

He sighs before releasing my hand. Maybe it's the Aether Cross, perhaps it is the pulse of Aether I accidentally launched at the Persei Guard, but I'm exhausted. Sitting on the rough ground, I take the time to eat and drink. Thankfully, the nutrition bars work quickly. When I tilt my head up, the small blue star is stacked directly on top of the larger orange one. We must be in a very different part of Argos. The sky had seemed much brighter with both large stars on either side of the horizon when we first landed near the guard.

I take the time to consider the Persei Guards' words, ignoring the 'whore' comment. The Harpyiai is searching for a light. Perhaps the Harpyiai being on Earth was just a coincidence. The Harpyiai was in Argos before Andrin got the task to go there. In such a large galaxy, it must be a coincidence.

Andrin helps me up when they return. We strap the backpacks on, and the visors go down. Andrin takes my hand, with Izar on my shoulder again. I squeeze my eyes to avoid the bright light, but I can still see it behind my eyelids. The spinning doesn't feel as bad this time, but I still stumble when we land. My body feels like noodles. Izar has to hold me by the shoulder so I don't fall to the ground.

"Are you going to be okay here?" Andrin continues holding my arm while Izar starts to unpack.

I pat his hand now that I have regained my equilibrium. "I'm okay. I'm just going to take in the sights. Enjoy a little walk on the dark side of the moon."

Andrin pauses before releasing my arm. "Is that another Earth joke?"

A smile breaks across my face. "You catch on quick."

He returns the smile before grabbing the rest of the pods. Izar and Andrin move quickly to finish the job. I take off my pack and take a slow spin around.

I thought Aether Crossing to another planet would be a lot more exciting. Maybe on a planet that has more than plain rock and steamy water, it would be more fun. The stones look just like Earth's rocks. The water pools remind me of travel vlogs of Iceland's hot springs. I'd been excited to try them on my next work assignment that was supposed to be on the island. I won't be touching these hot springs; the silver parasites give me the creeps.

I never thought being on another planet could be boring.

Just above the horizon, Persei B sits directly in the center of Persei A. A small pin prick of blue in the center of the orange orb. It is darker now, most of the light absent, except for the celestial glow and its reflection on the dark ocean. Here, the sea comes right up to the rock; there is no sharp cliff drop off. Leaving the packs in our landing spot, I head towards the shore—small puddles form in divots in the rock like little tide pools. Crouching down, more colors come into focus.

Iridescent purples and greens flicker in the pseudo-sunset. Shells. There are shells. The shells are moving. Tiny crustaceans are crawling along the small tide pool. Something curly moves too, dark curls like some type of vegetation.

There is life here. In this small tide pool, there is the beginning of a whole ecosystem. It's miraculous. Argos isn't barren after all.

There are so many tide pools here, between the ocean and me. It must be low tide for all these to be exposed. I edge closer to the sea, inspecting as many of the pools as I can. They are shallow, unlike the large, steamy pools where Andrin and Izar are depositing the neutralization pods. These must not be affected in the same way. Some are empty, but many harbor the same tiny creatures, and a few host another shiny, pearl-colored crustacean.

I carefully place myself at the edge of the receding tide so my boots won't get wet. The water is too dark to see more than a few feet out, probably because of the slate gray rock that surely lies below. I breathe in through my nose as I stare out at the great grey expanse. Instead of the briny salt air of the sea back on Earth, this air smells musty and old. I notice there is no wind, nothing to stir the stale air. Besides the movement of the tides, there is minimal movement across the water, no crests or troughs of waves. Much like the stale smell, the planet itself seems stagnant.

I turn back towards the packs, considering returning to them while my companions finish their tasks. Yet that idea seems just as dull as staring out at the flat water. Far off on the horizon, I can barely make out Andrin and Izar, moving from one water pool to another. As if sensing my attention, Andrin turns towards me. Instead of the charming smile I have grown accustomed to, he goes rigid in his crouched position. A moment later, he shoots up, his back rod straight.

A spray of water splashes up the back of my boots. I take a step further up the rocks to keep the waves from reaching me again. Andrin begins walking back towards me, raising his hands above his head. Despite his mouth opening in wide shapes to yell, he is too far away for me to hear. I continue my steps and decide to meet him halfway when another wave splashes against the back of my legs. I bend to wipe away the excess water that has reached the crease of my knees.

My blood chills. How are waves reaching the rocks when the sea is flat? There shouldn't be waves. My hand doesn't reach my legs.

Long webbed fingers claw into the soft flesh of my bicep with their wet talons.

Andrin's face burns rose gold from the exertion of his belting screams.

My eyes take in a thick arm, its smooth, silvery-blue scales connected to the hand just before it tugs. I slam into the ground on my side, landing hard on my shoulder, elbow, and hip. While the sharp pain ricochets up my body, another pull scrapes me along the rocks. The sharp stones cut into my flesh as I'm dragged across the surface. My head touches water. Cold. Very cold. My hair is instantly drenched, sending a jolt of panic through my body.

Move.

I have to move.

My head, my face, my only way to breathe is about to be pulled into the water.

I slam my heels into the ground and push with all the strength in my legs. I force resistance against the alien's pull, which causes a pop of pain in my shoulder that is connected to my captured arm. With a kick of my foot, I flip onto my stomach and tug back on my arm.

Mistake.

Big mistake. The enormity of my mistake is palpable as the thing comes into view.

Thing, being an accurate description.

Two heads release an ear-piercing scream and an overpowering smell of decay. The mouth of each head is wide open, revealing three long fangs jutting beneath short snouts. Between the long fangs are small, razor-sharp teeth that fill the rest of the mandible. The snarling, decay-scented jaws are bigger than my own head. Two sets of eyes track my every movement, one set far back on each head. The eyes blink. In a synchronized movement, three sets of eyelids slide over each yellow orb. Both heads are rounded, then slope into a large mass of the body that must be at least two meters long. Its torso is tube-like, except where it branches into the arms that are still gripping my bicep, hard enough to draw blood.

The red begins to seep through the white fabric of my suit. As if it can smell my blood, the alien's nostrils flare and its body contorts. It's like a grotesque combination of a leopard seal and an alligator.

A massive tail fin slaps the water. In a quick, yanking motion, its muscled form pulls us both closer to the water. It's nearly submerged. I plant my hand on the slippery rocks, desperately trying to keep my face out of the water.

I have no idea what this thing is, but if I had a guess, it would be one of the Scilla aliens they had warned me about before our Cross. My imagination floods my vision, the well-trained Persei Guard being devoured by these monsters after the Harpyiai had thrown him into the water: blood and flesh and teeth and water.

Andrin's screams clear the visual from my brain and bring me back to my current nightmare—Izar's with him. I just need to hold on. I have to stay out of the water. I might be able to fight the Scilla off for a short time on my own, but if it pulls me into the water, I'm done for.

Flexing my abdominal muscles, I draw my knees up so I'm kneeling. The sunset of the dual stars sets a glimmer of light against my vambraces. The metal vambraces. I take my arm and raise it above my head before slamming it into the claws gripping my arm. Ripping flesh and fabric away, the alien releases my arm. It screams again. Snarling a blood thirsty call, it whips both heads around furiously. The salty water sears, hot through my open wound. Another splash of water.

Footsteps. Pounding footsteps. Both Andrin and Izar run to my aid.

More splashes of water. Out of the water come two more Scilla. Six heads ready to bite my limbs off, summoned like sharks to my blood in the water.

One of the heads from the first Scilla snaps towards me, towards the hand still bracing myself to stay above the water. My blood pounds through my veins. Electric and alive. Something I might not be for much longer. I don't think, just move. I hold my arm up to protect my face, blocking my face with my forearm like Izar had taught me while sparring. Jaws snap down on my arm. Instead of pain, I only feel pressure. A screech of metal gives me relief. The jaw firmly latched onto my metal vambrace, instead of my weak flesh.

"Aurora!" Andrin's words are clear as he comes closer.

A cry of relief falls from my mouth. They are so close. Yet the other two Scilla are closer. The second head of the original

Scilla is even closer yet. The second head comes for me. This is it. The Universe is punishing me with a dramatic death for calling the planet boring.

No. No, I refuse to die in the jaws of a monster. I have travelled through space. A flood of indigent pride pushes past my paralyzing fear. I survived a galaxy exploding. Anger at this galaxy and those who brought me into this mess, away from my peaceful planet Earth, rushes to the surface. It will not end like this.

I will not end like this.

Light.

Bright light erupts from both of my vambraces. The jaw latches around the vambrace, then explodes. Purple blood sprays across my face and body. I spit the putrid clam-like taste from my mouth. The remnants of the creature's neck lay slumped like a limp noodle. The second head lurches to the side before it flops back into the water. Kill one head, kill the whole Scilla.

Relief floods me as the adrenaline still pumping in my blood forces shaky convulsions through my limbs.

Four heads scream. The other two water monsters splash frantically as they swim towards the rocky shore. There's no time for relief.

Hands with a familiar electric pulse grab my shaking form. Andrin slams the visor down on my helmet before lifting me over his shoulder. Then he runs us towards the packs. The pounding of his footsteps sends pain ricocheting up my spine as it absorbs the impact. Izar has already reached them and is running back towards us. Both he and Andrin still hold a spear in their free hands. Once the three of us collide, Izar grabs Andrin's shoulder.

Screams.

R. A. SANDS

Hundreds of those high-pitched Scilla screams.
I welcome the bright flash and the spinning.

CHAPTER 13

The landing is rough. The helmet is suffocating. Andrin slides me off his shoulder and sets me on the floor, where I can lean against the wall. I slap my hands repeatedly against my helmet, and he takes the hint to remove it from me. Slamming my head back against the wall of the charging pad, I gasp for breath. Andrin kneels in front of me, checking for damage. I don't have the energy to tell him it's only my arm. The slow thump of blood pulses through my open wound. Cold, I'm very cold. My hair and bodysuit are drenched in cold seawater.

Cold sea water and blood. My blood. The blood of an alien I killed. I have never killed anything before, aside from maybe a few insects that have gotten into my house. Before Andrin attacked me, I had never even hit someone outside of training. However, this is different. Killing the Scilla is different. Bone-rattling tremors rack my body.

"Pod 315 prepared for docking." The female computer voice announces.

Andrin wraps his arms around my torso and cups the back of my head before a sharp jolt rocks the pod.

Andrin can barely manage his own whisper as he says, "Close your eyes." It's not a difficult task to complete.

"Pod 315 prepared for decontamination."

A mist of liquid falls over us, before a gust of air and light shines around us. With my eyes closed, I assume it's like the ultraviolet decontamination light used in the showers onboard. I grind my teeth at the sting of the liquid on my arm. My guess, it's hydrogen peroxide, the way my wound bubbles. A few more beeps, and the pod's airlock door opens. Andrin tries to scoop me up in his arms, but I push him back.

"I got it," I argue with a clipped tone.

He lets me brace myself against him so I can stand on my own. I grind my teeth with the effort. My vision spots. My teeth slip, and I bite into my own cheek. The taste of blood in my mouth makes me want to gag. I am a murderer. I killed a living creature. I swallow the blood, refusing to let the growing crowd of aliens around us see me any weaker.

I ignore the sounds around me and stumble towards my room. I need to get clean, I need to sleep. Pretend that today didn't happen. Andrin helps me all the way to my room, but I hold my hand against his chest so he can't enter.

"Aurora, you need help!" I shake my head, and he continues to protest, "Izar went to get Philomena. Will you at least let her treat your arm?"

"Yes. Only her." I surrender.

Andrin's voice drops. "Aurora, I'm worried—"

I don't listen to whatever else he has to say. I turn from the door, uncaring if he has closed the airlock or not, as I begin to tear off my clothes. The white spandex is soaked and dirty, peeling off my skin like a used bandage. A howl rips from my throat as I pull it down my injured arm. Tears in the fabric have bonded to my clotted blood already. As I tear it from my flesh, the wound begins to weep blood again.

I'm trembling, hard enough that I begin to shake. I seethe as I force my fingers to press the shower buttons. The hot flash of water burns as it hits my skin. My teeth grind together as I attempt to muffle my cries as the soap coats my body and washes away the seawater and filth.

I killed that thing.

I killed the Scilla.

I had to. It was going to rip my arm off. It was going to pull me into the water and maul me like the Persei Guard. Tears streak down my cheeks like blood down my body.

I killed an animal today. Something with a herd based on the screams of the others in the sea. It could have been a parent. It could have been a baby Scilla.

I deserve the pain in my arm for taking a life.

I hold myself up against the metal wall of the shower while the tornado of air dries me. The ultraviolet light reignites the fire in the wound of my arm. My body shakes like a leaf. I stumble out of the bathroom to see a frightened Philomena standing in my room. I want to collapse with grief, pain, and relief when I see her.

She holds out white linen clothes and carefully helps me dress before sitting me on the bed. My eyes sting with unshed tears as she pulls my right arm from my body. I can't look at the wound while she tends to it. A stinging sensation follows a misted spray, then she wraps my arm in gauze. In an effort to distract myself, I look out the window at the stars. Algol and its two-star system are mocking me in a technicolor blur.

"You were not careful, Princess," Philomena chides.

"No, I was not." A scratchy laugh leaves my throat. "Why— why do you call me Princess even when I tell you not to?"

Her spindly fingers pause, only for a moment. I turn my head enough to see her large eyes watching me. Her mouth is parted, as if deciding whether to tell the truth or not.

I attempt another method of questioning. "Does the name Roa Mēdeia mean anything to you?"

The name sounds strange yet familiar. I know it belongs to me, but it still doesn't quite feel like mine.

"Yes. She is the lost Princess of the Andromeda Galaxy," Philamena says carefully.

The Commodore's message sparked all of this. When I saw it, I knew. I saw the message and knew it was the one that referenced me. I knew my given name was Roa Mēdeia. With Philomena's insistence on calling me Princess, I knew it was no accident. I just need her confirmation to know for sure.

"Does that have anything to do with why you call me Princess?" I release a hiss as her hands tighten on my arm. "Is it because I am Roa?"

Her eyes flash in surprise. "How—"

I grit my teeth as I turn back towards the window, my body in too much pain to enjoy my small victory. "I'm nosy, you know that."

"We were sworn to secrecy. Not everyone knows, but—" She continues her treatment of my arm. "But I am loyal to you, Princess. To you, and your fallen Galaxy."

I can't believe it has taken me this long to put it together. Especially with my Aether manipulation. Andrin can manipulate Aether because he is the heir of a constellation, close to a Gigas bloodline. Between the Aether and the Commodore's interest in me, I shouldn't be surprised I'm some type of royalty in another galaxy.

"Thank you, Philomena. Can we keep my knowledge of my true identity a secret between us?

"Of course." She finishes her movement by my arm and stands. "How else may I serve you?"

My eyes are already drifting shut. Pain, exhaustion, and guilt flood my bloodstream now that the adrenaline has worn off. She answered my most important question. This entire time, I have been asking why. Why did Andrin take me from Earth? He says it is because his father told him about me. Why did his father, the king of an entire constellation, care enough about me to send his son to retrieve me personally? I have a hard time believing it is so that his son can play hero.

A lot of resources have been spent to track me down, all based on a theory about what Aether capabilities I might possess. What is the real reason the Imperial Commodore is searching for me? Surely one alien girl from a destroyed galaxy cannot mean much to the Commodore of an entire flourishing galaxy.

"Just one thing. I want to send a message back to the Commodore."

Philomena leans in towards me. "What is your message?"

I open my mouth, but my eyes have already slid closed. They are heavy. So heavy.

Fire crawls inside my wound. Tiny pinches nip at my nerves. A gasping scream rips me from my sleep. My body is hot. I am burning up, my linen clothes soaked in sweat. The pain—

There is something wrong with my arm. The wound thumps with my racing heartbeat. It is beyond the lacerations from the claw marks. There is something inside of me. I sit up, tearing the gauze away from my arm. The scabbing wound rips open again. The surface wound is nothing compared to whatever eats at my muscles and ligaments. I scrub away the blood with the crumpled gauze in desperation. It crawls out.

A tiny green gem crawls out from my wound.

I don't recognize the blood-curdling scream that leaves my lips. I tumble out of the poor excuse for a bed and half crawl towards the door. The airlock handle is significantly heavier when I'm weakened and can use only one arm. The red lights in the hallway blur my vision further. I brace myself against the wall, desperate to find help.

Finally, someone enters the hall. I cannot make out what they are saying. The language is too difficult for my weary brain to decipher. My mouth gaps like a fish. The barrel-chested alien runs away.

I slump against the wall. More of the green gems crawl from my wound. Shiny green and red lights. It's like Christmas time in America.

"Aurora! What is—what—"

Then I'm floating. Green, Red, and Gold. The colors blur in the hallway until I'm lying down again.

"I'm sorry, this is going to hurt," Andrin's soft voice whispers in my ear.

Liquid fire engulfs my arm. I snarl and try to push him away. He only holds my arm still as the wound bubbles. Oh god. Oh—the pain is—the green gems crawl out of my wound like people fleeing a burning building. Grinding my teeth together, I hiss through the pain. I peel my eyelids open to see Andrin kneeling beside me, his golden features furrowed in concern.

"You should have let me treat you when we first got back. This species isn't even supposed to be on Argos, but I would have caught it if you let me help you," Andrin huffs. "They wouldn't have hatched and fed if you had let me check your wound in the first place. If you weren't so impulsive—"

Shiny green bugs the size of ticks crawl out of my wound, which bubbles with crusted, silver blood.

"I didn't do it because I'm impulsive." I hiss between deep breaths.

Andrin picks each bug out of my wound with a pair of tweezers as they surface. It's a quick movement of pick, crush, drop into a silver bowl, wipe the tweezers with a rag, then pick again.

"You are impulsive." He mutters.

A noise I can only equate to a snarl escapes the back of my throat. "Yes, I know I'm impulsive. It's not why—"

Andrin cuts me off. "What I can't figure out is why you were so angry with me about it that you wouldn't get properly treated for a wound your impulsiveness led to."

Now, I interrupt back. "It wasn't because I was angry with you. It was because of me."

A string of curses leaves my mouth as he pours the silver liquid from the brown bottle again, and my vision swims. Nearly hyperventilating, I drop my head back on the pillow.

"You're angry at yourself?" He asks in a quiet voice.

I answer in a grave whisper. "I killed it. I killed that thing."

I feel him wipe my skin around the wound dry before wrapping it repeatedly.

"You're punishing yourself." Andrin sighs. "You had to kill it. The Scilla are a vicious species; you're lucky you walked away at all."

"But if I had stayed away from the water, if I weren't so curious, if I had just stayed on this stupid Orbital Station, none of this would have happened."

"Maybe, but what's done is done. You have to accept it was necessary and let yourself heal." He covers me in a blanket, my tired eyes unable to stay open to inspect my surroundings.

His words don't comfort me. I had killed the Scilla without meaning to. I just wanted to survive. I thought I wanted to hurt the Harpyiai too, but can I really? The Aether that courses through my veins is dangerous. Maybe all the aliens in Galaxia aren't interested in using my power, but in stopping me. To kill me before I become a monster.

The screams of the Scilla echo in my head as my weak body pulls me to an unconscious oblivion.

A pinch on my arm startles me awake before a soothing warmth washes over my body. A soft blue light fills the room as my eyes drift closed again.

CHAPTER 14

Saffron and sea salt. I wake and stretch my stiff body. The sheets feel cool and silky beneath my dry hands. I blink my sleepy eyes. My sheets should be scratchy. I'm not in my bed. My body is no longer in searing pain. I feel—surprisingly well rested and reinvigorated.

I am definitely not in my bed. The door to the bedroom is open, and the view of a familiar living room helps fill in the blanks. I'm in Andrin's bed. Thankfully, alone.

"Andrin?" I call out, hoping he's the only one out there.

I hear a shuffling from the other room before a shirtless Andrin appears in the door. His dark curls are bed ruffled. He stretches in the doorway, his arms flexing as his stomach grows taut.

"How are you feeling?" He asks with a sleepy voice.

My eyes shoot to his face, a blush rising on my cheeks, knowing I have been caught staring. "Fine. Weirdly good, actually."

Andrin smiles, the sleepiness leaving his features. "That's good. It means the medicine did its job."

"Thank you for helping me yesterday. I'm sorry I took your bed."

He sits on the edge of the bed, close enough to touch me, but doesn't. "That was the least of my concerns. You really worried me, you know."

I wince. "I don't feel well enough for another lecture."

Andrin chuckles. "Fine, the lecture can come later. Can I make sure everything is healing right? Especially with the parasites I pulled from your arm in the middle of the night. Let's just hope I found them all. You don't want to know what will happen if one of them reaches maturity inside your arm."

I nod, too disgusted and ashamed to retort with my usual witty remark. I lift my arm and watch as he undoes the bandage.

"What were those things?" I ask.

"The thing that clawed your arm or the things that almost ate you from the inside out?"

I purse my lips, deciding I prefer it when I'm the sassy one. "The bugs."

"Parasites. Another invasive species that must have started thriving in the water on Argos, thanks to the Scilla that keep it acidic. The ramifications of allowing the Scilla to live are vast for the Algol system. Without that water source, planets within the Algol system will have to pull resources from other systems or halt their production and trade with the rest of the Constellation."

I open my mouth to speak, but the sight of my wound makes my stomach curdle. Thick ridges and valleys of flesh make a map down my upper arm. Where raw bloody flesh should have been, gunmetal grey stalactites grow out of my skin instead.

"Gross! What's happening to my skin!" I exclaim.

Andrin holds my forearm to keep me from moving. "It's okay, it's just silver nitrate. The claw wounds went deep. I used it to cauterize and disinfect your wounds. They do this on Earth, too."

I only grunt in response, still looking at the very alien-like things sprouting from my skin. Andrin takes a small bottle and sprays cold vapor over my arm. He grabs a new set of bandages and starts to rewrap my arm.

With enthusiasm, he remarks on my progress. "With how fast your metabolism and regeneration have been progressing, I think you'll be healed up in no time."

He pats my forearm before his fingers slide down, until they are intertwined with mine. My eyes widen at the gesture. When I search his face, a slight rose gold hue dons his cheeks. His hand warms my chilled fingers. Beyond the physical warmth, the affectionate touch is jarringly comforting after such a chaotic experience. I ignore the extra crackle of Aether in the space between our skin. He has been nothing but lovely to me since I arrived here. I mentally cringe, since he abducted me and brought me here. However, I seize every chance to direct my anger at him as a form of punishment for my kidnapping and exposing anything extraterrestrial.

"I have to tell you something," Andrin says, pulling me from my thoughts with a squeeze of my fingers. "We aren't going back to Earth."

Hot anger instantly boils my blood. "Why not?"

Andrin dips his head. "After what happened on Argos, my father was very upset. He considered it a mission failure."

I grind my teeth. A mission failure, because I almost got my arm bitten off. They must have been close to finishing deploying the neutralization pods when I was attacked. How could it be called a failed mission?

"He is sending me to Sarpedon, a planet near Epsilon. There is an issue with the power plant there. To make it to

Sarpedon, we have to restock the Orbital Station on the colony planet Seriphus. Seriphus is all the way in the Delta Persei star system. I can't bring you back to Earth yet."

My jaw aches from grinding my teeth. "Why not? Just go there after dropping me off."

"There aren't any other spacecraft capable of the mission. All others are either fulfilling requisitions for the Imperial Fleet or are broken. He overrode the navigation system. It's partially a punishment for me. When I failed to eradicate the Scilla, it was a failure to keep our Constellation safe, to make sure it would prosper." Andrin squeezes my fingers tighter, his eyes search for mine pleadingly. "Generations of my elders kept the Constellation safe before me. It is my birthright and duty."

The conviction in his voice plays at my heartstrings. He has no control over where we are going now. That is partially my fault. I needed to know what that Persei Guard knew, so I convinced Andrin to let me come along. Then I wandered my way into danger. Guilt gnaws at my stomach. My determination not only resulted in a death but also created consequences for Andrin's entire Constellation.

I just wanted to know more about the Harpyiai. If it were the one keeping me from returning home. That's all I want, to go home and keep my family safe. Which means I need the Harpyiai far from me. Maybe I won't be able to fight her myself, since clearly the Scilla was too much for me to handle. So I'll contact the Commodore. I will get him to call off the search for me so everyone in Galaxia will leave me alone. Which means I first need to find Philomena so she can send my message.

Andrin has his mission, and I have mine.

Andrin's eyes continue to search my face. I don't know whether he is seeking forgiveness or understanding. Then his head tilts, his brow furrows. His free hand sweeps across my forehead, pushing my hair aside.

"Aurora, your eyes." The shock in his voice sobers me.

I ask, "What?"

Andrin holds my face in both of his hands. "They're glowing. They look like—they are glowing like little stars."

"Is it a bad reaction? Am I okay?"

"It could be—" Andrin pauses. "Maybe it's because you're getting used to Aether manipulation. It might be a manifestation. You're becoming more powerful."

Curiosity and anxiety fight for dominance in my stomach. I want to see what else I can do, what I am capable of. I will be on this dumb Orbital Station until Andrin is done with Sarpedon. The better I get at Aether manipulation, the better my chances of surviving any future alien encounters.
"Can I try using that orb again? I couldn't do much before, but I can feel the Aether inside me now. I think I can do more."

Andrin's smile returns to his face. "It's still in the living room."

I move quickly to the living room, spotting the golden orb already perched on the coffee table. There is a spare pillow and a rumpled blanket on the couch. I do my best to ignore the mental image of Andrin's oversized form sleeping on the couch while I slept in his bed.

Andrin joins me in the room and hands me my vambraces. They have several dents, minor in diameter but deep. Teeth marks, from the Scilla.

"I picked them up after my call with my father, in case you wanted them. I can also get you a new set."

"No, no, I want these. I've earned these battle scars." It will also serve as a reminder of the consequences of my actions.

I slide the vambraces on, a tingle of Aether shooting down my arms to the tips of my fingers. I pick up the orb, rolling it between my hands.

"The Aether you used when the Scilla had a hold of your vambrace was impressive—raw, unfocused Aether. We want to try to focus it. Try thinking of how you felt when the Scilla attacked you."

A spike of fear rises up my spine at the memory. A faint hum fills my ears.

"I think it's working. Keep thinking about the attack." He presses.

As if my wound is responding to my memory, my arm aches. I close my eyes and force myself to imagine that thing. The Scilla. Those claws had ripped out chunks of my skin. Better than those teeth getting hold of me. The massive jaw that opened like a snake, wide enough, it seemed, to be nearly unhinged.

My heart races. The orb in my hands begins to heat. My vambraces glowed, like I am sure the orb would if I opened my eyes. I just knew that if I pushed the building Aether inside me, it would—

"Aurora, look." Andrin's voice breaks through my thoughts in a whisper.

I open my eyes and see the orb.

Glowing.

Floating.

A ring of pulsing golden light hums around the suspended form, mimicking the beat of my heart. As if the Aether pumps through my blood and straight to the orb. As I watch, the pulse slows, the glow weakening. I move quickly, lunging for the sphere as it drops from the air. I catch it in my shaking palms, and with a hiss, I let it drop.

It burns.

Like grabbing a curling iron with my bare hands. I am cursing when Andrin grabs my shoulders.

"That was incredible," He praises.

I raise my palms, showing him my blistered hands. The look of awe on his face makes me forget the thrum of my heartbeat against my open wounds. I smile back. Small, then wider, and suddenly I'm laughing. Laughing hard enough, I gasp for air.

"I did that!" I exclaim.

"You did! You're magnificent!"

Andrin grabs my face in both of his palms. We are both smiling, ear to ear. I feel so alive. I reach to touch his hands when I flinch back. I am grateful for the pain, as it brings me back to reality. Andrin registers the pain on my face and gently grips my hands.

"This, we can take care of with nano bots," He says.

He uses the fancy gel on my hands, nanotechnology, leaving them perfectly healed. Excitement surges through my system. I am powerful, I can feel it, I see it. Perhaps there is something special inside me.

"Let's make some magic."

Andrin's face twists. "It's not magic. It's Aether. Advanced science."

Ignoring yet another cultural miscommunication between us, I continue. "So, let's find a way to make this *Advanced science* without scorching my skin again."

We both stand in the middle of the mat; I pick up the orb again. It is cold, and my hands feel smooth, like only a few layers of my calluses remain.

Andrin explains, "This time, let's try to limit the amount of Aether you're channeling into it. The amount that was flowing in could have been too much, and that's what caused you to burn. Which makes sense, it was your first time trying to channel, and we didn't know how much you could conduct. This time, instead of a firehose, let's try a drizzle."

I nod. "Drizzle, got it."

I close my eyes and roll the orb back and forth between my hands. I think of Argos again. Instead of the attack, I think about being there, on a different planet. Something good. Walking around the barren, rocky ground. Seeing it expand across the horizon, then dropping off to a dark ocean, mirroring the three stars in the sky.

A hum sounds in my ears while the orb starts to heat. I focus on the memory of the pretty scene—the excitement of being somewhere completely new. The hum rings like a memory of a lovely song. My eyes open, and the orb remains in my hands with a soft glow.

Excitement.

The pleasant memory and the impending excitement create the Aether, which provides a night-light glow from the orb. I can make light!

I beam at Andrin. Pride shines on his face. The orb glows brighter. My satisfaction in accomplishing my goal, and Andrin's approval. My feelings. They are the energy source. The fear from the attack was strong, powerful enough to explode the head of the Scilla alien. The memory had brought back fear. Instead, focusing on the memory of being on the planet was powerful enough to channel the Aether inside of me, too.

Calm. Blank, calm thoughts. I release a slow breath. The humming song slows, then fades, and finally ceases. Very gently, I place the orb on the ground. When I stand again, I throw my arms around Andrin's shoulders.

"This is the coolest thing ever," I squeal.

Andrin chuckles, "Even better than Aether Crossing?"

I pull back enough to see his face, green eyes glowing in mischief. "Maybe tied. Once I can Aether Cross on my own, we'll see which wins."

"I thought you would be sleeping in after your injury." Izar's biting tone shocks the smile right off my face.

R. A. SANDS

CHAPTER 15

"Are you ready for your real training?" Izar stands with his arms crossed in the doorway of Andrin's living room.

I quickly remove my arms from Andrin and add space between us before I head towards the grumpy-looking male. Wordlessly, he hands me a training spear and stalks off. Somebody woke up on the wrong side of the UFO today.

I have to jog to keep up. He does not slow until we reach the training room. He taps a spot on the mat, and I take the silent order to find my stance there—a sharp sting flares on my thigh.

"Ow!" I shout.

I spin to Izar, eyes wide in shock. The mosaic patterns of his striped skin are set like stone, his face devoid of emotion. A sweep of his muscles and the training spear's shaft smacks into my other thigh.

Without a response from Izar, I add, "Seriously?"

His arms raise, preparing another strike—this time, I intercept. The shafts of both of our spears clank against one another. Izar doesn't pause—another swing. I block him again. Then another comes towards my side; I block, but the angle slips the spear from my right hand. He does not slow down. I barely have the spear back in my grasp before he aims for my head.

"What is your problem?" My voice is shrill and exaggerated.

No response. Our sparring continues. Apparently, he has decided that kicking my ass is how he is going to work through whatever has pissed him off this morning. Fine. I will let him work through his anger like he has helped me before. It doesn't mean I'm going to let him beat me to a pulp.

I block his next hit and launch a counterattack. I swing towards his legs, and he blocks. It's a volley. Torso, limbs, head. Each of us is trying to meet our mark only to be foiled by the other. I'm dripping sweat. I can taste salt in my mouth. It makes my hair stick to my face and down my back. My callused hands are slick, making the spear's smooth wood slippery enough to lose my grip. Izar slams his staff against mine, and it clatters to the ground. Panting, I try to catch his gaze. The glowing topaz eyes pulse with light beneath a furrowed brow. I guess we are not done yet.

His spear is raised once more. For my head this time. On instinct, I drop to a low crouch. The spear hisses through the air above my head fast enough that I feel a breeze through my hair. Just as my fingers reach my spear, Izar kicks it away. Fine, if I don't get a spear, neither will he.

I dive between Izar's legs, tackling him by the shins with my shoulders, forcing him to the ground. The fall loosens his grip enough for me to kick away his own spear. Then we are grappling on the ground. His hands and feet are quicker without the spear. His strength surpasses mine, but I am more agile—though he is swift, I am faster. Tumbling across the floor, my body aches. His hits come faster, and I barely block a third of them. I move to kick his flank, but Izar grabs my ankle.

In a sharp twist, he yanks my legs, forcing me to flip. I'm face down on the mat, only long enough to leave a sweaty imprint before his arms slide around my neck. He puts me in a chokehold.

A tight chokehold.

I smack his arm, calling for mercy as my trachea is being crushed. Yet he does not let up. Is he angry enough not to realize this could kill me? As my vision starts to blur black on the edges, I feel a sharp spark of pain in my chest. My Aether is flaring up. My skin grows hot. I'm not sure what will happen if I'm touching someone when my Aether erupts from within me. The last alien in contact with it had its head explode. My lungs burn from the lack of oxygen. The Aether is feeding off my fear. Not only my increasingly growing fear that Izar might not let up before I pass out or die, but also the fear that I might explode both of us before he does.

I whip my head back hard and fast enough that I feel the pressure of Izar's cat nose crunch. His arms release. Gasping, I push away from him. I roll until I can crawl, gaining distance to the other side of the mat. My skin still pulses hot, sweat sizzling on its surface. My heart racing, adrenaline on standby to save myself.

"What is wrong with you? You could have killed me!" Anger and disbelief squeak out of my sore throat.

Izar's hands cover his nose, but his eyes seem to focus on me. "You didn't seem to care if you died on Argos."

My head spins. "What? What are you even talking about?"

Izar stands, my arms brace against the mat in case I need to flee. Instead, he heads towards the wall of the training room. I watch as he grabs a towel and holds it against his face. A topaz liquid colors the rag. Blood.

"You left yourself completely defenseless on Argos. No spear. No situational awareness. Just wandering around on a foreign planet where you had no idea what dangers awaited you," he rants.

I protest, "If it was so dangerous, why was I even allowed to go?"

Izar rolls his eyes. "Because you told Andrin you wanted to go, and the Prince will cater to any of your desires. I thought training you to defend yourself would help keep you somewhat safe, but apparently, Earth creates dumber lifeforms than expected."

"Hey! You've already vented your anger on that mat, and I'll have the bruises to show for it for days. I apologize for disappointing you. I'll train harder and stay alert next time."

Izar removes the rag from his face. Only a small smear of blue sits below his nose now.

"I'm not disappointed. I was afraid for you. You got lucky being able to channel your Aether. Andrin and I wouldn't have gotten there in time. He barely did after." Izar motions to the now bloody patch on my arm.

Izar's tone is solemn as he adds, "You could have died. I can't let that happen again."

I roll my eyes despite the small smile that stretches across my lips. "You have a crappy way of saying 'I'm glad you're okay'."

"I am glad you're okay, Aurora." Izar doesn't return my smile, but he doesn't seem nuclear anymore. "But you need to be more careful. The galaxy is relatively new to you. Things might be different from what they appear."

My thoughts flash back to the dark waters of Argos. Seemingly beautiful but hiding Scilla. My arm feels itchy. His words echo Philomena's warning. I give Izar a grave nod.

"If you're still willing to train me, I'd appreciate the preparations for all the other monsters in the galaxy."

I mentally cringe. Still feeling conflicted about killing the Scilla. It had attacked me, and I had defended myself. Would the choice always be so easy?

Izar walks to our spears and tosses me mine. "We aren't monsters, Aurora. We're all just different aliens."

I laugh, "That remains to be seen. I have had more interactions with monsters." I roll the wood shaft in my hand and get into a fighting stance.

Izar doesn't match my stance. His forehead creases deeply enough that a stripe of color disappears as he silently assesses me. I roll my shoulders and shift my weight, uncomfortable in the silence.

"Galaxia is not a galaxy at peace. The Emperor is a fair leader, but his reign is expansive and impossible to regulate every Constellation. There have been instances in which Constellations have violated Galaxia's laws. Scorpio broke one of the most serious laws, not to interfere with a developing world. Your definition of monsters could include Harmakhis."

I push my stray hair out of my face. "Izar, I don't think you are a monster."

His jaw sets firm in a challenge. "The developing world Harmakhis interfered with was Earth."

My breath catches in my throat, but Izar continues to speak.

"On Earth, a voyage of Harmakhis found an advanced civilization in the desert. They traded ideas and technology."

The image of a sphinx flashes in my mind, and the anthropomorphic artwork of ancient Egypt. Finally, my recognition of his features falls into place. Izar and his species could easily resemble Egyptian God drawings of human bodies with cat-like heads. If the Harmakhis had enough influence to be regarded as gods, they must have made a substantial impact.

"Did the Harmakhis build the pyramids?" I keep my voice void of the confusion and disturbance I feel about accusations of alien contributions to ancient civilizations.

Izar huffs an exasperated sigh, "No, Aurora. The pyramids were already being built before the Harmakhis arrived, but they gave them technology that pushed the slaves past Human capabilities. They overrode their bodies for the sake of production; they turned Humans into machines until they died. When the Empire learned of it, they were furious and punished Scorpio severely. My point is, past Harmakhis have done heinous things, just as Humans have done in their history. That does not make either species monstrous. Actions are choices, not characteristics."

"I think our choices are what make up our character." I grab Izar's hands in mine and force him to meet my eyes. "Every choice I have seen you make, how you talk, and how you care for others, shows the strength of your character. You are not a monster."

Izar sighs and squeezes my fingers before releasing them. "Thank you. I will help you with everything in my power to keep you safe from those that are monstrous."

He grabs the spear again and taps the mat for me to resume my stance. Whatever is out there, next time, I will be ready. I will make the right choice.

"Princess! Princess!"

I freeze at the sound of Philomena's trilling voice. My eyes dart around the hallway, ensuring we are alone, before I turn to face her. It is late enough that most crew members are sleeping, and the red lights have turned on.

I whisper-yell down the hall, "You know I don't like you calling me that."

Her small mouth purses. "Would you rather have me yell out Roa for all of the station to wake up?"

I huff. "Of course not."

The look of victory on her face makes me want to laugh. Until I remember she had been chasing me down in the hall.

We both lean close as I whisper, "What's wrong?"

"Oki talked to someone in the communications team. He gained access to a secure messaging line for you to the Imperial Commodore. I tried to tell you when you got back from Argos, but you passed out. What message would you like me to pass to him?"

My thoughts swim. I have been so focused on finding a way to contact the Commodore that I haven't thought this far ahead. At least I haven't come to a final conclusion of what I want to say for my first galactic email.

What do I want to say to the person who sent a message to the entire galaxy and put me in danger? Maybe he wants me to be in danger. Perhaps he wants me hunted down, like the Harpyiai is doing, or wants to stop me before I can cause more destruction.

Yet the message was vague, an order to report all sightings; it didn't include capture. I still don't understand why the request to find me was sent out after all this time. Twenty-six Earth years seems like a long time to me.

"Tell the Commodore, I am the one you are seeking information about. And I demand to know why." My voice is firm, determined.

She gives me a puzzled look. "Do you want to tell him you are Roa Mēdeia?"

"No." My eyes meet Philomena's, wide with her devoted disposition. "If his intentions are honest, he will know it is me. If not, it's best he doesn't."

Philomena nods in understanding. "I'll have the message sent immediately." I watch as she prances down the hall. I do not know what I have done to deserve Philomena's loyalty, but I am grateful.

CHAPTER 16

Thirteen days have passed, or at least thirteen sleep cycles. The transit between star systems, even within a constellation, is long without a Star Gate—thirteen days of training, eating, healing, and travelling. While Izar's mood towards me has improved, he still seems grumpy with Andrin. I think he blames Andrin for my injury on Argos.

Part of his sour demeanor may stem from the length of our trip. It's affecting me. Although I crave control, I have never truly mastered it. I compensate with rationality, but as my temper shortens like a flickering candlewick, control slips further away, and I feel it might snap completely. I'm restless. The taste of exploration I had on Argos left me hungry for more, despite my near-death kiss with fate.

Which is why my Aether has been simmering under my skin since I woke up this morning. Today, the Orbital Station, as they are forcing me to call this floating UFO, will be landing. It'll land on Seriphus, the colony planet where the Orbital Station will refill its supplies before the next mission. Landing an entire station requires twenty times as much energy as staying in orbit. However, to bring supplies and additional fuel aboard, the Orbital Station must dock. Which means I get to step foot on another planet.

I'm up before the red lights turn white, dressed in a fresh white spandex spacesuit. My trusty vambraces grace my wrists, and my feet easily slide into the chunky boots. While I twist my hair into two French braids, I notice my white-blonde hair seems paler, nearly matching the white of my suit. There used to be various tones of yellow disbursed, but now each strand is almost translucent. I brush the braids over my shoulders before pulling on the thick, grey, hooded wool cloak.

The air of the Pilot House is chilly, although not as cold as the arid tundra of the quickly approaching planet. I wave to the few aliens I recognize from my meals in the cafeteria, members of the navigation and piloting teams. I sit in the last empty seat at the back of the room and strap in. Andrin and Izar are in their own seats, control panels and screens in front of them. Seriphus is larger than it appeared yesterday when it first came into view—a pale-yellow planet with lines of mountain ridges. The Orbital Station begins to shake as it enters the atmosphere. My fingers dig into my harness-like seatbelt, testing its holding strength.

The smooth, calm, computerized female voice narrates our descent. Times, distances, and speeds as we drop into the atmosphere and sail towards the designated recovery site. The mountain ranges turn from thin lines to prominent ridges. Suddenly, they are towering above us. I refuse to look down towards the impending ground.

"Orbital Station Rho is now approaching Seriphus berth Gamma. Standby for docking."

An abrupt jolt sends my teeth clashing together as the entire station comes to a halt. My internal organs did not get the memo that we are stopping. Out the window, I can see the long expanse of land around us. Flat yellow ground, with cracks fracturing the surface for miles. Andrin places his hand on my shoulder, and I look up.

"Ready to see another planet, Little Astronaut?" The delight in his voice matches my own.

I beam at him, my excitement beating my nausea. I unclip the harness and follow Andrin. I am under strict orders from Izar to wear the helmet and keep a spear, at least in collapsed form, with me always. After our fight following Argos, I don't press the issue. He's right, there are threats all around that I can't even imagine yet.

We reach the airlock when Andrin pauses. "We need our helmets out there. The helium levels are toxic to us."

I give him a fake salute and slide the helmet over my face. After checking my own helmet, Andrin presses buttons.

"Pressure neutralizing. Neutralization time, forty-five seconds." The animatronic voice reports.

I suck in a breath. My vambraces glow softly with my growing excitement. My hand reaches for Andrin's. His fingers lace through mine just as the airlock hisses open.

"Into the future," I murmur.

Cold air prickles my exposed skin. Despite the wool cloak, I can feel the wind rustling around us. The fractures in the ground look much larger up close. Taking a step out of the airlock, I have to lengthen my stride to avoid the fracture. We're in a large valley, and all around us on the horizon is a circular mountain range. There are a handful of buildings, all the size of large jet hangars. A few tanks and silos are scattered amongst them. Beyond the small compound are rows and rows of solar panels. They stretch until the mountain ridges sprout from the land.

"Do you want a tour?" I barely nod to his question but move my feet. "Let's practice Aether Crossing. It'll make the tour more efficient."

Excitement and apprehension battle for dominance in my stomach. "Yes to the tour, but I don't know about Aether Crossing. It hasn't been going very well for me." The thought of vomiting in front of this many new aliens adds an extra twist in my stomach. Especially if I have to keep my helmet on, I doubt the smell will come out easily.

Andrin squeezes my fingers. "You can do it. Practice makes perfect, that's what they say on Earth, right? I believe in you."

His white-toothed smile shines brighter than his golden skin. I turn away and let out a deep breath. I have a feeling he won't let it go. I plaster a fake smile on my face and turn back to Andrin.

"Might as well give it a shot."

Andrin's smile grows as he releases my hand, jogging a few paces away. "Let's start small, try to get here."

It's only thirty yards away. Close enough that I can easily visualize the spot. The Aether under my skin feels frantic, like a million marbles jumping around inside a pinball machine. I try to create the wormhole, but I can't focus my Aether enough to make a single point. My skin heats the longer I try. Andrin's smiling face begins to drop. I push more Aether to the point, willing it to work. Instead of a wormhole, a fiery hole stabs between my eyebrows—the world sways.

Andrin's hands grip my biceps. I blink frantically as I desperately try to inhale through my nose. When my eyes meet his, they look dejected. I shove his disappointment down into the little box inside my chest where I keep mine.

"It's a beautiful day for a walk." Andrin offers.

As if on cue, a gust of wind whips one of my braids against both of our visors. Walking seems to be the better option for my health.

Andrin's long legs stride more easily across the broken terrain. I'm thankful for the increased cardio training Izar has built into my routine, which helps me keep pace. The first hangar we pass has crates and boxes stacked on all the walls. Aliens of all sorts move throughout the hangar; some I recognize from the Orbital Station, and a few are new. Only some of them are wearing their own helmets. Three barrel-chested and short-limbed aliens move crates on their own on the main floor. Up on the shelves, there is a large cephalopod that looks like an octopus, its orange, suction cup-covered flesh moving from shelf to shelf. I try my best not to gawk at the new species.

"These front four hangars store food supplies. Dry storage and frozen. It's challenging to keep fresh food on a planet that doesn't produce it," Andrin explains.

I nod. "Makes sense. I know a lot of island or remote countries struggled with the same supply chain issues back on Earth."

Andrin chuckles. "Yes, I suppose on the scale of how we're able to travel, that is a good comparison. It's also why you must hate the food on board."

"I don't hate the food." My voice comes out high-pitched and defensive.

Andrin gives me a doubting look, which makes me snicker. Instead of protesting, he leads us between a set of hangars, all with their doors closed.

"Some store spare parts and equipment for Orbital Stations or other travel craft. There are also self-defense weapon systems in case the colony gets attacked."

A wave of worry rushes over me. "Does that happen a lot? Attacks?"

My skin prickles, this time not from the chill of the frosty air. My vambraces hum again, heating under my cloak. Izar's warning is fresh in my mind. Andrin shakes his head and tightens his hand around mine.

"No, not often. There are small pockets of Belemytes that are sometimes reported in the waterways of the mountains. They're more of a pest than anything else. They fly in packs like birds. Can exist in the water and air. We wouldn't bother with them if it weren't for the damage they do to the dams and aqueducts we have in the mountains to source water for the colony."

Andrin points to the large circular tanks. He explains they are part of the water treatment plant. Beyond the tanks, like fields of wheat, the lines of solar panels reflect gold.

"This is why Seriphus is so important to us. This part of the planet is never in darkness; at least one of its two stars always shines. We have power shuttles that go between here and Mycenae, carrying batteries. They're used to keep the planet and most of our spacecraft powered."

"Does the Orbital Station use it too?" I ask.

"It can. It also has its own fission process, like your nuclear power plants back on Earth. Our technology is simply more energy-efficient. We'll take a recharge on our stores and for our less vital equipment to help lessen the load on our main power plant."

I can only hum in response, my brain in overload as a flood of information washes over me. We walk through the fields of solar panels until my legs start to ache. We have been touring Seriphus for what feels like hours. The stars have shifted across the sky, offering only an estimate of the passage of time. The time-relativity factor is difficult to grasp. Especially when my body feels so fatigued, yet the stars keep the sky as bright as high noon. It reminds me of the disorienting forty-eight-hour trip I took in Alaska during the summer, when it was always sunny outside. Andrin catches my glance back towards the Orbital Station.

"You look tired, let's get you back." He offers.

Thankfully, he slows his pace too. While there is some housing in the colony, we will still stay on board the station. Sleeping with a helmet on isn't ideal for my beauty rest. Back in the airlock, decontamination begins once pressure and air levels are neutralized.

"Your Aether expenditure might be draining your reserves. I think it might be holding you back."

I turn my face as I take off my helmet to hide my embarrassment. "Well, I'm trying my best, that's all I have to give."

His hand grasps my arm, right where my scratch marks from the Scillia used to be. The wound has healed, but thin white scars remain on my pale skin. I take a deep breath before turning back to him.

He defends himself, "I didn't say it to insult you. I think you're making incredible progress. Unprecedented. However, I think I can help you get even better with the shot I mentioned. The one most aliens start taking as children, Astrobleme."

His eyes are shining with excitement and awe. He really does believe I am capable of more. Something is my gut twists. The idea of some alien substance in my body, even if I am an alien, makes my skin crawl. I turn my head so I don't have to watch the disappointment that is about to appear on his face.

"Thank you, but I'm okay."

His hand falls from my arm. "Why?"

I cringe from the dejection in his voice. I open my mouth, but a voice like the wind through tree leaves breaks the silence first. My eternal gratefulness for Philomena grows. I rush to close the distance between us. Her large eyes somehow appear wider with excitement. She grabs my arm with her spindly fingers, and I let her lead me out of the bay.

She doesn't slow her hurried movements until we reach the cafeteria. There are a few aliens in the room, preparing for dinner. Oki enters from the kitchens, a chunky tablet in hand. He bows his head deeply before handing over the tablet. It reads in plain English, the green lettering standing out from the black screen.

I cannot express how relieved I am to have received your message. I wish to offer you residence and protection within the Capital of Sagittarius, in honor of your parents' noble sacrifice. Send your precise coordinates, and the Imperial Fleet will escort you to the Capital.

My tongue feels like sandpaper in my mouth. I can't speak. The Imperial Commodore wants to honor my parents: my alien parents, my dead alien parents, from the Andromeda Galaxy. Yet I don't want sanctuary. I just want to go home.

I hand the tablet back to Oki. "Please tell him, thank you, but I'll pass. The Persei Heir promised to return me to Earth. If he wants to help me, he can revoke his message and keep anyone from ever searching for me again."

Oki and Philomena look to each other, conflict clear in their eyes. Oki opens his mouth, ready to protest, but Philomena places her hand on his thin arm.

"As you wish, Princess," She says.

I return her deep nod. "I'm grateful for your help, both of you."

I don't let them argue any further. I've made my choice. We will finish up on Seriphus, make a pit stop on Sarpedon, and I am going back to Earth. I can't cut it as an alien, but I have been Human-passing my entire life. I may be the last remnant of Andromeda, but perhaps it is better if the only thing remaining of the galaxy is the distant light in the night sky.

CHAPTER 17

It's freezing at the mountain's summit. I suppose I shouldn't be too surprised; it's always cold atop Earth's mountains. The mountain wind whips around us violently. The heavy wool cloak feels as effective as a bikini. As we walk along the ridge, I have to huddle into Andrin's side since I require extra warmth. He brought me up here so I can see what is beyond the mountain ridges—wind turbines. Hundreds, or even thousands of feet tall, wind turbines encompass the windward side of the mountains and valleys beyond. The wind turbines apparently require less maintenance than solar panels, so it's easier to install more of them over greater distances. They all funnel into an energy pipeline that runs on a grid back to the colony. The entire planet is an energy farm.

I shiver against Andrin's side. The view is impressive, but I'm glad he didn't make me physically hike up here. I woke up feeling energized this morning, and when Andrin suggested another attempt at Aether Crossing, we were both surprised at my success. So, we Aether Crossed in small intervals. He helped guide me every few meters to make sure I didn't fall into a cavern. So, not only am I cold, but drained. Andrin will most likely have to Aether Cross us both back down the mountain.

Andrin quickly bounds up the next few ridges, only turning back to wave me forward. "One last climb, I promise the view will be worth it."

I nod and concentrate, and a bright flash of light fills my vision before I land on wobbly legs next to Andrin. When I look up, the nauseous feeling drains away, making way for awe. The mountain ridges give way to a deep valley. Cascading down the mountains, mossy waterfalls flow into the lake reservoir below. The emerald lake holds strong against an arced gray metal wall, a dam.

I open my mouth, but instead of my voice, a blaring alarm explodes around us, rattling my bones. The helmet does little to muffle the sound. Instinctually, I throw my hands over my ears and cower. Andrin moves in front of me quickly to shield me with his body as he keeps a vigilant lookout.

"What is that?" I shout, but my words sound hollow in my own head.

Finally, the alarm seizes, yet the ringing in my skull continues. Andrin stands, his spear instantly extending at his side. Slowly, I straighten and extend my own spear.

"It's the colony's alarm system. It should only be used if the colony is under attack."

"Under attack of—" The words freeze in my throat.

Beyond the dam, a cloud of red rises from the mountain ridge. Thousands of tiny flapping wings. Like a horde of locusts. The siren blares again, rising and falling like a tornado siren. My heart hammers in my chest, mimicking the alarm.

"Belemytes." The name is an exhale on Andrin's lips.

The small reserve of Aether still in my blood fizzles with my fear. "You said they fly in packs and are nothing more than pests."

Andrin shakes his head, fear creeping across his features. "I've never seen this many before."

The Belemytes dive toward the dam. From across the lake, they look like small bugs, but the distance must be distorting my perspective. A horde of thousands of red arrows, amassing like a plague of locusts, pelts the wall that retains the lake. Sharp, metallic dents echo through the basin.

"I have to go. I must stop them before they destroy the dam. Seriphus needs that water."

"Andrin—"

I reach for him, but the white flash of light blinds me. My booted feet slip, and I slide a few feet down the uneven mountainside. I drop the spear on instinct to catch myself, the stone digging into my palms. The spear tumbles further down the mountain before lodging itself between rock ledges. A string of curses leaves my mouth at my irritation, but to my relief, the spear hasn't fallen into one of the caverns that riddle these mountains. I climb down the hill, keeping my torso pressed against it.

My cloak flaps violently as the howling wind drowns out the piercing alarm's oscillating sound. Once I reach the landing, I collapse the spear and secure it to my body harness. Somehow, the way back up the mountain looks even further. I focus on the Aether inside of me, but it doesn't so much as spark. It was dangerous to use so much of my Aether reserve while galivanting across the mountains. I curse my impulsiveness and naivety, which keep getting the better of me. If I don't get it together and become more vigilant in these unfamiliar worlds, my luck will run out.

I guess I'll have to climb back up. My braids repeatedly whip the visor, blocking my view. The rough rocks scrape away small strips of flesh from my hands as I use them for climbing wall holds. The air chills me to the bone, my fingers feeling raw and my muscles stiff as I hoist myself back up the mountain.

I'm panting. My heart is hammering. The wind continues to blow. The sirens rise and fall. The metal wall tings with the assault. A thousand tiny wings flap. It's overwhelming—my brain pounds against my skull from overstimulation. I squeeze the heels of my hands against my temples, but the helmet blocks me. I force my eyes back to the dam, to Andrin.

His golden skin pokes out from the white suit as the light flares from the spear, shining like a beacon amongst the flood of red. I watch in awe as he moves, a fluid dance as the tip of the spear shocks the Belemytes from the sky. Then a larger form rises from outside the dam.

Red and winged—not the small Belemytes but a female figure with wings that resembles an angel. I squint, trying to focus my eyes. Her wings are deep red, and her skin is covered in the same color feathers, despite her female form. A Harpyiai.

My Aether surges alive under my skin. Not just a Harpyiai, the Harpyiai. The one who has been searching for me. It has to be. The one that hunted me on Earth and is the reason Andrin took me. She is here. Like a moth to a flame, she rises past the Belemytes and soars towards me.

A miniature swarm of Belemytes follows her, as if under her command. They shoot forward, flying faster and diving towards me. On instinct, I take my spear in hand, careful to keep a controlled grip on my weapon. The tube expands to its full length, the spear's tip locking into place via overlapping metallic scales. The pointed end glows blue in my hands, my adrenaline already building up the last of my Aether reserves.

With the spear ready in my hands, the guilt I have carried since Argos leaves me. I will not let another alien take a chunk out of me again. Especially not her. If any blood is drawn today, it will be hers. The spear sparks bright blue with my flare of determination. The light calls to the Belemytes, and they soar faster through the air, passing the Harpyiai.

They are the size of my hand, tubular, with sharp fins and a stream of tentacles behind them. Their red color shines brightly in the sun, like demon flying fish. I posture my spear forward and high, ready to take out the fastest approaching aliens.

Wind.

Sirens.

Wings.

From the opposite side of the mountains, four hovering machines rise. The gold skin and white uniforms of the riders tell me they are Persei Guards. The hovercrafts zoom through the air towards the dam. The red swarm blocks my view.

The pounding of my blood in my ears is the only sound louder than the sirens. I suck in air through my nose. Then I let it burn inside me, feeding the fire of my Aether. Burn. I release my breath, my Aether burning bright across my skin.

As the first few come in range, I slash the air, a beam of light laces out a foot. The Belemytes in the air near the light plummet to the ground. A very effective weapon, apparently, although it reminds me of a bug zapper.

I move, following a rhythm that blends Aikido and Izar's training. I let the Aether flow with every ounce of concentration from Andrin's training. I let my body dance as the Belemytes fall to the ground. The Harpyiai keeps her distance. Assessing me.

My eyes desperately dart to the dam below, searching for Andrin, four sets of Persei Guards, and the blue hue of Izar amongst the sea of red. Andrin and the other golden-skinned

Guards fend off the remaining swarm of Belemytes, while Izar stands alone by the metal wall. My companions won't be coming to my aid anytime soon.

My split attention costs me. Some of the Belemytes have closed in, picking at my cloak with their sharp beaks. There are too many. They ram their beaks against the visor of my helmet, and I stumble. My boots roll over what I can only assume are the exoskeletons of fried aliens. I land first on my butt before my back slams into the jagged mountain. I refuse to let go of the spear this time.

I am Roa Mēdeia.

I am the last of my kind.

I will not falter.

Countless insect-like birds swarm me. I jab my spear above my head, desperate to beat them off. I'm covered in the pests. My skin flares with heat, my Aether pulsing with the beat of my heart. Blue light flares, from beneath my cloak, from my hands, and inside my helmet. The Belemytes zap off my skin, falling around me like cicada shells.

The Harpyiai's head cocks to the side, her beady eyes squinted in scrutiny. Her wings flap slowly, powerful gusts overpowering the mountain winds as she gracefully lowers herself above me. I try to push myself off the ground, try to ready myself to fight her, and stop running away. My limbs refuse to cooperate. I can't move. I have exhausted my Aether and bodily energy from that pulse of light. Once again, I have left myself defenseless when I need my Aether the most. Straggling Belymetes continue to probe and nip at my prone form.

"We thought you would be stronger than this," Her beaked face clucks at me. "Perhaps Ketos was wrong about you."

Confusion and fear grapple for dominance in my depleted form. She tilts forward, her claws outstretched as she reaches for me. A resounding baritone clap echoes through the mountains. The Harpyiai's head snaps towards the dam.

From my spot on the ground, I search desperately for my companions at the dam, afraid of what I'll find. The metal begins to creak and groan.

Metal-on-metal grinding.

Then, a click.

A forceful zap shoots across the wall, like the snap of a rubber band. The mass of Belemytes on the wall plunge into the water. Not for another attack, but in death. Electrocuted. Izar turned the dam into a gigantic electric fence, an industrial-scale bug zapper. The second the wave of Belemytes hits the water, they sizzle again like oil in a frying pan. I look away, nausea threatening to empty my stomach as vapor that I am sure is not steam rises from the water.

There's another white flash; a pair of boots stands guard before my form. The Harpyiai releases a shrill call before soaring into the sky. Andrin's spear fights off the remaining Belemytes. I try to stand, to push myself up, but I'm still drained. While my limbs refuse to cooperate, Andrin doesn't falter.

With a red flash, the Harpyiai disappears in the sky.

The sound of the dam ceases, like the power has been turned off. Andrin makes quick work of the last remaining Belemytes. Three of the hovercrafts take off, circling the emerald lake before flying back over the dam. The last hovercraft flies towards us, a Persci Guard with Izar seated behind. Izar jumps off, landing beside me.

It's quiet then. Only the sounds of our panting and distant waterfalls break through the mountain wind. All around us is a sea of red, red exoskeletons of the now dead swarm. I get the sickening feeling that if they step anywhere, I would hear a crunch.

I cry out, "I can't move."

Andrin's arms slide beneath my knees and around my back before I am lifted into the air.

"Andrin, we need to go. The Defense Unit is searching for the Harpyiai, but we need to get her to safety," Izar warns.

Andrin and Izar share a look before Izar grabs his shoulder—the familiar light flashes.

CHAPTER 18

I'm still immobile in Andrin's arms as we land beside the Orbital Station. Everyone around us falls back a few feet in shock. Andrin passes me off to Izar, who quickly heads to the cargo bay's airlock.

"Get her some food and rest in my quarters. We're leaving as soon as the Station can get off the ground," Andrin orders.

As Izar carries me inside, I look behind to see Andrin yelling out commands. The blaring alarm sounds, echoing through the valley. The aliens move quickly, and some even running into action.

Izar rushes me inside to Andrin's rooms and lays me on the couch. I can see aliens rushing around outside through Andrin's living room window. Machines and the stout aliens move cargo to the Orbital Station. Empty pallets are carted away and pushed inside the hangars. The entire colony seems to be beginning to lock down. Anyone not moving supplies to the Orbital Station rushes inside the station or to the surrounding buildings.

"Launch procedures commencing. Time to Launch, five minutes." The familiar female voice blasts over the announcing system.

Izar inspects me, arms crossed. "You look ill."

"Thanks," I mumble. "I used a lot of Aether today. Andrin had me Aether Cross up the mountains before we even got to the dam. I think I'm entitled to look a little run down."

Izar's mosaic brows crease. "You need to be careful with your energy expenditure. Think about how your Aether responds to everything you do. It's a part of you."

"I didn't think I was going to fight off a million alien mosquito birds today." I shoot back defensively.

There is a bite in my voice. The fizzle of Aether that has replenished my reserves sparks in irritation. Being annoyed always seems to elicit the most powerful Aether responses. When a knock sounds at the door, Izar quickly thanks whoever is at the door and returns with a tray of food.

Izar gives me a warning look. "Stay here. Make sure you're sitting when we take off."

"Good thing I can't move my limbs anyway." I roll my eyes and watch as he disappears behind the airlock.

I watch the chaos outside the window while the food goes untouched. It's as if my limbs are asleep, tingling, and out of control.

The animatronic voice continues its countdown. Notification of all hatches and exits being secured. The Orbital Station gets noisy as internal equipment spins up.

The station launches.

It tilts, weight shifting as whatever holds us in place releases its grip. When the voice announces underway, the Orbital Station shutters and gravity shifts. The force like an airplane taking off hits me, but instead of a horizontal force, I feel it along the vertical axis. The ground shifts out of my view from the window. The surface of Seriphus dips below my sight. We are parallel to the mountains for only a moment.

I see it then, the squad of hovercrafts zig-zagging through the sky chasing a blur of red.

The Harpyiai.

She dives and corkscrews through the air, as agile as a hawk—a flash of red light blooms from where the Harpyiai flies. Before the light fades, the Orbital Station shoots into the exosphere.

Seriphus takes shape out the window. The sphere shrinks, and its two stars come into view. We are moving fast. Faster than we did to get to Argos. Perhaps the Orbital Station's refueling allows it to go faster. The three celestial bodies are smaller than basketballs by the time Andrin returns to the room.

He looks disheveled in the artificial light. His curls are stuck up on one side of his head as if he has been running his hands through them. He drops his own wool jacket on the floor. When his gaze falls to mine, I can see the relief and exhaustion. He conducts a brief inspection of me before his eyes fall to the food tray.

"You didn't eat," Andrin says.

I try my best to sit up, but my body still feels stiff. "I can't really move."

Andrin's eyes flare again. "Still? I thought that with rest, you would feel better."

His concern only doubles mine. It only reassures me that I'm making the right decision.

"I want to take Astrobleme," I declare.

His spine stiffens. "Are you sure?"

My body refuses to move. I reach for the Aether inside of me, but the fizzle won't even respond now. The Harpyiai was so close. I could have had her. I'm lucky she didn't get me instead. I clearly wouldn't have walked away victorious.

"Yes. Next time the Harpyiai comes. I want to be ready for her."

He nods, slowly assessing my features. Then he crosses the room and heads for the interior ladder. He disappears down the steps before returning minutes later. He holds a small, rectangular case in his hand.

"What's down there?" I ask.

Andrin looks over his shoulder before he sits on the coffee table in front of me. "It's my office. My living quarters are directly above it for ease of access."

I hum in response. Maybe I should have looked around more while I was snooping through his office. Andrin opens the container to reveal syringes and vials of luminescent blue liquid. He helps me remove my cloak and motions for my arm. I try to roll up the spandex-like sleeve, but it barely reaches my forearm. Determined, I take off my vambraces, unzip my suit, and roll it halfway off my body so my arm is free.

Andrin clears his throat, keeping his eyes focused on his hands instead of my bandeau-covered chest. He cleans my inner elbow with an alcohol pad before grabbing a syringe. He takes the needle, presses it past the vial's barrier, and pulls the plunger—the liquid moves and shimmers, as if it were alive. Before I can second-guess, he sticks the needle into my vein and pushes the plunger.

The hot liquid burns through my veins. Starting at my inner elbow and coursing up my arm. It moves beneath my pale skin. I feel the needle removed from my skin, and I inspect my arm. A thin smear of the liquid and my blood mingle on the surface of my skin. It triggers the wisp of a memory, but a burning pain cuts off my train of thought. My skin glows blue where I feel the fiery liquid spreading beneath the surface.

It's heading towards my heart.

As if it were the liquid from glowsticks pushed through a piping system, bending and twisting beneath my flesh with each beat of my heart, the glow spreads further. My breathing quickens. My heart burns when the liquid reaches it, then glows beneath the thin bandeau top.

Lub, dub.

It spreads further. Flashing through every vein in my body makes my pale skin glow. It travels through my body as if every cell is reaching for the Astrobleme.

Lub, dub. Lub, dub.

The glow pulses in the rhythm of my heartbeat.

I feel good. Very good. Alive. Familiar. Like it is meant to be in my blood. Like I have felt it before. I turn back to Andrin and smile. When he sees my smile, the concern vanishes from his face and is replaced with his own. I am beaming.

"I feel so good," I giggle.

I quickly stand, bouncing on my toes with my blooming Aether. I spot the golden orb from across the room and grab it. I roll it between my hands, feeling a jolt of electricity jump from my left hand, through the orb, and back through my right hand. It shimmers in a pale golden light with effortless ease. My smile widens, pain aching in my cheeks. I spin around to show Andrin, but my smile dims slightly. His gold skin looks dull. Like he is made of real metal that has oxidized, he used a lot of Aether today, too. A thought creeps into my head.

"I know you said you don't need Astrobleme beyond once a year after childhood, but do you ever take it when your Aether reserves are low?"

Andrin shifts back, collecting the used materials into a black biohazard bag. His face is pensive.

"Sometimes it's used before missions. In the past, it was used to replenish forces during battles," He says.

Mindlessly, I grab his hand and continue to inspect the coloration. "Do you think you should use it now? You don't look as shiny as normal. And I feel great now."

Andrin laughs, staring at the remaining materials. His hesitation makes me pause. Maybe Astrobleme is rare or expensive. I also insulted his appearance. Before I can apologize, he's prepping another syringe and injecting it into his own inner elbow. While my skin glows blue, his ripples back into shining gold, like a tidal wave washing away the tarnish. I take his hand in mine again; electricity buzzing grows between us. When he turns to me, he looks rejuvenated, but the pensive expression remains.

I'm about to tell Andrin he looks attractive again when he speaks.

"Would you like to shower in my room? I know I could benefit from getting cleaned up."

I laugh, taking my hand back to play with the orb. "Sure. I feel rough after today."

I toss him the orb before finding my way into his bathroom. It's bigger than mine, but the shower works the same way. I scrub my skin under the hot water until I can't feel the remnants of the Belemytes' beaks picking at my skin anymore. My skin has settled, my paleness returned, but the heat remains in my veins.

I put on the linen shirt and shorts left on the counter for me. They are baggy and smell like saffron and sea salt. Andrin's clothes. I inspect myself in the mirror, but pause.

It's not the sight of his clothes that stops me, but my eyes. My normal bright blue eyes are glowing as vibrantly as the Astrobleme from the vials.

A knock on the door makes me jump.

"Are those clothes alright? I can send for another pair," Andrin asks.

I push the door open and slide by Andrin, his chest inches from mine. "No, I think they fit pretty well. The shower is free."

Andrin remains in the doorway, his head twisted over his shoulder. His cheeks turn rose gold when I catch him watching me as I look over my shoulder.

He clears his throat before mumbling. "I'll be out in a second. Eat some food."

On cue, my stomach growls. I stifle my giggle and head back to the living room and the tray of food Izar had brought in before launch. With little interest beyond survival, I pick at the food cubes until I uncover a familiar waxy wrapping. I tear it open like a toddler and take a big bite of the mochi ice cream. Instant pain shoots up my front teeth from the cold.

"I'm glad you found them." Andrin's chuckle reverberates through his chest.

I turn, ready to share my gratitude, but the sight makes the ice cream melt in my mouth. Andrin walks towards the couch, dressed in nothing but linen shorts, his glorious chest on display. He looks like a Greek God. His gold flesh seems carved by artists. My eyes roam up his torso to his face, where a self-satisfied smirk greets me. I refuse to speak and try to hide my embarrassment at clearly being caught gawking at a perfect display of the male specimen, so I throw the other half of the ice cream into my mouth. It does nothing to relieve my embarrassment as a moan slips from my lips.

Andrin's green eyes darken.

My already hot body heats again. I should have turned the shower temperature to cold.

He sits next to me, the sides of our thighs touching. It does nothing to cool my skin. I feel flustered like a high schooler holding hands for the first time. Maybe it's the Astrobleme pumping through my veins. It enhances my Aether, so perhaps it enhances emotions, too.

I can't deny that I find Andrin physically attractive. Despite the strange gold hue of his skin, his bone structure is strong, just as the rest of his muscular body. I can easily ignore his physical attributes; I should. His kindness is more difficult to ignore.

While I don't like that I'm here, he genuinely believes it will keep me safe. He saved me when he grabbed me before the other Scillas arrived on Argos, and again when he fought off the Belemytes. I don't want to be a damsel in distress, but he has been my hero.

"I think the Harpyiai made them attack. While you were busy with the dam, she came for me."

Andrin's hand grazes my jaw, bringing my eyes back to his. "I thought the same thing. When I saw her head for the mountain ridge, I was scared for you."

My skin sears under his touch. "I think the Harpyiai was more afraid of you. I guess I owe you thanks for saving me." My voice comes out breathy as our eyes remain locked.

"I believe the appropriate response at this moment is to decline with gratitude, as no thanks are necessary."

His hand falls from my jaw, taking a slow trail down my neck to my arm, before resting on my hand. The Aether in my body ricochets inside my veins. I can't focus. My mind goes blank except for the thoughts of his hands on my skin. The energy between us feels magnetic.

"But the right thing is rarely fun." I lean close enough that I have to look up at him through my eyelashes. "I want to thank you for saving me from the Harpyiai again."

My eyes remain on him. Taking joy from the transition of his emotions from concern to shock, to happiness, to hunger. I like where the emotion lands.

I lean in, my hand brushing his cheek. He's watching my lips now, waiting. When I kiss him, it's gentle at first, just enough to test the moment. The spark between us answers immediately. I smile against him before he deepens the kiss, his hands finding my waist and drawing me closer.

There's salt on his lips. The air feels charged.

He lifts me effortlessly, settling me against him, and I laugh softly as the world tilts. I pull on his shoulders to slide myself closer. My straddled legs fit perfectly on his hardness. He grips the flesh of my muscular butt in approval, forcing a breathy gasp from me.

My hands thread through his hair as we kiss. Static crackles beneath my skin where we touch, his dark curls lifting slightly with the energy building between us. My pulse races. His hands slide along my sides, grounding and unsteady all at once. His fingers trail up my thighs until they reach the edge of his baggy shorts before he lifts me again.

This time, my back lands on the couch, his hips firmly pressed between my spread legs. I plant my feet on the cushions to force my hips upwards, pushing them against his. He grinds his hips back in response. He feels so good. I can feel my skin heating, possibly from the energy building in me or the need growing between my legs. In a swift motion, his hands pull my calves over his shoulders and he slides lower down my body. When his mouth meets the apex of my legs, I release a cry loud enough that I throw my own hand over my mouth.

Andrin's chuckle against my skin makes me bite my hand. He is very, very, good at this. My own hair starts to float, static electricity in the room building with my own climb. His tongue moves swiftly, and his fingers—

The golden orb flies across the room, slamming into a bulkhead with a heavy thud. I turn my head towards the sound, but Andrin's unoccupied hand grips my jaw, keeping my focus on him. Those green eyes are alive with mischief. His speed increases. My entire body feels like it's on fire. In my veins, there's the slightest pulse of blue light that matches my rapid heartbeat. Faster. Andrin's hand slides lower, an almost invisible grip on the column of my throat, a golden collar. The air crackles. My hair lifts as if caught in a current, the Aether rising with every breath. When it finally crests, it breaks in a flash of light, leaving the room quiet and dim once more.

When my heart rate slows, I open my eyes again.

Andrin exhales slowly, his voice awed, "Magnificent."

I laugh weakly, still catching my breath, and sit up. He moves before I can, lifting me with ease and carrying me down the hall. His room welcomes us in a blur of motion and warmth, and when he sets me down, the tension between us finally eases into something softer, our movements savoring instead of starved.

Later, wrapped in the quiet aftermath, I let myself rest against him. The world feels distant, stars drifting behind my closed eyes.

As sleep pulls me under, I dream of light and endless skies— of constellations burning bright across an infinite dark.

CHAPTER 19

I wake up fully energized, alone, in Andrin's bed. The Europhic feeling of the Astrobleme has faded, but the energized feeling in my body remains.

I push myself out of bed, shower, and dress in the new workout clothes that have arrived. Andrin's not in the living room either. The space is empty and clean, and the food tray has been removed. The only thing out of order is the orb that still lies next to the dented wall. I had launched it across the room last night without touching it, without even trying to. The Aether must have repelled whatever makes the orb such a good conduit. I pick up the orb and toss it from hand to hand. There's now a dent in it, matching the size of the dent in the bulkhead it struck. Apparently, I had channeled a lot of power.

A spike of concern travels down my spine. That loss of control was unintentional. If I continue to grow my ability to manipulate Aether, I will have to develop my control. I have to be mindful of the damage another emotional surge could cause. While I like to think of myself as emotionally intelligent, I can be volatile. I always wear my emotions on my sleeve and rarely practice restraint.

The red lights in the hallway are still on, which means I could have only slept for a few hours. However, the Aether pushing through my body demands that I move; I cannot imagine going back to bed. On my way to the gym, I pass the cafeteria. Oki and Philomena are close together, and I smile, imagining their stolen moments between work. Before I can move on, she calls out to me. I follow their frantic waves and hurry into the cafeteria.

"What's wrong?" I whisper.

"The Commodore sent a message back." Philomena starts.

Her tone raises the hair on my arms. "What did he say? The suspense is making me nervous."

Oki responds first, "He said, '*Do not trust the Persei. The Persei gained their glory through sacrifice.*'"

Philomena grabs Oki's hands. Fear. Both sets of their bulbous eyes are wide. They have been around Persei longer than I have. They would know more about their species than I do—my conversation with Izar after Argos runs through my head again. The Imperial Commodore works for the Emperor. He would help uphold the Galaxia laws. The Commodore could be alluding to a similar situation as Scorpio, but for the Perseus Constellation.

Persei of the past could have done something monstrous enough for the Commodore to be concerned. Sacrifice? What kind of sacrifice?

I start to ask, "Did the Commodore—"

"Aurora. Are you ready to hit the track?"

Izar's words make me freeze. His voice is close. Close enough that he could have heard our conversation. We were discussing that the ruling species of the Perseus Constellation might be untrustworthy. Izar said his family is loyal to the Persei. Does that mean he is, too? How deep does that loyalty lie? As much as I don't want to run laps, I want to get Izar away from Philomena and Oki as fast as possible. I brush past Izar, but he is quick to catch up.

"Why are you discussing the Imperial Commodore?" Izar asks.

My steps falter. I want to vomit. He overheard. How much?

I make my voice light as I say, "Um, I'm trying to learn more about the galaxy. You know, since I'm new to the alien thing."

"Sure. This galaxy is called Galaxia, like yours was Andromeda." Izar grabs my arm to keep me moving. "And you should be careful about talking to anyone off the station."

My brows furrow. "Why do I need to be careful?"

"Because the King directed you not to have any contact outside of the station." Izar warns.

This time, I stop and ask, "Why?"

Izar looks around the red-lit hallway and pulls me to keep us moving. In his silence, the gears in my brain keep turning. Maybe the Commodore had a reason to warn me. If the King is keeping me from contacting anyone, perhaps I shouldn't trust him.

Who would I contact? They couldn't have assumed I would have found out about the Commodore. Who else do I have? My parents.

I pull Izar's arm to stop. "Could I have been in contact with my parents?"

The conflict on his face gives me my answer. He forces us to keep moving, nearly pushing me through the airlock.

"Are you going to stop me from contacting them?" I press.

Izar storms across the training mats. "I'm not going to stop you from doing anything. You need to be prepared for the consequences of your actions. Now get on the mat."

Izar beats the alien goo out of me. Hit after hit. Starting with hand-to-hand, then with the spear, and when he breaks my training spear, back to hand-to-hand. The only highlight is that the taste of the sweat and blood is slightly more flavorful than that of cube food. I think I might even have a broken rib. While I'm already on the ground, Izar's barefoot descends. I barely roll out of the way in time before it hits the mat, right where my face had been.

"Will you calm down? Are you actually trying to kill me right now?" I exclaim.

Izar storms away a step. "Get up."

"No! I yield, okay? Whatever point you're trying to prove, it's been proven," I protest.

Izar spins, his topaz eyes blazing. "I don't think you've learned anything since you got here."

Now I bristle. I push myself off the floor, bracing my ribcage. I refuse to get scolded while lying on the ground.

"I've learned plenty. I couldn't manipulate Aether before, yet I just took on an entire horde of Belemytes on my own."

Izar quickly fires back. "Except you didn't. You burnt yourself out and needed Andrin to save you."

I turn to hide my hurt at the truth of his words, but he continues his assault.

"Are you always going to rely on someone to save you? Or only on your Aether stores when you're in danger? It's lazy and dumb. What if you run out of Aether again? What if you're overwhelmed and can't control it?"

I spin around to yell back at him. "I'm getting stronger, my Aether can be an asset! I can do more!"

Izar gets in my face, his sharp teeth flaring. "Do you know what a Super Nova is?"

Despite the strange topic change, I don't back down. "No, I don't. What does that have to do with—"

"A Super Nova is what happens when a star dies. When a star runs out of energy, its core depleted of fuel, it collapses in on itself," Izar hisses. "If you push yourself past your limits and drain your Aether, you will collapse, you will die. Aether comes at a cost."

We both let the words sit between us. The level of passion in his speech leaves no room for argument.

Once his heaving breaths slow to a stabilized rhythm, I speak. "Okay, fine. No Aether usage while fighting. No going Super Nova."

"Good, no going Super Nova." Izar bows his head for a moment; when he looks up, mischief has returned to his eyes. "Now back into the ring."

Izar continues to pummel me, although with less personal wrath. The idea of power keeps circling in my brain. The Harpyiai's words repeat in an echo; she and Ketos thought I would be more powerful.

"Have you heard of anyone called Ketos?"

Izar stumbles, his usual precision faltering as his elbow swings too high above my head. "Repeat that," he demands.

"Ketos? Is that another constellation? Or species? The Harpyiai said something about Ketos."

I have to pull back my own punch when it is clear Izar isn't focused on our sparring anymore. His entire body is off balance as his face scrunches in confusion. He shakes his head slightly before he finally answers.

"Ketos is the name of a Gigas. The primordial beings are more like forces of nature than aliens, we told you about when you first came aboard. The Gigas are supposed to have been created somewhere between the Age of Zero and the creation of Galaxia."

A pain begins to form behind my eyes at the wave of information. "What is the Age of Zero?"

"The beginning of everything." Izar continues shaking his head. "That does not matter, though. Ketos is just part of a bedtime story told to juveniles to ensure they behave. The Gigas don't exist anymore."

The steadiness of his words is not enough to sound convincing. Izar's distress only deepens my own. He abandons his fighting stance to drink from his canister. I do the same, still trying to comb through the tangle of information in my own head. The Harpyiai working with an archaic Gigas seems less likely than most things I have encountered during my time aboard the Orbital Station. I must have misheard her, or the name refers to someone else.

I am still chugging the bottle of electrolytes when Izar holds a pair of black holsters in front of me.

My eyebrows knit as I ask, "What are those?"

"A peace offering, for my earlier antics. They're daggers made from the strongest metal in Galaxia, from the Capital of Sagittarius."

I take the holsters and unsheathe two identical daggers the length of my forearm. They are lightweight, and the handles fit perfectly into my palms, the etched hatching adding grip. The same obsidian-like metal of the handle sharpens and gleams down a long blade. I twist the blades in my hands, and as the lights hit the metal, they shine in colorful hues. A rainbow of colors glimmers like oil in sunlight. The blades feel even more natural than the tanto blades Shihan Hikaru had let me hold on my last day in the dojo.

"I thought they'd be easier for you to use than the spear," Izar explains.

I flash a grateful smile. "They're beautiful, thank you."

"I won't stop you from contacting your parents," He whispers, almost incoherently.

I pause my inspection of the blades to look back at him. "Really?"

He gives me one stiff nod. "As long as we keep it between us, I can help get a message to them."

Relief floods my system. "Thank you, you don't know what that means to me."

"Family is everything." He turns, heading towards the airlock. "Keep those daggers on you. I am sure you will find a need for them when you convince Andrin to let you onto Sarpedon."

A devious smile breaks across my lips. Of course, Izar would assume I would want to find a way to join another adventure. He is right, of course; I surely won't be missing my last opportunity to step foot on another planet. One last hurrah before my homecoming can't hurt.

CHAPTER 20

The next afternoon, a meeting is called in the Pilot House as we approach Sarpedon. My last planet before my return to Earth. It's uninhabitable, the lone planet orbiting the Epsilon star. Only select places are stable enough to land on Sarpedon. Its crust has not yet solidified; a molten lava layer covers most of its surface. One day, the lava planet will become a terrestrial planet, but that won't happen for hundreds to thousands of years. That thermal energy emanating from the planet's core is why we are travelling to it.

I slip into the back of the Pilot House as Andrin briefs Izar and his piloting team. Andrin explains the mission objective. A problem arose with the new infrastructure for harnessing geothermal energy. A group of engineers and manufacturers on Sarpedon is meant to run the power plant, yet all communications and signal systems have gone silent. The King, Andrin's father, diverted the Orbital Station's navigation system to bring us here to investigate the radio silence. There is concern that something failed with their communication equipment, or, even worse, that an accident severely injured them and the plant. Since it is such a vital asset to the Constellation, Andrin was tasked directly with ensuring the mission's success.

As soon as Andrin exits the Pilot House, I follow him down the hall. "Hey."

He beams at the sight of me. "Aurora, hi."

I lean against the wall and look up at him. "I was wondering if I could ask you for a favor." I blink my eyelashes for extra effect.

His Adam's apple bobs. "Can it wait until after Sarpedon? I need to prepare."

I grab his forearm just above his vambrace. "Actually, that's what I wanted to talk to you about. I really want to go. I want to visit one last planet before I go home."

He runs his hand through his curls. "I don't know Aurora. It could be dangerous."

"You said it's probably just a communication system failure, right? And if it is dangerous, I could help you and Izar. You've both been commenting on how incredibly my powers have developed."

I squeeze his hands, smiling up at him. I watch as the hesitation dissolves and his resolve breaks.

He sighs. "Only if you take another shot of Astrobleme before we go."

I smile so big it is almost painful. "Deal!"

I throw my arms around his shoulders before planting a kiss on his cheek. He is stunned long enough that he barely wraps his arms around me before I am pulling away and running down the hall.

"I'm going to get dressed!" I announce.

Since apparently my desires are predictable to everyone but Andrin, Philomena already set out a clean, white space suit on my bed. This special material adapts to maintain a moderate internal temperature while withstanding extreme external temperature changes. An added benefit to my comfort since my body temperature tends to skyrocket when I utilize my Aether. It will keep me from sweating, no matter how much Aether I expend. On a planet as hot as Sarpedon, sweating poses a larger risk than overheating. Sweat can quickly evaporate into steam, burning off flesh faster than I could die from dehydration or overheating.

I pause with the material just above my waist when Andrin knocks on my door, syringes in hand. The sight of the blue liquid makes my skin run hot. My fingers tingle with anticipation of the euphoric feeling that followed my first injection. my thoughts darken, and concern about my sudden shift toward accepting this foreign material in my body cools my desire for only a moment before the needle meets my arm. Andrin administers a shot to both of us; our skins glowing like blue and gold beacons, all other thoughts forgotten. After removing the needle, he presses his thumb against my wound. Lifting my arm to his mouth, he plants small kisses up until he reaches my neck. I already split my hair into my braids, so he has full access to my flesh.

"You're glorious," He murmurs against my skin.

He captures my smile with his lips. I kiss him back, grasping the hair at the nape of his neck.

"Thank you for including me," I mumble between kisses.

"I'm glad I can bring you along. You're an asset." He gives me one last kiss before pulling back. "Now, as much as I'd love for you to wear the suit like that, it's time to pack out."

I smack his shoulder and pull the suit over my shoulders. Andrin holds his hand out for me before we slip out the door. Once we reach the bay, we finish dressing out. Head to toe, heat-protected, and armed. Izar waits for us at the charging pod airlock. I smile at him, but he only nods in return after seeing the daggers strapped to the outside of both of my thighs. I had been worried the metal daggers would melt on Sarpedon's surface, but Izar doesn't seem to share the concern.

"In case anything happens. Don't hesitate," Izar instructs.

I nod, my giddy mood dimmed slightly. "I promise not to falter."

Izar seems satisfied with my answer because he turns back towards the airlock and opens the door for us. A chill runs up my spine as the three of us step inside. Something is wrong with Sarpedon. Whatever that is, we'll be face-to-face soon.

The Charging Pod launches, and the gravity around us evaporates. I wiggle my toes inside the boot that remains latched to the ground. This will be my last planet, my last adventure—a cold pit forms behind my sternum. I will have to give up all this excitement to get my Earth life back.

The automatic voice guides us through the trip. "Pod 125 has arrived at the Drop Off Point."

I take Andrin and Izar's hands in both of mine. "Time for one last trip into the future," I say.

My eyelids close moments before the Aether Cross flash.

I open my eyes when the brightness beyond my eyelids darkens. The spins have mostly ceased, and the Crossings feel no worse than mild motion sickness now. I focus on Andrin's hand still clasped in mine until my vision stabilizes. When I finally look up, a gasp escapes my lips.

We are standing on a grated platform. The frost along the platform railing confirms that we are in Sarpedon's mesosphere. This is the top platform of the power plant. The steam and superheated water will be pumped all the way up here for cooling. Then it will be pulled back down by gravity once it condenses. The tubes that hold the water are massive in height and width. Miles high to reach all the way up here, with a diameter of half a football field. Over the side of the platform, all I can see is the base of the plant and a sea of red lava between plates of black rock. Soon, they returned to me from where they had been inspecting a communication panel mounted on the side of the superstructure.

Andrin speaks first, "There is no signal. From the transmitter or receiving end. It looks like there's no power to the plant at all. We will have to go down to the base."

My vambrace clinks against his as I grab his hand. "I'm assuming there is no elevator."

I hear a chuckle from Izar beside me before he grabs my hand too. The surge of Aether inside me tells me we are about to Cross, so I close my eyes.

The landing is rough, the surface is uneven. Probably because the rock plates are floating on a magma surface. The heat is nearly suffocating. Despite the temperature-controlled suit, I can feel it around me. The stench of sulfur leaks through the immense ventilation system of our helmets. Andrin and Izar release my hands as they move towards the building entrance. Watching my steps very carefully, I follow behind. The plates shift beneath my feet, some more than others. The childhood game of *'floor is lava'* did nothing to prepare me for a real lava floor.

They type in a code, and the airlock opens. Once through the other side, we pause. Something is very, very, wrong here.

It's dark. The long tunnel is lit only by dull red lights down the middle of the ceiling. They seem similar to the nighttime setting of lights up in the Orbital Station, but only half of the installed lights above are illuminated. As we walk, the metal floor reverberates with the thuds of our rubber-soled boots, echoing down the long hall. Beyond a faint electronic buzz of the lights, it's silent. Not even the hum of an air-conditioning system, which should be imperative for a building with electronics on a superheated planet.

Strange shapes draw my eyes to the wall, but the light is too dim to make out the details. I summon light to sit in my hand and lean closer. There are dents and scorch marks on the metal walls. Andrin grabs my wrist and pulls my hand down.

"Put it out," Izar warns, his voice deadly stern.

I extinguish the light before I am yanked down the hallway. Izar and Andrin have both extended their spears as they move swiftly. With my free hand, I pull out my own spear. We round a bend and halt.

Bodies.

There are lifeless bodies on the ground. Aliens of different species and forms lay haphazardly at the entrance of another door. Izar holds his hand up before advancing. I don't dare speak a word. Every inch of my skin is covered with goosebumps. I can feel my braid trying to rise beneath my helmet, its static electricity growing.

Izar motions us forward, and he disappears into the doorway. As Andrin pulls me along, I inspect the bodies we must step over. Some of them look like the massive stout movers from Seriphus. Or they would, if they still had all four limbs attached. There is the body of one land-octopus alien. I would assume it would also be orange if it did not look like grilled calamari in its current form. As we enter what appears to be a large control room, others are there. Numerous Asprutan, the same forest spout species as Philomena, are scorched. There may be other species, but I do not recognize them. Maybe because I have never come across them before, or because they are decimated beyond recognition.

They are all dead; at least fifty lives lay wasted on the industrial floor. These must be all the engineers and maintainers who are supposed to be running the plant. Andrin pauses before one that looks human. Human but with seared golden skin, a Persei.

After assessing no immediate danger, Izar collapses his spear and motions from the largest desk in the center of the room. I collapse my own spear and move to meet Izar. I stumble for a moment, and Andrin still stands frozen, his hand locked tight around mine as he stares at the fallen Persei. I want to comfort him, but imminent danger takes priority. I squeeze his hand and gently turn his helmet towards me with my free hand.

"Andrin?"

He blinks, fast enough I almost miss the water in his soft green eyes. "It is fine."

He stalks forward, now pulling me behind him with an even tighter grip on my hand. Izar inspects a set of screens with keyboards below, similar to the control panels in the Orbital Station's pilot house. The console is black, yet only one screen is damaged.

"There's no power. I think the entire base is running on reserve power, which explains the red lights but lack of ventilation," Izar whispers.

"We need to get it started again. We need to know what went wrong," Andrin demands.

"I can try." Their eyes shoot to me.

They exchange a glance before Andrin speaks, "Aurora, I don't— "

I stand up straight, determined to convince them. "Let me try. At least the console. You two have been Aether Crossing us around. I have more than enough Aether. I am on edge, caught in the thriller-movie tension of this deserted building. I have a charge I feel like I need to burn off."

They look at each other again, as if in a silent argument. Finally, Andrin nods toward the console. I step toward it, my vambraces already glowing. I place my hands on the console top above the screens. I have no idea whether this will work or how I would make it work. I just have a feeling. I let the feeling build, drawing on my anxious energy. There, my Aether sparks from the tip of my right ring finger and sends a bolt into the console.

"By the stars—" Izar's shock prefaces the light.

The console clicks. The hum of an exhaust fan starts. The motor inside the console struggles against the building's heat as the screens light up. Izar doesn't waste a moment before his fingers are flying across the console. A series of videos fills every screen. Security cameras. He keeps pressing the buttons, rewinding the footage until the rooms are illuminated again.

Izar points to the far left screen. "There."

We watch the hallway video feed. The lights are on, and aliens move around as if it were a regular workday. Until a red form storms down the hallway. Everyone scatters to get out of her way. The Harpyiai.

"What is she doing here?" The fear leaks through my voice.

Andrin shakes his head. "I don't know. I don't understand. She—"

Izar interrupts, "Look."

We turn back to the screen. A black blob charges through the open bay door. The engineers and maintainers scramble in panic. This black alien is one I haven't seen before. It looks reptilian. Flanked in black scales, stalking forward on all four haunches, a serpent-like head swinging in front of it. Two of the barrel-chested aliens rush forward to attack it, but both are stopped in their tracks by an eruption of fire from its jaws. An

Aspurtan runs to the wall, slams a switch, and causes the light to go out across all screens.

"What is that?" My voice is shrill.

"It's an Ignos." Andrin's hand wraps protectively around my hip. "I thought they were extinct."

Izar scoffs, "Apparently not. What do you want to do? Abandon the station?"

Andrin shakes his head as he continues his conversation with Izar above me. I cannot stop staring at the footage. The strobing lights pulse through the silent video feed like a vintage horror movie. The Harpyiai argues with Persei aliens in the very same spot we stand now. The Ignos continues its destructive path forward. It reminds me of a demonic Komodo dragon or of a fantastical wingless dragon; I really wish that fairytale creature had remained fictional.

The Ignos throws one of the octopus-like aliens across the control room as it breaches the inner chamber. The alien hits a wall of electronics and slides down with sticky slowness, fluid leaking from its form. The Ignos releases a torrent of fire towards the alien and—

The camera feed cuts out to grey pixels. Whatever equipment was behind the octopus alien must have been a power distribution center. I look towards the space where the equipment should be, but a wall of scorched metal stands in its place. The screens that held camera feed show only static, the proof of where the Harpyiai went, disappearing. I hope the Harpyiai got scorched too.

The timing is suspicious. She came here before Seriphus. Both planets are used to generate massive amounts of power for the Perseus Constellation. She and Ketos, whoever that is, are searching for a light. Which must be an energy source.

Earth, and three planets in the constellation that the King has sent his son to, seem too improbable to be a coincidence.

Andrin's voice breaks through my thoughts. "We can't just abandon the station. My father won't let us within a light year of Mirfak if we fail at this."

"Just tell him the base was destroyed. There is nothing else we can do," Izar argues back.

Andrin continues to scheme. "We just need to get the generator started. Once the generator starts, it activates the water circulation, and the turbines generate power, which is fed back into the generator. If we can give the generator a kick start, the plant will run. We can send a new plant team to keep it running afterwards."

Izar scoffs, "What is your grand plan to turn on the generator to complete your mission, Taxiarhos?"

I flinch. Izar only calls Andrin 'Taxiarhos' when he's furious. They continue to whisper-yell above my head until I push against their chests to separate them.

I interject, "What if I can do it?"

They both freeze. Izar seems to follow my train of thought first.

"No. Absolutely not. That will take far too much Aether."

"I can do it. I'm fully charged with Astrobleme. If this is the Harpyiai's work, I want to be part of ruining her plan." I turn to Andrin. "You said so yourself, I am an asset. Let me be an asset."

Andrin does not give Izar time to argue back. "Fine. Pull up the schematics."

"Andrin," Izar protests.

"Pull up the schematics or go guard the door, Syntag," Andrin commands.

Izar shoots Andrin a lethal glare, but does as he's told. After pulling up the plant blueprints, they both explain the plant layout to me. The plan is to get to the water circulation pump and start it. If I can start the pump, the water will begin circulating through the magma, where it will be superheated, then continue to the turbine and generator, and finally be cooled by the mesosphere before returning to the molten surface. The pump is outside of the base, on the opposite entrance we came in. There are intake and discharge sides with butterfly valves I must open. Then I will have to open the electrical panel, deliver a strong enough shock to give the pump a kick-start without frying it, and throw the switch.

Shouldn't be hard at all.

It's not as if I only learned how to manipulate Aether a few weeks ago.

Izar types a message that will wait in a cueing system, standing by to be transmitted as soon as the plant restores power. The three of us head back towards the door through the thin path not littered with dead bodies. I take note of Andrin's refusal to look at the fallen Persei as we pass this time. As we walk towards the open bay, my hair stands on end. My Aether warns me first. A scrap sounds behind us. Izar pauses, and Andrin stops a moment later. Slowly, we all turn towards the noise.

A seething Ignos bellows a roar that echoes down the hallway.

"Run!" Izar shouts.

I don't hesitate. My booted feet pound across the steel floor as I propel myself towards the open air. I hear Andrin and Izar sprinting behind me, keeping pace just a few meters behind.

"Go to the pump. Start it. We will hold it back," Andrin commands.

Andrin and Izar both skid to a halt at Andrin's command. I look over my shoulder, ready to protest and fight alongside them.

"Go! Watch out for the heads!" The gleaming topaz of Izar's eyes sends me back into motion.

I push myself harder—my arms pumping. My legs move faster than I have ever pushed them before. I nearly stumble when the structure gives way to rock plates. The sudden movement of the plates beneath me causes me to tumble halfway to the ground. I catch myself with one hand on the toasted rock before I push off like a sprinter.

Leaping from rock to rock, I stay near the base of the structure. Along the wall, I see the massive pump, the size of a small house, with pipes on either side. I sprint to the closest pipe valve first. The valve handle is enormous, the length of my entire arm. I try to pull, but it barely budges. I duck under the handle and push. I throw my whole body weight against it until it finally gives way. I glance back towards the bay for any glimpse of my companions.

Instead of my friends, I see an Ignos. A terrified part of me hopes it is a different Ignos. If it's the same, that means—

It sniffs the air before its head snaps towards me. It releases a horrid roar—time to move.

I run around the pump, desperate to get to the other valve. I press my body against the lever, willing it to move. I don't have to look over my shoulder to tell that the Ignos is closing fast. The slapping of its scaled tail against the rock tells me it's close enough. I push against the handle and flex my thighs to brace myself on the ground with as much force as I can. I look between the lever and the Ignos stampeding towards me. A pained squeal comes from the level as it rotates a few inches. The Ignos opens its jaws, so close to me now.

I can see it, a flame forming in the back of its throat. I duck before the flame can exit. I roll out of the way of the Ignos just in time for it to throw its own body against the lever. The lever pops open with a rattle and groan. I'm back on my feet before the Ignos can turn around. My fingers find the button of my spear, and it extends to its full length, the tip glowing like a beacon of blue.

The Ignos charges again. The open jaws spill flames at my feet. I leap back, almost falling over the ledge of a plate. My left boot feels sticky, like the thick sole is melting. The Ignos rallies its head back for another flame. I leap over the scorched ground and try my best to gain distance. I need to get to the pump without getting the pump or myself roasted like chestnuts on an open fire.

My only option left is to stop the Ignos before it can stop me.

Running in a zigzag pattern, I dodge the Ignos' fire. I count as the assault continues. Five seconds. It takes the alien five seconds between each flame to recharge. Each flame spray only lasts a single second. Deadly, but not hopeless. The Ignos starts to catch onto my pattern, just as I wanted it to. When it takes aim again, I skid to a halt.

The massive beast cannot stop as quickly. Its hind legs dig into the rock, tearing up the ground as it does. The momentum is exactly what I hoped for.

As the massive lizard halts, it spikes itself right onto the end of my spear. I channel a burst of Aether through the glowing point. The neck splinters open, black scales and black blood spurting out from the open wound. The head splatters to the ground, jaw still ajar. The body slumps to the ground after.

Whipping the black goo off my face mask, I quickly return my attention to the pump.

I only make it a step before I hear movement. The sound of scales dragging across the rock. My head turns back, my eyes unwilling to see the monstrous sight behind me.

Watch out for the heads.

Izar hadn't meant fire.

From the bubbling black goo, scales grow. Scales grow and branch out in two directions.

I start running.

I run before I can see the source of the now identical two roars of the Ignos. Where are Andrin and Izar? If they couldn't take down one Ignos together, what chance would I stand alone? Why do so many aliens have multiple heads?

Pump.

Get to the pump.

Start the pump.

That is my job. I make a mental promise that if we all survive this, I will thank Izar for making me run all those laps. I don't slow my steps. With full momentum, my body slams into the side of the pump. Now I need a door, a door to an electrical panel.

Fire sears the metal beside my head. Way too close. I roll to the side so I can face the Ignos. My suspicions were right, two heads. I duck while the second head shoots fire. Two heads, five seconds of reload each, one second of firepower, seemingly one after the next. Which means I have only three seconds of safety before I get flame-sprayed. Cutting off the heads clearly won't help me. I don't like working with exponentials.

My Aether rallies inside my blood, waiting to be called upon. If only I knew what to do with it. Over my shoulder, I see a metal plate, dented and jutting from the smooth face of the pump. There must be electrical components on the other side of the panels. All I have to depend on for survival is a hope and a wish. So, I really hope I'm right.

Of course, the Ignos is in my way. Its tail slams into the side of the pump. I need to finish this before it can cause irreparable damage to the pump. Otherwise, it won't matter how much Aether I push into it. I raise my spear and stab into the chunkiest section of the tail, forcing it to push past the crunch of scales and into the meaty mass. On pure instinct, my Aether shoots down the end of the spear. With a roar, the Ignos' tail flops to the ground. The Ignos takes a step towards me, but wobbles. The tail helped stabilize the creature; now it's off balance. I send another wish into the universe that it can't regrow a tail like salamanders.

I make my move, charging towards the metal sheet. It's half-fastened to the wall, half-free. I think back to when Andrin cut through the swarm of Belemytes; his spear blasted Aether like a knife blade. I focus my thoughts on the end of my spear; the Aether blade is replicated.

With a quick slash, I shear the metal sheet clear off the wall. It clatters to the ground, still sizzling where the heated metal's rough edges. My spear is vertical again, just in time to hit the chest cavity of the lunging Ignos. It reels back, spear still lodged between its scales, and it rips the spear from my hands. I take the daggers from my thigh holsters and hold them in a fighting stance. They are too short. The heads or their flames will reach me before I can get it. Flames spray from the metal panel all the way to my feet. Without thinking, I pounce forward, a dagger stabbing into the eye of one head. Another weapon is lost as that head rips back in agony. It swings its injured head around in distress while the second one prepares for another attack.

My Aether wells up inside of me. The least I can do before I get fried is start the pump. Even if I die, I won't let the Harpyiai win. I lunge for the opening in the pump and slam my right hand against the exposed electronics. I can't feel a single volt of electricity through the system, which might have been something I had considered first if I were not about to get barbecued. I push my built-up charge into the pump, willing it to work.

For just a moment, I look into the sky. A black sky streaked with orange, smoky plumes. Pits of blackness slip between the clouds of lava exhaust filled with a million little stars. I wish on every star in the sky that my Aether can start the pump with a random electrical shock mid-circuit, rather than create an explosion instead. The system takes and takes from my energy reserves.

My stationary moment costs me. The uninjured head has recharged. It aims right at my face. My eyes snap shut as I hold my left hand out, a hopeless form of protection. The heat is searing. Rippling in waves over my skin. Yet the flames don't reach my flesh. They are halted mere inches from my hand. The heat of the flame is flowing into me.

I'm absorbing thermal energy.

Thermal energy. Heat. Fire.

Fire needs fuel, oxygen, an uninhibited chemical chain reaction, and, of course, heat.

I am stealing the heat from the flame. A spark of energy bolts from my right hand across the electronics. If I can take thermal energy from the Ignos' fire, maybe I can use it too. The fire from the uninjured head dissipates, but the daggered eye head readies to take its turn. Flame takes form in its jaw, readying. With one hand on the panel and the other towards the Ignos, I ready myself too.

It releases its flames, but all I see is white.

The light diminishes. The pump behind me rattles and shudders to life. I want to breathe a sigh of relief, but the pump seems inconsequential now. The Ignos roils back, flame absent from its maw. I blink at my hand, lifted towards the Ignos. Not an ember or scorch mark to be seen. I've done it again. I absorbed the fire straight from the Ignos twice. Wishes on stars can come true.

My hand pulses. Warmth. I'm still charged.

The Ingos raises its injured head, rearing for another flame. I raise my charged hand. A double roar comes from the dual-headed lizard.

One more wish, I promise the universe.

Heat and flame billow out of the Ignos' mouth. I stand fast as a barrier around my hand keeps my flesh safe, waves of heat bending through the air like a desert mirage. I narrow my eyes at the beast, then I push back.

I push the charge of Aether in my hand back towards the open mouth. Aether sparks from my hand, a spike of blue light that suffocates the orange flame. It eats away at the orange flame until it dives down the Ignos' head, blue light cracking through every gap of black scales.

In a burst, it splits the Ignos' head in two. Without pausing for deliberation, I send a second line of blue light down the jaw of the second head, and a second explosion occurs. The Ignos sags to the ground. I pant, terrified that more heads will grow. My arms shake as I brace my palms on my knees. Black goo and steam seep out of the neck wounds before the form deflates. The mass continues to shrink until it is nothing more than a splat of black scales with my dagger and spear buried under the tar-like substance.

The adrenaline in my blood dips, and I drop to my knees. I have to gulp down air so I will not pass out. The pump is operable, and this Ignos is dead. My mission is complete twice over. My next concern is Andrin and Izar. I can't stop yet.

CHAPTER 21

My head spins towards the base's bay door. Still no sign of the Andrin or Izar. A second boost of adrenaline races through my system as I push off the rocky plates and take off towards the structure. My boot has, in fact, melted, which slightly throws off my balance. Despite it, I push harder. Just as I get to the bay doors, I see Andrin and Izar backing out of it, spears in hand. The first Ignos, now with eight heads, is behind them.

"Pumps on, time to go!" I shout.

Andrin spins to see me, relief flush on his face. I close the distance between us, Andrin grabbing my arm and Izar's before a flash of light takes over my vision. My teeth slam together as we land in a tumbled mess on the ice, frosted metal grates. The mesosphere platform shakes slightly now. The hiss of steam and the rush of water through the pipes are loud, confirming the plant is back in full operation.

Andrin throws an arm around my shoulders and kisses the top of my head. "You did it."

"Let's get out of here," Izar pants from beside us.

Andrin's face creases. "I don't know if I have the Aether to Aether Cross all three of us right now. Fighting with the Ignos nearly drained me."

I wiggle my gloved fingers. "I have more. I have enough to Aether Cross to the Charging Pod. I can get myself there for sure, I think I have some to spare to help you two, too."

Izar's mosaic skin crinkles beneath the vizor of his helmet, but Andrin nods as he says, "Okay, let's do this."

The three of us latch onto each other once more. Using his watch to pull up the homing coordinates, I concentrate on the numbers. I imagine the precise position of the Charging Pod, floating in orbit above Sarpedon. I can almost feel it around me while we stand on the frozen platform. I nod to Andrin and close my eyes. The flash blooms behind my eyelids, our feet touching down before I open them. The steadiness beneath my feet confirms we are on a flat surface. I release a shaky breath when I open my eyes. We are safely in the pod. I sag with relief, letting myself slide to the floor. I rip my gloves and helmet off and throw them at my feet.

"Let's go home," I gasp between panted breaths.

Only the sound of our heavy breathing and the automated voice fills our travel back to the Orbital Station. We go through the decontamination process, and I begin walking to my room. I'm desperate to wash the smell of smoke out of my hair.

"You did great today. Truly incredible," Andrin calls to me as he jogs, trying to catch up with me.

"Thank you," I say over my shoulder without stopping.

For once, I do not feel talkative. I'm not drained, but I feel hollow. I channeled a lot of power today. More than on all other days, combined. I had taken energy from the Ignos' fire. Without much thought, I had converted thermal energy into something usable. Something deep inside me warns me that it's unusual. I already knew my capabilities were more advanced than they should be, based on Izar's comments and the privacy reserved for my Aether manipulation training in Andrin's room.

As Andrin catches up to me, he tucks the loose strands of my hair behind my ear. "Are you okay?"

I put on a tired smile. "Yeah, just drained. I want to get some sleep."

Andrin nods. "Go to bed. I have to send a report off to my father before I can call it a night. Do you want a shot of Astrobleme before bed?"

Maybe that will cure my hollow feeling. The liquid always fills me with a sense of renewed life force. I nod and give him another faux tired smile before he heads in the opposite direction. Once clean, I slip under the scratchy sheets of my bed, but Andrin has yet to arrive with Astrobleme.

My power has grown significantly since my first day on the Orbital Station. I had a reason to fear the Harpyiai. Now, she should fear me. Today I defeated an Ignos on my own. Tomorrow, I will be on my way back home.

With the hiss of the airlock, my eyes barely flutter open. My feigned fatigue has turned real. Andrin enters and kneels beside my bed, taking my arm that sits above the blankets. I cannot keep my eyes open long enough to watch him. The sting of the syringe and burn of Astrobleme in my blood tells me it is done. Without a word, Andrin departs. Despite my closed eyes, the blue glow of my skin illuminates the room. Once again, the sense of de-ja-vu washes over me as I drift off to sleep.

CHAPTER 22

"What do you mean we aren't going back to Earth!" Everyone in the Pilot House cringes at my outburst.

"Aurora, I'm sorry. My father overrode the navigation system again. We already started the journey back to Mycenae." He tries to grab my hand, but I slap it away. "Aurora—"

Out of my peripheral vision, I see Izar hold a hand against his chest to stop him. "Let her cool off. I'll make sure she doesn't try to Cross out of a Charging Pod again."

I scoff at the thinly veiled promise of being babysat. Andrin remains in the Pilot House while Izar jogs to meet me.

"Let's hit the mats. That usually does the trick when you're feeling pissy," Izar jests.

A near growl leaves my throat. I make Izar open all the doors. I'm afraid that if I touch any metal right now, I might electrocute the entire station. Maybe I should.

As we pass through a set of double airlocks, Izar whispers. "You got a message back from your parents." He slips a paper to me.

My hands shake as I take it, my anger temporarily deflating to a painful longing. I had asked Izar to send a simple message for me, since he said they would receive it by email. I told them I was sorry it had been so long since I'd called, but I was on a remote job with limited connectivity. I told them I would be home soon. I wish my entire message hadn't been a lie.

Aurora,

You know better than to drop off the face of the planet without so much as a phone call! You're lucky we didn't contact every embassy in the world!
But your mom and I both hope you are enjoying your latest adventure. Your mom worries when you go so long without contact, so please try to get in touch again soon, Little Traveler.

Dare to do,
Dad

Waters crests within my eyelids. I read the note ten times before I summon the same heat I had felt on Sarpedon. I focus on a pinpoint-sized spot until it starts to smoke. The smoke turns into a charred spot before it ignites. In seconds, the ash and smoke are drawn through the airlock's air purification system.

When I meet Izar's eyes, his eyebrows are raised, but he says nothing. The note from my parents doused my temper, but only slightly. Without another word, I push onward towards the training bay. We run through sparring drills, neither of us pulling punches, but our movements are emotionless.

"What weapons would you like to start with today?" Izar asks, trying to ease the tension we both still hold.

I glance around the training bay, and a few aliens are using the facilities.

Izar matches my suspicious movements with his own. "What happened at Sarpedon after you left Andrin and me for the pump? Something has been different with you since we got back."

I step closer to Izar and lower my voice to a whisper. "I'm missing one of my daggers."

Alarm rises on his colorful face. "Did someone steal –"

"No. I used it. Yesterday."

I can almost see the gears turning in Izar's head while he silently thinks through the events that took place yesterday. His features darken when he arrives at a solution.

"You came across another Ignos." He determines.

I hold the silence between us for a beat, unsure of how much to tell. "Yes. I was able to kill it."

Izar's eyes snap to mine, shock evident in his expression.

"Andrin and I couldn't handle one when it was both of us." His voice is low in warning.

I nod my head in agreement. "I know. That's why I didn't want to say anything."

"You used your dagger against it, yet you still had enough time to turn on the pump."

"Yes," I whisper.

Izar nods, reading between the lines. "How?"

I open my hands. "Heat. I stole the heat from its flame."

Izar freezes. "Does Andrin know?"

A shot of guilt rips through me. I don't know why; I feel strange about what happened on Sarpedon. Instead of running through my string of complicated emotions, I shake my head.

"For our egos? Aurora, come on. Why?" Izar presses.

I run my tongue along the inside of my teeth. "Not for your egos. I did it with my Aether manipulation. It was different. It didn't feel safe."

Izar nods, giving the space another inspection for eavesdroppers. I think of my growing capabilities. The extent of my power, I've started to hide. The more I've trained, the more I can feel it, like there is a force alive inside of me.

"I haven't met anyone capable of all that. You're getting more powerful. Can you control it?" Izar asks.

I let myself think of the Aether that boils my blood just beneath the surface of my skin right now. Completely invisible. Under my control, but only for now.

"Yes." The half-lie tastes sour on my tongue. "Most of the time."

Izar's arm lands on my upper arm, causing us both to stop. His topaz eyes flare with light.

"I'm worried about you going Super Nova. I know you think the Astrobleme has been helping you, but if you can't control your Aether, it might only be creating a bigger problem."

I consider his words. I know he has been unhappy with Andrin giving me Astrobleme. Yet it has been helping. I have gotten significantly stronger, though perhaps a little unstable. It has to be worth it. I won't have to worry about aliens taking advantage of me if I'm more powerful than they are. I can live peacefully on Earth without worrying about the Harpyiai or Ketos. The thought of being near the Harpyiai still makes my stomach churn.

"What do you think the Harpyiai was doing on Sarpedon?" I ask. "Why attack it?"

Izar shakes his head. "I don't know. It's been something I've been trying to figure out, too."

I let the silence settle between us. A million questions demand my attention. I'm supposed to be going home. Yet an itch in my brain keeps pestering me, begging me to understand Galaxia. Now, the Commodore's warning about the Persei shouts for my notice. If the King is making me go to Mycenae, I might have to rely on my only other alien contact with resources.

Suddenly, I blurt. "Hey, I gotta go."

Before Izar can protest, I'm jogging out of the gym. Sweaty and still strapped with my single dagger, I search the entire Orbital Station for Philomena. I finally find her in an industrial-style laundry room I've never been to before. She's sweating from the steam, and guilt instantly stabs my chest. She's been taking care of me this entire time, and I haven't made nearly enough effort to help.

"Princess, what are you doing down here?" She asks.

"I need you to send one last message to the Commodore for me. They aren't taking me back to Earth. Tell the Commodore, if he really wants to find me, I'll be on Mycenae."

Her eyes widen. "Is everything okay?"

A puff of air leaves my chest. "I don't know."

PART 3

R. A. SANDS

CHAPTER 23

Philomena dresses and styles me to meet the King and Queen of the Perseus Constellation on Mycenae.

Home planet of the Persei species.

Ruling planet of the star Mirfak, capital of the Perseus Constellation.

She styles my hair with golden clips, dusts gold over every inch of my skin, then applies thick black eyeliner and mascara. She wraps me in layers of white linen until the strips resemble a beautiful yet revealing dress. Despite the erroneous effort, it is pretty. I look gorgeous.

I've missed feeling pretty.

The off-white-to-white baggy linens and spandex have not been flattering. I'm luminescent now. After admiring my appearance for the millionth time, I strap on my single dagger thigh holster, slip on the golden vambraces, and put on my leather sandals. Beautiful and powerful.

As I enter the Pilot House, I nod to the familiar members, unwilling to make small talk. I refuse to meet Andrin or Izar's eyes, but I can see they are dressed in a similar flamboyant fashion. The large window reveals the approach to a wondrous blue-and-green planet.

Mycenae is only a third of the size of Earth, but it has more surface area covered by water. Its land is made up of many islands and islets, connected by channels. The automated voice counts down our descent. The lower in altitude we go, the more amazing the view gets.

Pillars of pearlescent skyscrapers built upon white rock shorelines jut into the sky. Smaller, white block buildings come into view; polka-dotted like old relics in a new world. At the very edge of the peninsula, perched on a cliff, is a massive palace. Iridescent pillars create open corridors, with lush green gardens surrounding turquoise pools. It's like an Olympus made futuristic.

We dock outside of the central Acropolis, between where the green countryside and city converge into the skinny peninsula. Docking stations with hangars and many more buildings surround us, making up Mycenae's main Space Station. We are to debark here and be escorted to the palace, where a royal reception is planned, a very formal welcome home for their Crowned Prince.

The bay door is already lowered by the time we arrive. A stream of aliens lines the bay, and Andrin is to exit before anyone else. He walks ahead first, Izar half a step behind on his right, I on Izar's left. As Andrin passes, the aliens along the procession bow their heads deeply. The outside air feels instantly sticky compared to the cold, dry air of the Orbital Station. I swear I can smell the sea salt from the coast only a few miles away. Inside, my Aether crackles. Anxious, alive, charged. I focus my breathing into a slow, rhythmic pattern, taking special care to keep my skin pale and static electricity away from my perfectly styled hair.

Andrin steps onto Mycenae soil, Izar a moment after him. My steps falter, falling behind. A slow exhale of breath. An even charge lies under my skin. I lift my leather sandals and step foot onto Mycenae. I grab both of their hands and wait for Andrin to Aether Cross us. With a bright flash, we are transported. The light dissipates, and Andrin steps forward again, releasing my hand. Izar drops my hand but doesn't leave my side.

An arch of pearlescent towers awaits us. White and purple sweeps of fabric hang in swags outside every white-sandstone window. Lush green foliage with small white flowers crawls up the sides of the first floor. A set of massive wood doors opens before us—a crowd of gold and white looms within the courtyard.

"Remember what you are capable of," Izar whispers to me, "Don't trust anyone."

I gape at Izar, but he presses his hand against my shoulder blade, urging me towards the entrance, his face void of emotion like the sphinx statue he resembles. I shift my head forward as music begins to play ahead of us. Andrin is halfway down the procession before we enter. I swallow, schooling my face and centering the Aether blooming in my chest. On my exhale, I step onward, into the capital of Mycenae.

Music flows around us. String and wind instruments play an upbeat, loud melody. I breathe in through my nose and gently out through my mouth, keeping my face still, my lips barely parted. The thick scents of sweet flavors and rich food fill my nose, making me salivate. At the end of the long tunnel of white-clothed, golden-skinned Persei, two thrones sit on a dais.

Seated on the thrones are Andrin's father and mother, the King and Queen of the Perseus Constellation.

His father looks startlingly similar to Andrin, except for the dark, curly beard shorn tight on his jaw. Their faces are almost identical, barely showing signs of age, except his father's skin is bronzed like worn gold, and a few wrinkles crease his face. His face also lacks Andrin's ever-present smile, and his eyes are a cold brown. The Queen sits next to him, on a notably lower throne, and has a mane of curly hair like Andrin's. Her skin still shines bright gold, and a slight smile forms on her plump lips as our eyes meet. Neither of them looks old enough to have a child as old as Andrin; his mother could pass as our age.

As we walk down the aisle, the Persei bow their heads. Izar and I keep our pace behind Andrin, stopping when he does at the foot of the dais. The music cuts in as we take our last steps. When he bows his head, I do the same.

A booming voice jolts me through the silence. "By the Stars, the Crown Prince of Persei, Taxiahos Andrin, has returned home. May we thank our Golden Elders! Rejoice all and share in our happiness."

Noise fills the open courtyard, as suddenly as it had ceased. All around us, conversations come alive as the Persei resume their movement throughout the courtyard. I feel eyes watching us where we remain at the foot of the dais, despite their split focus.

"Son," Andrin's father's booming voice speaks again. "Come closer so we may see for ourselves that you have returned safely from your travels."

I have to physically swallow to stop myself from laughing. Andrin has returned relatively safe. I never asked to join the intergalactic transit, but my safety was most at risk after leaving Earth. I'm running out of fingers to count my close calls since my abduction. Andrin steps forward, his mother squeezing his shoulder, before he and his father move close enough to speak quietly.

"You look well, Syntag," The Queen notes in her silky voice.

Izar nods deeply, a sly smile on his face. "Thank you, your Majesty. You look lovely, as always."

The Queen turns her attention to me next. "You must be the shining star they brought back from Earth. What is your name, dear?"

I copy Izar's nod. "Aurora, your Majesty." It may not be my birth name, but it is still my name.

The Queen holds out a hand, beckoning me closer. I close the distance until she reaches towards my hair, pushing a strand behind my ear. She tilts her head to the side as she inspects my features. A light shines in her eyes.

"By the Stars, welcome to Mycenae. I look forward to getting to know you, Aurora." The Queen holds the side of my face long enough to make me uncomfortable.

I jolt against her grasp as the King calls out, "We shall talk more in the family dining hall after the festivities. Enjoy the symposium and show our guest to her new quarters."

The King's words were spoken loudly, so that the public could hear them. Andrin nods at his dismissal and grabs my hand, leading us out of the open courtyard. Apparently, enjoying the symposium means letting everyone else enjoy the food and drinks; we are to go to our chambers. I follow Andrin's lead, keeping my head high despite the stares and whispers that follow us.

He leads me up a grand staircase, the polished sandstone reflecting the sunlight beaming in from the windowless sills. My head swivels around as we ascend. More of the same architectural designs I saw outside, but at every corner, a new detail is engraved into stone or metal. He leads me down a long hallway on the fourth floor before stopping in front of a tall door. It's made of pearlescent metal, with a retina scanner embedded in the frame.

"These will be your chambers. Your retina is already registered for all the rooms in the palace you might need access to."

My eyebrow quirks upward. "How did you get my eyeball information?"

Andrin laughs, "We were in the Orbital Station for over a month. The technology is advanced."

My brows dip as my eyes narrow into slits. "Wow, I wouldn't have guessed advanced technology would be involved in operating a *spacecraft*." Attitude heavily punctuates my last word.

Andrin leans forward and lets the system scan his eye. There is a metallic click, and he pushes the door open. The room is split into three sections. At the entrance is a sitting room, a fainting couch, and a library. To our right is an open bathroom, complete with a hot tub-sized bathtub and a rainfall-style shower. To the left is a massive bed and an open door revealing a walk-in closet. The room would be impressive enough, but the windows run from floor to ceiling, all open and exposed, gauzy curtains swaying in the light breeze. The room overlooks the turquoise ocean and cityscape stretching down the coastline.

"Whoa–" I gasp.

Andrin's chuckle tickles my ear. "I'll take that as approval."

"Very fancy," I mumble, turning towards the room again.

"I'm glad you like it. My rooms are on the fourth floor in the same wing," He says.

I turn, my eyebrow quirked at his forwardness. A rose gold colors his cheeks.

"I—I just meant—" He pulls two blue vials and syringes out of his pocket. "I also brought these."

My Aether itches my fingertips at the sight of Astrobleme. I hold out my arm. He quickly administers a shot to both of us before discarding the remains in a trash can. As the blue glow moves through my system and colors my skin, I take another look around the room.

"These rooms are very nice, but aren't they a little unnecessary? You agreed you would take me back to Earth after we stopped here so you could acquire a new spacecraft," I remind him.

A knock sounds on the door, saving him from any further explanation. I breathe through the excess Aether in my system and will my complexion back to its naturally pale state. Izar seems momentarily shocked to see us both exit my bedroom. He quickly settles his mosaic skin into a teasing smirk.

"I see you were getting the Royal tour of your rooms. Sorry to interrupt you with boring obligations," He jests.

I fight the blush on my cheeks and push Izar's shoulder. He bows his head to Andrin as he exits behind me. As we walk down the hallway, the formalities return. Andrin is in front, although his hand still clasps mine. Izar and I resume our places behind him. We only pass a few Persei and a handful of Asprutan, who bow their heads as Andrin passes. It must be very strange to walk through your home with such formality at all times. Although I suppose, if you grow up your whole life being treated as royalty, it would feel normal.

When we reach another massive door, the two Persei guards who stand watch on either side open it. I remind myself to keep my eyebrows neutral as we pass. Apparently, family dinner is still a formal event. With the doors open, I can see down a long hall, with an almost equally long, but mostly empty, table. At the very end, on a higher seat than the rest, sits Andrin's father. Andrin and Izar bow their heads, so I do the same. I'm sure my neck will hurt if I have to be here for more than a day. At least there is no full bowing or curtsies.

The King's booming voice breaks the silence. "Come, join us, my boys."

His invitation for just Andrin and Izar to sit seems purposefully dismissive of my presence. Yet upon the King's invitation, I follow anyway, and the heavy door thuds closing behind us. Forty-three steps, that's how far we walk to get to the end of the table where the group of four is already seated.

On the King's right, a much older version of Izar sits, with a female more feline and orange in appearance to his right. Izar's parents, I would guess, since they look similar and the familiar way they greet him. Izar's father is the King's advisor, I remind myself. The King's Strategoi. The only member of the king's Guard who ranks higher than Andrin. Just as Izar will be promoted once Andrin ascends to take his father's spot as ruler of the Constellation.

To the left of the King is the Queen. Andrin moves forward to take the seat next to his mother while Izar sits beside his own. I accept the only spot left with a place setting, a seat next to Andrin—the furthest from the King. Despite his summons for my presence, when the King's eyes settle on me, they are filled with disdain.

Additionally, his invitation for just Andrin and Izar to sit was purposefully dismissive of my presence. In some regards, I suppose I should feel like I am intruding. These parents have not seen their sons in at least three months, and yet I am interrupting their reunion. Except I was not invited to this dinner; I was summoned.

Furthermore, the King knows who I am. He knows I am Roa Mēdeia. Even if he thinks I am still ignorant of my own identity, he shouldn't be so blatantly dismissive of me. Earthly royal customs may differ, but I cannot imagine they are so foreign that blatant disrespect toward another Princess of a Constellation, even one that is gone, is aper poi.

Despite my internal fuming, I paste a pleasant, passive smile on my face and take the seat next to Andrin. As if spurred to life, seven Asprutans simultaneously step forward and fill our glasses. I thank the one who pours what looks like red wine into my glass, and her eyes jump to mine in surprise. The widening of her already bulbous eyes almost makes me flinch, but Andrin's hand taps my exposed knee beneath the table. I shift my gaze to him and see a slight shake of his head. I've messed up some custom. A pang of annoyance hits me. Andrin should have warned me of the Persei customs—or I suppose I could have asked. With an internal sigh, I resign myself to the fact that I will apparently need to ask for a refresher in etiquette after dinner; it would be best to remain silent for now.

The first course is quickly set before us. The room is quiet, like being a guest in someone's house after witnessing a fight. I'm careful not to do anything unless I see Andrin do it first. The King takes a bite of his food, then nods to the group. They all nod back. Only a beat behind, I join them. Then the King raises his glass, the red liquid sloshing around.

"May we honor the Golden Elders and continue their legacy," The King proclaims.

Everyone repeats the phrase, raising their own glasses. My mild annoyance grows to teeming irritation. I want to kick Andrin for his failure to provide instructions for my preparation. Finally, they all begin to eat, drink, and talk. I remain silent. Taking a sniff of the glass before I drink it, I'm relieved. Wine, thank goodness. It tastes decadent on my tongue. Maybe it is a superior wine, or perhaps it is because I haven't had a glass in over a month, but it is one of the best I've ever had. The first course comes and goes, a salad replaced with a chunk of what I think is animal meat. I suddenly realize I'm terrified to ask what type.

"It's similar to beef." Andrin's lips tickle my ear as he whispers to me.

A chuckle escapes him at my silent sigh of relief. I cut off a piece and placed it on my tongue. A soft moan hums behind my lips. I missed real food. I'll never touch another chunk of bland sponge food ever again.

Andrin's lips return to my ear. "Be careful with the noises you make, or I won't care that my parents are seated next to us."

I almost choke on the food, forcing me to grab the glass of wine again and swig a mouthful to help me swallow. I shoot him a glare, afraid any retort would come out too loudly.

"Aurora, that is what you call yourself, correct?" The King interjects in a near-mocking tone.

I stiffen and replace my glare with a polite smile as I turn towards the King. I can't tell if he's toying with me, purposely using my Earth name. Is it a game? A test? His features are challenging to read.

I reply with melodic sweetness, "Yes, your majesty."

He hums as if in thought. "My son reported you had no recollection of how you got to Earth."

It is a statement and yet a question. "Yes, your majesty. I was adopted by my foster parents when I was just a baby. I had been surrendered to a hospital. It was always assumed my parents had died in a car accident."

He hums again. "Was there any indication you or your guardians had that you were not human?"

My eyebrows scrunch before I can catch them. "No. On Earth, only crazy people think aliens exist. I guess not so crazy in hindsight. We always thought I was just human. I was gifted, but not that special."

Yet another hum. "Interesting. Especially considering how special you are."

"Yes, well, both of your sons have done a great job training me and helping to develop my Aether manipulation. I'm sure I can keep myself safe now when they return me to Earth." A bitter bite has soured the tone of my reply.

"Ah, yes, Earth, the developing world of the Orion Nebula. You're lucky my son found you in time. Foreign species aren't even supposed to visit ones that haven't developed space travel on their own."

"Humans have discovered space travel," I interject.

"Only within the past century. Earth is known to be so underdeveloped that any type of history of interference is wiped from the world's history. That's what happened to the Harmakhis." Izar and his parents exchange various uncomfortable looks. "The Persei were lucky enough to keep our Golden Elders as part of your Greek history."

There is silence throughout the dining hall. A chill smothers the simmering Aether beneath my skin as tension settles in the air. I hold the King's stare. While Andrin's eyes may twinkle with joy and mischief, the King's are poisonous slits. My Aether begins to boil, a warning. Andrin's hand on my bare knee squeezes, begging me to break eye contact. Except for a defiant part of me that refuses. I used to respect all the customs I encountered on Earth. Since I awakened this Aether source inside of myself, I feel raw and challenging. I refuse to lower my gaze. Especially when he knows I am also a royal from a different galaxy. Just because he doesn't know I'm aware of it doesn't mean he can treat me any less than.

Finally, the King speaks. "I'm sure they have taught you much that your Earthly knowledge never could have provided. I'm glad they kept you safe during your recovery to Mycenae. We were so worried the Harpyiai would reach you first. My son told me of her attacks against you. You wouldn't want to put your Earth family at risk, would you?"

I bristle at the threat to my parents. That is what it was, a threat and an insult to my home planet and my family. I may be from the Andromeda Galaxy, but Earth is my home. My power comes from my alien origins, but I have honed them myself.

"I don't know about safe," Izar's voice cuts through the tension. "I did beat the stones right out of her on the training mat on almost a daily basis."

The room exhales at the comedic relief.

"Izar, I did not raise you to fight females!" His mother chides him.

Andrin laughs as Izar's feline grin rises. "She would have to win sometimes for it to really be called a fight."

The dining hall explodes in conversation and laughter. I could kiss Izar in thanks for relieving the tension in the room. Andrin and Izar regale their families with tales of their travels. My heart clenches seeing the pure joy on both of their faces. Their mothers' love and concern. The pride in Izar's father's eyes. I keep mostly silent, observing the love in their interactions. The King stays almost as quiet as I, both of us eyeing each other in suspicion.

He is the reason I am not on my way back to Earth or home with my parents. Why? Why should he care if the

Harpyiai are after me? From my correspondence with the Commodore, I can ascertain that they failed to report my location as the original message demanded.

After the dessert course is cleared from the table, the King rises. We all rise with him. He holds out his arm, and the Queen loops hers through his. She seems sweet, passive, but kind. I wonder if their personalities balance for the royal couple. Andrin doesn't seem to have either parent's personality.

"Andrin, meet me in my office," The King calls in a faux casual manner over his shoulder without missing a step.

Andrin lets out a sigh beside me, but squeezes my hand. "I'll stop by later."

"Okay." My volume is still quiet, as if I were any louder, I would disrupt the balance.

"I'll escort her back to her rooms," Izar offers.

Andrin nods to Izar before heading towards the door his parents exited through. Izar holds out his elbow as an exaggerated prop. I let out a dramatic sigh but lace my arm through his, grateful for the lighthearted mood. He escorts me out of the original doors we entered through, the opposite of where the royal family departed.

We have already climbed one set of stairs when Izar breaks the silence. "So, they're weird for Earth standards too, right?"

I snort. "I was wondering if that was just me. I assumed that's how things are here."

Izar rolls his head from side to side. "Yes and no. Dinners like that are always awkward. Normally, I'll eat with my parents or Andrin. It's rare for all of us to be together."

Mirfak, the planet's star, has set, leaving the stone hallways in shadows. The only light from inside the palace comes from dim solar-powered lights dotting the walls every few meters. The flimsy curtains billow like ghosts as they catch the sea breeze. The eerie hall does little to relieve my tension from dinner.

"When we first got here. You said not to trust anyone. What did you mean?"

Izar's nails dig into the skin of my forearm, and I jerk back. His eyes are wide, giving me one sharp shake of his head that tells me not to speak. My stomach twists. Is there hidden technology amongst the ancient-looking architecture? Or are there guards simply lurking around the corners of the halls?

I give him a slight nod and peel his bony fingernails back from my forearm. The black nails are tipped with red, but my skin quickly closes, the Astrobleme in my system still ready to cure any minor flesh wound. Once fully healed, I loop my arm back through his, and we continue walking without another word.

We're almost to my door when Izar adds, "If you need any resources for any questions you may have, I'd be happy to locate them for you. Not all this world's knowledge is available for public inquiry."

Izar's coded message is too cryptic. I can't decipher it. Clearly, I should be distrustful, but of what, who in particular should I be most worried about? Do I really have to worry about the King so gravely? Yet there is something else, something else he wants me to ask—another piece of knowledge he wants me to seek out. The chill settles deep in my bones. The Aether crackles on my skin, making Izar jump slightly.

"Sorry. Side effects, I guess." We stop in front of my door, and Izar releases my arm. "When I find out exactly what questions I have, I'll put in my library request."

Izar lets out a half-hearted chuckle. "Be careful of wandering around alone, too."

He does not need to repeat his warning. Not to trust anyone here. Besides aliens actively seeing and hearing things, his cat-like attack only increases my suspicions that there are microphones and cameras all over the high-tech palace. It may have the appearance of Ancient Greek luxury, but it is reminiscent of an Orson Welles society.

I give him a half-hearted wave. "Thanks for escorting me back so I could receive your ominous warning."

Except Izar does not laugh at my jest. "Figure out how to operate all the barriers. They can keep things out, or in." Izar warns.

I open my mouth to ask him what he means, but he has already created space between us. Izar throws his hand up as he begins to walk down the hall.

"I'm two doors down from you. Try to keep it quiet."

I flip him off even though he is facing away. Two doors away lies a long stretch of these massive rooms. For good measure, I take a quick scan around the hall before I scan my retina and slip into my room. I count to five hundred, then open my door.

Big Brother watching or not, I will find out why the King wants me here.

CHAPTER 24

Sneaking around the palace is easier than the Orbital Station, especially at night. Only dim solar-powered lights illuminate the stone passageways every fifty yards, which leaves plenty of dark alcoves for me to duck into to avoid Persei Guards or Asprutan servants.

I am not entirely sure what I am looking for, but I know if the King made Andrin bring me all this way, there must be a reason. I do not attempt to open any door with a biometric scanner; I do not want to risk triggering any alarms. I am already taking enough risks by wandering around on my own.

I've been wandering around for a little more than an hour. For a short time, I had been silently stalking a guard and tucking into alcoves on the rare occasion that he turned. I had to give up my hope that he would reveal anything interesting about the palace when the watch turned over to a far more diligent guard. Which is probably for the best because my body protests every time I twist myself into the small spaces to hide. My muscles feel tight, and my joints stiff; the gravity on Mycenae must be heavier than Earth's and the Orbital Station's. My nosiness refuses to let me end my search despite my fatigue and lack of success. I have mostly opened closets or doors to other hallways and servant passageways.

I am about to give up my snooping when my Aether flares. I pause, then continue walking. It banks back, as if it's calling to something. That is a new reaction. As I approach the set of double doors, my Aether flares again. There's a biometric scanner on the side of the door, but it won't be necessary with the thick wooden door cracked open. I peer through the narrow opening, careful not to put any pressure against the doors themselves.

A blue glow emits from the room. My skin flares to answer the color. Along the walls, there are hundreds, maybe thousands, of jars and vials of luminescent blue liquid.

Astrobleme.

I can't resist pressing against the heavy wood door to expose more of the room. I grind my teeth together as the wood scrapes against the stone floor, but don't let it deter me. There are stone tables covered in beakers and trinkets, like a science laboratory. Two pearlescent pillars divide the room. Yet the most astonishing thing is a gigantic crystal in the center of the chamber, directly under the oculus of the domed ceiling. It's a jagged, raw gemstone that pulses with an internal light. A light that pulses at the same frequency as the Aether in my skin.

"You failed to inform me how powerful she has become."

The King's bellowing voice makes me freeze. I pull my head out of the room and hold my breath to focus my hearing.

"I told you; she's progressing." Andrin's voice responds.

Their arguing is coming from a closed door at the end of the hall. Very close to me. Slowly, I pull my head out of the now obviously ajar door and take silent steps towards the source of voices.

"Progressing? I had to hear from the Strategoi that she attacked the guard stationed on Argos. Imagine my surprise when Izar's father informed me after you left that detail out of your report from your uncompleted mission to sterilize the Scilla hatchling pools."

Vomit rises in my throat. Sterilization of hatchling pools? Andrin had said we were neutralizing the water so the other planets could drink it. The Scilla are terrifying creatures, but— I thought we were cleaning the water, not trying to exterminate an entire species. Andrin starts to defend himself, "I—I didn't know. She was just learning then. She more than proved herself on Sarpedon. She restarted the power plant."

The King grunts. "And for that, you think she has earned a place here? That she is powerful enough to deviate from the reason I sent you across all of Galaxia to find her?"

"Oi! You!"

I freeze. My spine stiffens at the sound of a gruff male voice from behind me. Turning just my head, I look over my shoulder. A Persei Guard. Moving my way quickly.

I bolt.

I dash through a doorway to a servant's staircase and descend as fast as my feet will allow. I don't have time to slow myself down before I slam into a door. The force of my collision swings it open, my momentum flinging me to the floor. My hands barely scrape the stone ground before I push myself up and launch forward again. I'm outside.

I'm in a grove of citrus trees. My sandal-clad feet slap against the stone pavers. Ahead, I can see stone pillars with ivy and violet bougainvillea. I run through the pillars and find myself in a four-way intersection of tile floors and pillars. Trampled petals and fallen leaves make the smooth path slippery. I hear the Guard rustling through the trees the way I came, I dash to my left. I find myself amongst cypress trees.

Hands grab my arms, and I shriek.

"Aurora!"

My heart hammers in my chest. My vambraces spark with visible Aether when I hold them in front of me to force back my captor's chest. Andrin's chest. Only the concern in his face makes my Aether dim to a simmer. One of his hands falls to my waist as the other pushes hair back from my face.

Concern floods his features. "Why are you wandering around here alone after dark? It's easy to get lost in the gardens."

Gardens. I look around us again. I curse myself for arriving in a secluded garden with Andrin, again. It didn't end well for me last time.

His concern remains; his touch is tender. "Let's get you back to your rooms."

CHAPTER 25

Andrin escorts me back to my room, and my heart continues hammering in my chest. My head pivots between the instinct to run from the guard, the conversation I overheard between Andrin and his father, and the room filled with Astrobleme.

"I have a surprise for you," he says.

My frantic thoughts freeze momentarily. "What's the surprise?"

Andrin laughs. "You don't have to sound so foreboding. I have arranged for you to speak to your parents."

My mom and dad. Tears spring to my eyes, but they don't fall. I think back to Izar's words of the King forbidding my contact with the outside world. Yet Andrin defended me against his father, and now he has found a way for me to speak with my parents. Although he seems to be hiding the reason his father wants me here. My instincts have put me on edge, but Andrin has been supportive at every turn. My conflicting emotions battle for dominance within my head.

Hope beats out my skepticism when I ask, "How?"

Andrin smiles at the hope in my eyes. "Our satellites sometimes orbit at overlapping positions with that of Earth, so we have small windows we can directly send information across space in real time. You'll only have eighteen minutes of connectivity if you want to try."

I grasp his arms hard enough that he flinches slightly. "Of course! When? When can I talk to them?"

"The overlap only happens once every 28 days. There is an overlap tonight. We were lucky enough to arrive on time for you to speak with them today. It starts in a little less than an hour."

"Okay! I need to wash all this dust off, though. Do you have anything that resembles normal clothes? I think I can make them buy that I'm in Greece, but the rest is too much." I flutter my hands over my dramatic dress and ostentatious appearance.

"I can grab you some of my clothes; they will look baggy, but they aren't gowns." Andrin offers.

I squeeze his hands tightly, a lightness I haven't felt in weeks overpowering my chest. "Perfect."

He heads to the bedroom door but pauses, a mischievous smile on his lips. "Do you need help working this shower? Or perhaps washing the dust off?"

I playfully scowl. "No. Now shoo."

We're both laughing as he closes the door. The shower is much easier to figure out than the Orbital Station. I tie up my hair and remove the numerous layers of fabric before stepping in. I lather my skin in saffron-scented oils as I try to scrub the gold off. I'm closer to a splotchy red by the time Andrin returns with clothes. I quickly pull on the baggy shirt and shorts, hoping my parents won't question why I'm wearing clearly male clothing.

Andrin works on a holographic screen that he's pulled up in the miniature library of my room. The holographic technology will work like FaceTime. I just hope my parents pick up the call. I wiggle in my seat when Andrin aligns the signals to connect.

"You just need to be careful about what you tell them. They can't know about aliens or extraterrestrial travel. Humans tend to have a hard time understanding it." A teasing tone slips into Andrin's voice.

A slight ache in my heart forms, but I get it. I didn't exactly handle the news well either. I look down at my appearance. Andrin takes my hand, forcing me to slow my rushed pace. I try to shoot him a playful glare, but I can't. I'm too excited. While I traded two messages with my parents, I haven't heard their voices or seen their faces in so long.

"Okay, it should be in alignment in twenty seconds. Then you have eighteen minutes," He says.

I nod and release my breath. "Got it. Do you mind if I talk to them alone? I promise I won't mention any alien or space stuff."

"Of course." Andrin presses a kiss to my forehead before heading to the door. "I'll see you tomorrow."

I smile at him, but I am also counting down. When my internal countdown hits one, I hear the familiar chime of an outgoing call. Deep breaths. The image connects, and I hold back a sob. My mom's large gold-rimmed glasses over her monolid eyes are the first things to come into focus. Her eyes squint further, her light-brown skin nearly wrinkle-free despite her age.

"Aurora? Aurora!"

"Hi, Mom." I blink away the tears from my eyes, forcing my voice to sound joyful.

"Aurora baby! I missed you so much. Alan! Alan, get in here! It's Aurora."

From somewhere in the background, I hear a clatter, then the sound of rushing footsteps. My dad comes into view while he takes a seat next to my mom. The age shows more on my dad's face; his pale skin wrinkled deeply around his eyes and mouth from years of smiling.

"Hello, beautiful. Where have your adventures taken you now? It's been too long without a phone call."

My mom hits my dad across the arm. "Don't guilt-trip her. I'm just happy she called. Although he is right, it has been too long, sweetheart."

I laugh at their lighthearted interaction. Thirty-five years. They have been married for thirty-five years, and yet love still shines in their eyes. They always filled our home with love. Love for travel, for their German and Filipino cultures, for the rest of the world, a passion for food and language, but most of all, our family.

"I know, I'm sorry. Things have been—crazy. I'm on a different contract now, I'm in Greece."

They both ooh and awe. They ask me questions, and I reply with fake answers. They fill me in on how their lives are going. I can't help but interrupt them when a question pops into my mind.

"Why did you name me Aurora?"

My parents must have told me when I was little and full of questions. Over the years, it must have slipped my mind as unimportant. However, lately, I've been desperate to hold onto any piece of my identity I can.

My mom purses her lips, "The nurse who took care of you on your first night in the hospital named you. The woman who surrendered kept mumbling about the crash and the roads. The woman had run off after leaving you at the hospital, and a nurse tried to chase her down for more information. Except she had already disappeared when she got outside, and there was an incredible display of the Northern Lights that night. So, the nurse decided to name you Aurora after the beautiful sky."

Maybe the woman hadn't been speaking of the roads.
Perhaps she had been trying to say something else.
Roa.

The woman had been calling me by my Andromeda-given name. What relation did I have to that woman?

My internal clock ticks away. Fifteen minutes have already gone by. Sixteen, if I count the time it took for them to pick up. I only have two minutes left with them.

"I'm sorry the call is so short, but I have to go soon. I have a—a work thing."

The disappointment is evident on their faces. My stomach feels hollow.

My voice cracks as I say, "I miss you so much."

"We miss you too, sweetheart. Are you okay? Eating well? Staying safe?" My mom coddles.

"You look very healthy. Glowing. Travel has always suited you," My dad chips in to soothe my mom's concerns.

"Yes, I'm okay. Just a bit homesick. I'm eating plenty and staying safe." My thoughts turn sour at the idea of the Harpyiai. "Are you both good? Safe?"

A look of concern passes both of their faces. "Yes, of course. We aren't the ones jet-setting across the world."

Little do they know, I have travelled much further than across the world. With the pause in conversation, I can see the lack of faith in my words. Perhaps I give something away on my face. Concern tightens my mom's features. Neither of them is used to me asking questions about my life before my adoption. Outside of a few teenage years, I have never cared much about my origins. I should have asked more questions back then. I refocus my energy on how nice it was to talk to them, how happy I am to see their faces. I force the joy to appear on my face and in my voice.

"Okay. Just know that we love you. We're proud of everything you've done and how you're paving your own way in life."

"Thank you, Mom. I love you both so, so much."

"*Opta ardua pennis astra sequi.*"

A smile graces my lips as I repeat the Latin phrase to my dad. "*Opta ardua pennis astra sequi.*"

The call cuts out. Eighteen minutes.

I stare at the blank blue hologram until my eyes burn. I've wanted to get home so badly, but how could I bring this danger to them? The Harpyiai was able to track me down to Earth; who is to say she can't do it again? I have to end her before I return, or I will be running from her my entire life. I refuse to put my parents in danger. They loved me as their own child, they kept me safe, and I will do the same for them.

Suddenly, the air feels too hot. The steam from the shower keeps the air heavy and damp. I need to open a window and get some fresh air, or I feel like I might suffocate.

I move to my window. The sea is calm, the only waves in sight are those that gently crash against the rocky shore. The cityscape beyond the coast stands proud and tall. The pearlescent metal gleamed in the glow of Mycenae's two moons.

I find the barrier control panel and press buttons until it lights up. I push the button with an open symbol, but all I hear is a metallic shuttering sound from every window before the button flashes red. I push another button that looks like a set of shutters, and I hear the metallic noise again. Suddenly, small slits of golden moonlight leak through the now more apparent blue-tinted barrier. It's a polarized filter. A salty sea breeze flows in from the shuttered barrier.

I press my face into the shutters and stand in the moonlight until my eyes struggle to remain open. I've been awake for too many hours. While my body hasn't craved sleep much since I started taking daily doses of Astrobleme, I still feel drained. Fatigue only finds me when my Aether has been used. Except I haven't used my Aether since we landed, perhaps my alien metabolism has finally met its time limit and demands sleep. Maybe it's the relief after seeing my parents and knowing they are safe.

I clearly cannot trust the King. He brought me here for something I would have learned if that guard had not stopped me. Andrin is hiding things from me—at least my identity, and why the King wants me here. My guilt at hiding my growing power from him no longer feels as poignant. Tomorrow I will make Andrin tell me the truth this time—the whole truth. Then take me back to Earth, especially with Izar's warning blaring like an alarm through my head.

I need to get out of Mycenae before whatever the King has planned for me comes to fruition.

I push the button to close the window, but the metallic noise sounds again before the second light flashes red too. I gulp down air. I may have broken the high-tech, fancy windows. So much for Izar's advice on figuring out how to use them.

A loud knock on the door startles me out of my fatigue. I scramble from the flashing window and run to the bedroom door.

As I swing it open, a towering golden body blocks my path. It's not the golden Persei I'm used to. The male turns to face me, with a full beard on his face; his brown leather clothes match those of other guards I've seen. They are the only Persei that don't wear white here.

"Um, hi." My brain can now easily switch to their language.

"The Queen requests your presence tomorrow morning for breakfast," He grumbles.

Before I can respond, he turns and leaves. Any sense of relief I may have felt after contacting my parents disappears. At least it's with the Queen and not the King.

CHAPTER 26

Between the Astrobleme in my system and my anxiety for breakfast with the Queen, my sleep is fitful and short. I'm awake before Mirfak rises over the horizon. Philomena arrives at my door shortly after. She lays out a short white silk dress for me and helps secure it with delicate gold chains.

I run my hands over the dress in awe. "It's beautiful, thank you for finding it on such short notice."

"Anything for you, Princess. Now sit so I can do your hair."

Her tone this morning leaves little room for argument. While she braids my hair, I take in my reflection in the full-length mirror beside the vanity. My muscles have developed significantly in the past few weeks. I have always been slim, but lean muscle now fills out my form like a professional athlete. My pale skin looks like porcelain instead of sickly, as I have always known it. My eyes are what hold my attention.

They glow blue, as they do after every dose of Astrobleme. Yet the glow used to fade like the blue of my skin. Now, they retain the glow of sunlit sapphires. The vibrant blue seems far more potent than the eyes I grew up with. Crypts of green and gold speckle the blue collagen field, white furrows curve around my iris. Like everything else in my life, they seem more intense. Perhaps my blood concentration of Astrobleme is growing, and it will be permanent—a field of stars in both my eyes.

"Do you have any advice for my breakfast with the Queen?" I ask Philomena.

"The Queen will have a menu prepared for you both. It is proper to eat at least a small bite from every dish. It will be less formal than the Royal dinner you attended last night. You may eat in whatever order you desire. She, as the Queen, will be responsible for pouring the wine. It is a sign of hospitality and welcome," she explains.

"Wine? For breakfast?"

A trilling sound like laughter leaves Philomena. "It is watered down; it is closer to a juice."

I almost nod, but remember Philomena's spindly fingers are twisting my hair into an intricate pattern. "Alright. Anything I should avoid doing or saying?" I want to be more prepared for breakfast than I was for dinner last night.

Philomena ponders silently before answering. "Be careful of your word choice. Heritage and history are paramount to Persei. Especially the Royal family. Do not ask questions you do not want the answer to."

That response, on its own, raises questions. I am afraid of what the answers might be. Philomena ties off my braid with a silk ribbon before letting it cascade down my shoulder. The sea breeze blows in through my broken window barriers, sending a chill up my arms.

"Perhaps an overdress will be useful. The terrace will be windy as it is exposed to the sea," she says before disappearing into my closet.

She emerges from my closet with an organza robe-like dress, then slips it over my shoulders. The long sleeves billow out like the skirt before the nearly transparent material is tied with a sash around my waist.

Her bulbous eyes meet mine in the mirror. "You look beautiful, my Princess."

I turn to grasp Philomena's hands in mine. From my seated position, we're the same height. "Thank you, Philomena, for everything. I cannot imagine these past few weeks without your help. It has been a whirlwind, but you've been a much-needed friend."

She bows her head. "I have heard stories of the Andromeda Galaxy before it fell. A beautiful realm where fauna and flora coexisted. Where all species were allowed to flourish within their natural habitats, Andromeda's destruction was like losing an idea of paradise. I hope I will have the privilege to see you rule a world that hosts a similar haven one day. It is an honor to serve the daughter of truly honorable Emperors."

My mouth drops open. A knock resounds on my door before words can form on my tongue. She opens the door and swiftly slips through, leaving it open for me to see two Persei Guards standing ready to escort me.

Emperors.

Daughter of Emperors.

I'm not only an alien princess of a fallen constellation, but something far more important. I'm not just close to a Gigas bloodline; I was part of the most powerful bloodline in an entire galaxy. That is why the Commodore is so committed to his search for me. I should have unheard of power.

The guard's gruff voice jolts me from my thoughts. "Are you ready to be escorted to the Queen's Terrace?"

I tighten the sash around my waist and nod. "Lead the way."

My heart hammers in my chest as my head swims the entire walk to the Queen's rooms. She is already seated when I arrive. My two guards wait in the sitting room where the Queen's own guards remain, while I enter the terrace. I bow my head deeply as I close the glass doors, so it's only the two of us.

"By the Stars, Your Highness," I greet her.

The Queen gives me a soft, sweet smile. "By the Stars, Aurora, please take a seat."

A gust of sea breeze ruffles the fabric of my dress as I sit in the plush chair across the table from her. Philomena was right, a large spread is already at the table. The Queen pours me a glass of wine, and I drink when she does.

The breakfast wine is light and sweeter than the dinner wine. Notes of pear and honeysuckle remain on my tongue. I wait for her to begin eating before I sample the first of twelve small dishes. Hummus and crème dips, at least three types of breads and pastries, a variety of fruits, and a scattering of meat cuts are on small plates on the table.

It's not difficult to try everything. I place a hand on my stomach, worried my full belly will protrude from the loose fit of the thin silk.

"Are you enjoying Mycenae?" The Queen asks.

Enjoying it? I have been here for less than a day. The food is much better than on the Orbital Station. The planet is pretty, but I have only seen the palace and the gardens while I ran through them at night. Her husband sets off my fight-or-flight response like a fire alarm. Although this is the adventure of a lifetime, every part of my body is screaming at me to leave.

My lips form an automatic response. "Yes, of course, it is beautiful."

The Queen peers at me from over her wine glass. "It is beautiful. Yet you don't want to be here."

I almost choke on the wine as I swallow. "No, no, it's not that. I just want to go home. I never asked to leave Earth, and I'm waiting for Andrin to fulfil his promise to bring me home."

The Queen finishes her wine, then picks up the decanter to refill both our glasses. "I can understand that. I haven't been home since I was a young girl. I haven't left the palace grounds in 133 years."

133 years.

How long is a Persei's life span? Why has she not left Mycenae in all that time? I take another sip of wine to buy myself time. Start with the easy opening.

"You look phenomenal for being over 133."

The Queen laughs. "It's part of our genetic makeup. Our cells continue to regenerate at the same rate at which they die. You only begin to age towards death when your cells die at a faster rate than they are created."

My fingers mindlessly touch the soft flesh of my wrinkle-free cheek. I have never been afraid of aging, but that is the naivety of youth. She could have been alive for hundreds of years. Although I cannot imagine that asking a female's age is any less rude on Mycenae than it is on Earth.

I slowly chew on a bite of buttery, flaky pastry before asking, "How old were you when you first came to Mycenae?"

The Queen gives me a charmed look, clearly catching my roundabout question. Then her gaze becomes detached, as if she is looking into the past.

"I was twenty-three. I came with my sister. She was beautiful. Across the Constellation, Persei would boast of the beauty of the girl from an unimportant colony planet. They compared her to a beacon, her inner and outer beauty capable of illuminating the darkest of nights. She was to be married to the King. I was to be her doera."

Was. Clearly, she did not marry the King, or her sister would now be the Queen.

"What happened?" I prod.

She stares out at the sea beyond us. "Ketos. He killed my sister. I became the next prospect for the King."

Ketos.

It seems impossible that it could be the same Ketos the Harpyiai referenced on Seriphus, and yet—

I shiver at her ominous words. "Why did he kill your sister?"

The Queen tears off a piece of pastry and stares off at the coastline. "Ketos is one of the original Gigas, a byproduct of our universe's creation. A terrifying creature that combines the most ferocious aspects of water, land, and space. He travels throughout Galaxia, consuming Aether in its rawest forms."

"That sounds like ancient mythology." I counter, hoping Izar's explanation was accurate.

The Queen's eyes turn icy on me. "I am sure much of what you have learned since you left Earth sounds like a myth."

I cringe at my own outburst. So many Earth cultures are based on mythology, and I have always been respectful of their origins and beliefs. However, my words had slipped out on an impulsive stream of consciousness.

"Many of your Earth Grecians' history and so-called mythology came from Persei history and prophecy. From the Golden Elders and their legacy. Humans may be incapable of Aether manipulation and great feats of technology, but it does not mean they don't exist."

I have to physically bite my cheeks to keep my anger from slipping out. I hate it when these aliens talk poorly of Earth, my home. I have been enjoying the Queen's company far more than her husband's, but it is increasingly apparent that they share similar mindsets.

"I apologize; I didn't mean to insult you," I insist, "I am sorry that you lost your sister."

The Queen's features settle into sharp, determined edges. "I mourn the loss of my sister frequently, but it is better to be a Queen of a powerful Constellation than the slave of one."

The sweet wine in my mouth turns sour. "What do you mean?"

The Queen waves a dismissive hand at me. "I cannot expect you to understand when you have been on Earth your whole life. With time, you will come to understand that as civilizations advance, they need power."

I grit my teeth. I'm having a hard time justifying my desire not to insult the Persei culture when the King and now Queen have insulted mine at every turn. Did she mean she would be a slave on her colony planet? Subservient to the Persei here on Mycenae? Or did she mean she would be a slave to her sister as the Queen, while fulfilling her role as her doera. Philomena had called herself my doera. I assumed it meant servant. Had she meant slave?

I think about Earth's history once more. The Perseis ' influence on Greece; the Harmakhis' on Egypt. Both cultures used slaves and servitude, yet these so-called advanced civilizations did nothing to stop it. They used it to their advantage. It's not unreasonable to assume they condone similar practices in their own Constellations.

The food spread before me morphs into unappetizing lumps of lard and slop. I feel disgusted that I've been taking part in these archaic practices. The thought of all those in the palace who have been cooking and serving food, cleaning, and who knows what else, makes me feel oily in my own skin. Bitter anger fills me; an advanced civilization capable of space travel still relies on exploitation. I think of the Scilla hatchling pools, the Asprutans, and all the aliens working aboard the Orbital Station and on Seriphus.

I don't hide the bite in my retort. "I suppose I wouldn't know, since it seems my galaxy was destroyed before I could learn anything about it.

The Queen swirled the red liquid in her wine glass before meeting my eyes. "The Perseus Constellation has remained influential because the Golden Elders discovered what Ketos wanted. Every 133 years, we deliver it when he arrives."

My stomach gurgles in unease. "What does he want?"

"We offer him a sacrifice of our most pure and potent energy source. Our brightest light."

I freeze.

Sacrifice.

The Commodore warned me that the Persei gained their glory through sacrifice—energy, power-hungry beings willing to sacrifice others for glory.

That specific term is unsettling, brightest light.

That is what the Harpyiai has been searching for. That is why she was asking about the brightest light on Argos, for Ketos. She had failed to harness energy from the power plant on Sarpedon. Instead, she broke the system, or the Ignos broke it before she could. Which led her to Seriphus in search of an energy source on the supply colony planet, but she found me again instead.

Was she successful? I had seen the guards chase her away on their hovercrafts, then she Aether Crossed. She admitted she is working with Ketos, but for what end?

My curiosity battles my anger for dominance as I ask, "What happens after he gets his energy source?"

"We get our power from Ketos, from our sacrifices to him. The more powerful the energy source, the harder it is to contain. Any excess of his consumption rains down across the Perseus Constellation in an asteroid shower, and we harvest the matter to create Astrobleme."

My mind spins. The Harpyiai could use Astrobleme to become more powerful. Izar said the Harpyiai species hails from his home constellation, Scorpio. Maybe the rulers of Scorpius sent her. Perhaps they are trying to usurp the Persei.

Maybe the Harpyiai and the Scorpio Constellation are trying to take over Galaxia. If she knows who I am, she might be trying to use my pedigree as a political tool. They are escalating their rebellion, and the Perseus Constellation is in danger.

The Queen stands, tearing me from my mental rabbit hole. She moves from the table towards the terrace glass doors. Her skirts billow around her, flush against the windowpane, like the sea washing fabric to the rocks. She pauses at the door, turns just enough for me to see the haunted look in her eyes.

"The cosmos relies on balance. To obtain the power of Astrobleme, we must first accept that there will be destruction." A ghost of a haunted smile graces her lips. "When Andromeda was destroyed, the light was bright enough that almost every Constellation in Galaxia saw it. Perhaps, Roa, the brightest light Ketos seeks, will be his destruction in the end, too."

Roa.

She called me Roa.

The Queen slips through the terrace doors, then, like a ghost, floats out of the sitting room into the hall beyond. I'm up and moving quickly, keeping my pace as casual as possible, even though I want to sprint to my room.

Clearly, the Queen knows who I am, as I assume everyone in the royal family must. Her cryptic ravings sound like a riddle in my head as I repeat them. I can't determine her motives, but her tone gives me chills, her voice so full of gravity and sorrow.

She admitted Ketos transits here once every 133 years. She herself had arrived on Mycenae 133 years ago when her sister died from Ketos' attack. So, the Persei must know that Ketos is coming to Mycenae again, and soon. Which means the Harpyiai is not the only alien adversary I have to worry about.

"Aurora." Andrin's smile drops as soon as he sees my face.

CHAPTER 27

I jump at his sudden appearance. I had been so lost in thought as I stalked down the passageways that I hadn't seen him waiting at my door. He glances towards the guards that have silently been following me back from the terrace before quickly ushering me into my room. When he reaches for my arm, I shrink back. His eyes flash with hurt, but he instead opens my door for me with his own biometrics.

I quickly push past him, pacing up and down the room. "The Perseus Constellation is in trouble."

Andrin's face twists, "What are you talking about?"

"The Harpyiai and Ketos are working together." I stop my pacing to face him, but his bewilderment only deepens. "It has been 133 years since Ketos was last here! The Harpyiai is going to use the energy source to take over the Constellation!"

"Aurora, wait-" Andrin gets close enough to grab both of my shoulders. "Slow down. You aren't making any sense.'

I throw my hands up, spinning as I push him away. "I can't believe you're still pretending that's my name," I snarl.

"What—"

With whiplash speed, I spin back and cut Andrin off. "Roa. You know my name is Roa. Your parents know, everyone knows, and I figured it out myself, but I can't figure out why you haven't told me."

Confusion flicks across his face. "Well, it's just a name. You have always known yourself as Aurora."

"I also knew myself as a Human, which, clearly, we have established, I am not. So why leave out that part of the information? Is it because you were worried someone else would tell me who Roa Mēdeia was to Andromeda Galaxy?"

He opens his mouth, pauses, then closes it again. Still keeping secrets.

I continue to press. "Why were you so afraid I would find out that I am not just a Princess of Andromeda, but I was the last heir! Are you jealous that if my galaxy had not been blown to star dust, I would outrank you?"

His mouth gapes open and closed like a fish. "I didn't think it would matter to you."

I slam my jaw closed so quickly that I bite my cheek. "That it wouldn't matter who I really am or my position in my galaxy? Both are important. Both are part of who I am. You once asked if I was curious about my origins. Of course, I am! While you have been cozying up to me for weeks, you have conveniently left that part out. You didn't even give me the option to know more about myself. I shouldn't have been surprised to learn you kept the truth about Ketos hidden from me." The coppery taste of blood fills my mouth.

Andrin's head quirks to the side. "Aurora, wait, why do you keep talking about Ketos?"

I cross my arms over my chest. "Seriously? You are still calling me Aurora?"

He sighs, "Roa. What are you talking about? Why would I tell you about Ketos? He's a bedtime story to warn young Persei not to seek too much power. A way to explain how the

Persei have remained in power with their energy resources. He isn't real."

I watch his face, scrutinizing every micromovement. He believes what he is saying. My defenses shift.

"Not according to the Harpyiai or your mother. Ketos killed your aunt!"

Andrin's face twists like he is sucking on a lemon. "That's ridiculous. She's never told me that before."

My arms fall to my sides. "She said it happened 133 years ago, the last time he came to the Constellation. He comes every 133 years, so he'll be back here soon."

"My aunt died because she didn't want to be Queen, and she threw herself off a cliff." He throws his arms up in the air.

Silence settles between us. Frustration is battling for dominance between both of us. Finally, Andrin sighs and holds his hands up. He slowly walks towards me, as if I were a wild animal.

"It's just a story. Ketos consumes the light from Mycenae and hibernates until he is awoken by a brighter light."

"Maybe there's some truth to the bedtime story." I force my Aether to create a ball of light in the palm of my hand. "How do you think he's consuming this light?"

"I always thought it was some type of parable about summer turning into winter." Awe shines on his face. "You think she's telling the truth, and it's all real."

"Yes. She said Ketos distributes power after the sacrifice. The Harpyiai mentioned Ketos in the mountains of Seriphus, and I think she wants the power that the Persei normally get from Ketos for herself. I have a theory that she wants me only because the Commodore wants me."

Andrin's golden features twist. "You think the Harpyiai wants to use you as a bargaining chip with the Commodore?"

As if the thought of my power alone summoned it to the surface of my skin, my Aether crackles along my fingertips.

"I think it's possible. The timing is too strange to be a coincidence."

Andrin spins, running both of his hands through his hair. "Auro—Roa, you have to know that's not why I brought you here."

The desperation in his eyes makes me pause. They are wide and panicked.

My tongue is as dry as the sandstone of the palace as I dare to ask, "Then why did you? Tell me the full reason, not the half-truths you've been feeding me, as if I'm too stupid to see their faults."

Andrin paces back towards me, he takes my hand and refuses to let go. "When I was first sent to get you from Earth, it was because I was following my father's command. To keep the heir of Andromeda safe to help gain the Persei's favor in Galaxia. It was to protect and serve my Constellation. As soon as I saw you, it was like staring into a star. After getting to know you and seeing how incredible you are, for the first time in my life, I knew what it meant to be in the presence of a star. All I want is to protect and serve you."

My skin is hot, despite the sea breeze that flutters my thin clothes. My brain refuses to articulate a single word.

"Roa, I'm in love with you."

My Aether flares out in a wild spark before suffocating. Andrin takes the moment to close the distance between us. He wraps his arms around me tightly. His lips claim mine. I force mine to move against him while my brain struggles to work. How can he love me? I have known him for such a short amount of time.

I freeze. I want to trust him, but hesitation churns my stomach. Andrin slows his movements when he notices my lack of participation. When he pulls back from the kiss, his eyes plead with me. I want to trust him, but there needs to be transparency between us.

"You should have told me. About my name and being the Heir to Andromeda."

"I know. I'm so sorry. I don't know for sure why the Harpyiai is after you, but you're right, that does make the most sense."

"I'm worried I'm not safe here." His face falls even further.

"I promise, I will do my best to keep you safe." He pulls away slightly to pull Astrobleme vials out of his pocket. "I'll do what I can to keep you powerful enough never to be afraid again. I will protect you."

My face must give away my desire for the blue liquid. He leads me to bed and has me sit. He administers a shot to each of us. My skin glows blue again. I adjust the translucent sleeve back down when he removes the needle.

"Are you cold?" Andrin's eyes are on the barrier, still stuck partially open.

"Um, a little. I got it stuck last night."

Andrin gives me a soft smile. I smile back because the Astrobleme makes my blood feel warm and viscous. He goes to the panel and presses the buttons, but the alarms still show the same.

"I'll have to send someone to fix it later. That's beyond my capability."

"Okay." I nod dismissively, absorbed in the feeling of Astrobleme.

The blue begins to fade, but the feeling of the pulsing Aether remains in my blood. It's euphoric. Andrin returns to my side, taking my face in both of his hands.

"I love you, Roa," He repeats.

I have grown attached to him, I'm attracted to him, but I don't love him. I can't find words to respond, so I kiss him. His kiss is hungry in return. I can't give him my words, so I let him take my body.

CHAPTER 28

Andrin leaves before Mirfak is high in the sky. As I take a bath overlooking the Mycenae coastline, my thoughts turn back to the Queen's sister. The one who threw herself off a cliff to avoid a crown, or was killed by a boogie monster. The fear in my blood doesn't dissipate at either possibility.

I need answers.

I rise from the water, a small wave crashing over the shell-encrusted rim as I hurriedly wrap a towel around myself. I remember a friend's offer to help me gather information. I dress in the short silk dress and sheer robe again before restoring my metal accessories. I strap my lone holster to my thigh, the metal of my single dagger humming against my bare skin. The leather peeks out from under my short skirt. Maybe I should be hiding it better, but I like displaying that I can be a threat in multiple ways. I swing open my bedroom door, only to be greeted by the backs of two Persei Guards.

"Good afternoon," One grunts, his tone gruff and lacking pleasantries.

"Good afternoon. Excuse me, I need to speak to Syntag Izar. He promised me a tour of the library."

I slip between the two guards while they give each other a confused look. Moving swiftly, I arrive in front of Izar's door and knock loudly. After a few seconds, there's no answer. I bang my fist against the door again, louder this time. Izar finally opens the door, his face scrunched in a hiss.

"What do you want? It's so early," Izar groans.

I roll my eyes. "It's the afternoon. I want that tour of the library now."

His annoyance shifts to confusion. "What are—"

His gaze falls to the guards behind me. He surveys me again and must see the urgency in my eyes. Slowly, recognition settles into his features.

"Oh, yes. I'd be happy to show you all the incredible tomes the greatest historians and intellectuals of Perseus have acquired." Izar slips into an overly formal and mildly condescending persona.

I plaster a fake smile on my face. "Great. I'll wait here."

To his credit, he doesn't look at the guards again. "Of course. Let me get changed and I'll escort you there now."

Izar holds his word and returns to the doorway within a minute. Billowing pants and a vest hang haphazardly from his body as he begins down the hallway. Our pace is slow and steady. Slow enough not to draw attention, but fast enough that I don't burst out of my skin. Izar leads my two trailing guards and me down below the ground level to a subterranean library. It's vast, with ceilings thirty feet high and aisles that slope deeper into the ground. The air is cold and dry, the space hidden from Mycenaean heat. Rows of shelves rise high, a maze of tomes. There must be thousands of books in here.

Izar shifts closer. "What are the answers you seek?"

His tone is hushed, barely loud enough to be called a whisper. I suppose the library allows us to talk quietly without seeming suspicious. I have to think of my guards and what they will report back. I don't know the intention behind keeping an eye on me.

I lean in close to whisper, "Remember our conversation about Gigas? I want more information about one in particular."

The mosaic spaces between his eyebrows crinkle. "I'll see what I can find."

As he steps through the aisles, he pauses, looking around the stacks. He turns back towards me, eyeing the guards who still follow a step behind. He points towards a stack two rows over.

"You should check down there, see if anything calls out to you," he says cryptically.

Izar slinks away with the grace of a cat. The two guards remain near me, one guard on either side of the stacks. I feel a sense of being trapped, the book stacks stretching high above me, only a few feet apart from each other. I read the spines of the books as fast as I can. Some take me longer, as my brain struggles to grasp the curves and points of other languages. Finally, I see something that catches my eye—a sun-bleached pale purple with a single title.

The Andromeda Galaxy

My Aether sparks as my fingers roll over the spine. The silver ink absorbs the Aether like a vacuum. I glance towards the guards on either side. They both look incredibly bored. Good.

I grab two books from the shelves around the lavender book—another glance towards the guards. The taller guard is scuffing his boot along the floor. The shorter one looks up at the ceiling, as if it might fall on him. Top-notch guards. I grab the lavender-bound book and shove it between the two others in my hands. I pull them close to my chest and use the flowy fabric of my over-dress to conceal my finds.

I walk back with a faux-casual purpose toward the central aisle, where the taller guard stands. As I walk past him, they both slide into coordinated steps behind me. Izar rounds the corner six rows down, his topaz eyes glowing bright in the dim light. He gives me the slightest of nods. He meets my pace, and we walk towards the staircase up to the main floor. In a smooth shift of weight, Izar passes me the two books in his possession. A deep, bone-chilling emptiness starts in my fingertips and creeps up my arm. The books nearly fall out of my arms at the strange sensation, but I force my face to remain stoic. I slide it beneath my own find, between the decoy book sandwich.

The afternoon sun shines through the palace's skylights as we step onto the ground floor. My heart is racing. The books feel heavy in my arms. They feel like the weight of every decision that has come before me. They feel like the weight of every decision I will have to make.

"By the way, you should be careful where you wander about in the palace. Apparently, an intruder was spotted in the King's wing last night. That's probably why the King assigned guards to all the palace's guests. For their protection," Izar warns.

My blood chills. My eyes meet Izar's, and the fierceness of his gaze holds me. Izar knows my mischievous, nosy tendencies well enough by now to have identified me, even if the Persei haven't yet figured it out. He taps the books in my hands with his pointed nails.

"The Persei will do anything to protect their own interests. You should do the same and protect yourself."

He quickly steps away from me and disappears into his own room. The metallic taste of electricity sits sourly on my tongue as I struggle to hold in my Aether. I don't release my breath until the door is firmly closed and I count to ten in my solitude. I toss the books onto the fainting couch as if they were on fire. I should be more careful with my Aether, or else they might actually catch on fire. Something tells me these books are a limited edition.

Once I've calmed, I push aside the two decoy books and hold up Izar's selections first. It's a bland tan medical textbook. I open the table of contents and stop when I see the word Astrobleme. Opening the indicated page, I see that potent word again. Administration starts at puberty. Shots once a month, as the young Persei grow. Once puberty is complete, the shots should only be administered once a year.

Warnings follow.

Astrobleme is a DNA synthesizer made with active ingredients of meteorite deposits, including Astrogren with calcium-aluminum-rich inclusions (CAIs) in a saline solution. Side effects may include increased heart rate, decreased blood pressure, insomnia, and irritability. Astrobleme overuse may result in kidney or liver failure. In severe cases, Geaefication may occur.

Irritability? Well, I've always been short-tempered. Yet even for me, I have felt more excitable as of late. As for insomnia, I can't remember the last time I slept more than a few hours at a time. It seems strange for me to experience such extreme symptoms while I've only been taking Astrobleme for a few weeks, since the day we left Seriphus. Could I already be having side effects from it? What is Geaefication?

I read through the rest of the chapter, but nothing else is beneficial. No further mention of Geaefication. I reread the section on Astrobleme two more times before stuffing it between the decoys.

Curious about what else Izar brought me, I picked up the second selection. It is a grey-bound book, made from crude, dry, and cracked leather. I cringe at the thought of what type of alien skin made the book binding. The words are embedded with black ink, a phrase the Queen had said.

Brightest Light of Persei

This must have my answers about Ketos.

The same bone-deep chill I felt in the library makes my fingers ache as I run my fingers along the inky words. Most strangely, it feels like the book is—alive, somehow.

I take another deep breath and open the cover. It's all handwritten. The pages are yellow and crisp with age. They feel brittle, as if they will fall apart if I turn a page too quickly. There is no table of contents, so I start at the beginning.

The date is at the top of the page, 532 BGE. It consists of a single line, handwritten in scratchy ink.

A syphon, as old as time and as powerful as the stars, will come from the sea and lay waste to land.

I continue flipping through the pages slowly. Only minor details are given. Fire, flood, famine. 532, 399, 266, 133. All 133 years apart. On the fifth page, I find only the date for GE. There is a slightly longer passage there.

STARRY EYED

They will capture the syphon and enslave its essence. Feed the syphon light, and Persei will prosper. A gift will only yield what it is given.

There are thirty-eight more accounts of destruction. It has to be Ketos. Each new account describes only the location of 'the light'. The book documents where they got the light from every 133 years. Coordinates scrawled across each page. Coordinates not from Mycenae, but from across the Persei Constellation. Unless my brain isn't translating correctly, the sentence's tense seems wrong; it is neither present nor past. The writing sounds like it's foretelling the future.
 Prophecies.
I flip to the last page of the book. Perfectly full, as if the author knew before writing exactly how many pages they would require. The top of the last page says "5054 GE."

RIGHT ASCENSION: 14h 21m 20.64s
DECLINATION: +78° 52' 08"

This location makes me pause. It is the same format as all the others, but this one is in a vastly different location. All of the others had been within seconds of each other in ascension and declination. This set of coordinates is separated by hours.

When the hunter's arrow shatters the siphon of time, the light shall fold upon itself. The stars will weep in silent decay, and the old sky will turn to dust. Yet from the void where shadows danced, a new dawn shall carve its path – borne upon the echoes of a forgotten sun.

It sounds like translated texts from the fifth century. A broken rhyme. My blood chills. The book is written in the future tense. The Queen had said that Earth's Greek mythology is based on Perseus' history and prophecy. This book was made to predict the coming of something great and evil.

Ketos.

An ear-piercing screech rips through the air. I turn at a neck-breaking speed to see a light, bright as a star, searing across the sky. It's an enormous asteroid, shooting across the Mycenae countryside. The asteroid blocks out Mirfak, sending the planet into momentary darkness despite the blinding light it emits. It burns my eyes. Like a solar eclipse, light and dark are battling for dominance.

I hold my hand above my eyes to shield them, watching as the asteroid soars over the cliffs before plummeting into the ocean. A cavernous void follows the asteroid deep into the vacuum as it strikes the water. Water swells along the coast from the sudden surge, then is sucked from the shoreline into the void.

As the light of an asteroid disappears, overtaken by waves that magnify outwards. The waves travel, amplifying until they resemble a tsunami. A tsunami that will surely bring destruction to the pearlescent city, located on the peninsula.

I drop the book and run for my door. I have to tell someone. The guards. Izar. Andrin. The King. There must be an alarm system. Like a tsunami storm warning. A way to get people to higher ground.

Except the wave is already crashing towards the land. So many citizens of Mycenae will die. Most aliens can't Aether Cross. We have to help them. Before the buildings collapse or the flooding takes them.

There are no guards at my door when I fling it open. I sprint down the hallway, but the ground gives way beneath me. I tumble, a mess of limbs and white fabric as the palace stones continue to shake. An earthquake. From the asteroid. It continues to shake the world, longer and harder than any earthquake I encountered in California.

Despite the shaky ground, I plant my hands and push myself up. This earthquake could trigger another tsunami or cause additional structural damage. My fear for those in the peninsula's lowlands grows.

I'm almost to the grand staircase when I dare look out the exposed palace windows to check the scale of destruction. Instead of water- or broken pearl-colored buildings, I see red. Red feathers.

Claws tear into my flesh as my world flashes with red light.

CHAPTER 29

The light clears from my eyes, and the claws of the Harpyiai release me. I'm falling. The rush of wind is deafening. I spin uncontrollably down, picking up velocity.

As I spin, I see blue. Pale yellow. Ocean, and sandstone.

She has dropped me to fall to my death and tumbled by the crashing waves against the rocky shoreline until I'm nothing but a speck of sand. The rocks are fast approaching; I may just be crushed on impact.

Something sharp shears into my ankle. A scream rips out of my throat as I flip in the air, being held by only the muscles and tendons of my ankle. I strain my neck to see what has a hold of me, the Harpyiai. The talons of her feet dig into my flesh. She continues our descent, using her massive, red-feathered wings to slow our plunge. I have to push through the layer of organza that flaps around my face so I can look back towards the rocky shoreline.

With a quick jolt, she jerks us to the side, and she opens her claws, tearing my flesh further as she releases me. My limbs flail, and my organs rattle inside my body. Blue, yellow, brown, white, red, blue, yellow, brown. The colors of the world flick across my vision as I spiral towards the ground. Pain ricochets from my shoulder and hips as my body smashes against the grassy cliff outcrop. My vertical momentum halts, but I continue to spin, rolling down the slope through the dried vegetation.

Fiery pain emanates from every cell in my body. I'm gasping for breath when my body finally halts, slamming against a boulder. I roll myself to my back, salt and copper burn my eyes and tongue. Blood and tears. Wincing, I wipe the blood and other debris from my eyes so I can see. My left hand is already swelling. Twisted and broken in grotesque angles.

The unmistakable flap of wings draws a string of curses from my mouth.

An inhuman howl tears from my throat as I throw myself to my knees and push off the ground. My legs wobble, but my footing is sure. A horrendous purple spreads from one of my knees, already doubled in size. I flick my lone dagger out of my thigh holster and release a war cry as the Harpyiai descends.

Her wing smacks into my side, sending me stumbling, but I send some of her feathers flying with a swipe of my blade.

I let myself get distracted. I've been training this entire time so I could go home and keep my family safe. So that I could keep us all safe from the aliens that want to harm me. I've gotten too wrapped up with Andrin and his family and their strange secrets. I literally ran right into the Harpyiai's clutches.

I won't be distracted now, one of Izar's first lessons.

She stands on her two powerful legs, her clawed feet dig into the ground. I'll have a hard time knocking her off balance. If I can injure just one of her wings, it might be enough to cripple her temporarily.

I let my Aether bubble under my skin, let it build a charge.

She lunges for me, wings spread wide and beaked head bowed. I push my arms to the right before ducking left. The bottom feathers of her right wing slap across my face as I raise my dagger over my head. A piercing caw bellows from her beak. With a swift flex, she backhands her wing, hitting my back and sending me sprawling face-first.

My dagger tumbles from my broken left hand. I roll my body and kick off the ground to land in a crouch. My Aether sparks across my skin now, ready to consume.

I push Aether through my left hand, a wall-like pulse against the Harpyiai, sending her flying backwards as I had accidentally done to the guard on Argos. She skitters back, wings flailing wide as she tries to compose herself. I can't help but clutch my hand to my chest, vibrations like a jackhammer ricochet up my broken bones. I grab my fallen weapon in my usable hand.

I look up just as she charges me again, and I focus my Aether, then Aether Cross. My landing is clumsy, and my brain spins. The moment of disorientation costs me as she grabs my braids and yanks me to the ground. A blinding light ignites from my chest. Her beady eyes shutter, and I lunge.

I slice through her shoulder, my blade striking true, but the Harpyiai snaps her wings closed, with me inside. With a flash of red light, the world disappears.

When the light subsides, I surrender to my nausea. I let my vomit cover us both as we fall from the sky. She opens her wings like a sail, and I plummet. My drop is instant and fleeting as her claws scrape up my thigh and the sides of my inverted form. My scream feels like knives through my throat, following the burn of stomach bile and blood.

She flies us over the ocean side of the cliff now. Maybe she hopes another wave will wipe me from the planet for her. I wanted to defeat her, kill her, so she couldn't kill my family or me. I've been so naive to think my weeks of training are any match for the rest of this alien universe that is determined to kill me. Now, I need to fight to survive.

I release the tie at my waist, and my overdress flies upwards, catching in the wind. The Harpyiai flails, her wings thrashing as she tries to tear the material from her face and features. She doesn't release her grip on me, and it costs us both meters toward the water. Maybe I can cut off her foot when I'm close enough to the rocks so that I won't die from the impact. If I were to do it right now—a massive wave slams against the rocks— I would drown or crack my skull open.

Closer, closer, we are dropping altitude so quickly. Maybe a few more seconds, and it might be a safe drop. The talons loosen their grip on my ankle.

I won't get a few more seconds.

I try to twist up, pulling my torso to reach her taloned feet and hold on. Now, it's too late. I'm plummeting. Too high up and falling too fast. I let out a cry of fear. I can feel the spray of the ocean. I force my flailing limbs to close around my head and tuck into the fetal position.

I'm a coward, I'm weak.

I close my eyes before the impact can come.

CHAPTER 30

My body's desire not to drown launches me back to consciousness as a wave rolls over my limp form. I twist to my stomach, coughing up the ocean water. Blinking, I can barely clear away the blackness in front of my eyes. My vision is limited to a narrow tunnel, but I can see the ocean beyond me and the jagged rocks of the cliff-face beneath me. I move my arms to push myself up, but my broken left hand and right arm refuse to bear weight. I hiss out a breath, desperate to take stock of my body. My right side took the fall this time. My shoulder is on fire; at minimum, it's dislocated. Hopefully, the muscle and ligaments aren't torn. The metal of my vambraces are bent awkwardly into my skin, not breaking the flesh but enough to tell me it absorbed some impact. My hip feels stiff, bruised, or damaged.

Another wave washes over me.

My body shivers involuntarily from the cold splash over my burning skin. I only got a little bit of water in my mouth and eyes this time. I'm at the bottom of the cliff, at sea level, when the waves crash over the rocks. I have to move; I have to get out of here. Every micromovement sends pain searing through my nervous system. I can't focus; my Aether feels like lightning bolts jutting through my bones.

I press my right hand to the slippery rocks below. A deep inhale, I push up as I exhale. The air leaves my body in a roar. My torso is lifted from the rocks, but only in time to see a flash of red.

The Harpyiai's talons grip my neck, slamming me back against a rock. My head knocks into the stone, and I blink away the darkness again. With a hand still gripped against my throat, she squeezes the broken bones of my hand as she yanks my left arm away from my body.

Something cold and hard clicks into place over my vambrace. She releases my left arm as my vision returns, then switches to my right arm and jerks it away. Another scream escapes me. Dislocated for sure. She locks a metal shackle onto my right vambrace. She wants to chain me to the rocks.

"What? You like to play with your food before you eat it?" I hiss towards the Harpyiai.

Her bird head swings towards me. It cocks to the side as her beady eyes narrow at me. She comes close to me, leaning her beak right into my face.

"You're not food for me."

She launches into the air. Feathers slapping my face as she skyrockets upwards. She's off balance, her uninjured wing flapping twice as fast. At least I gave her a flesh wound.

My victory is short-lived as a massive wave barrels me. I can't cover myself from the force of the wave while my arms are chained apart. I'm gasping for air, shaking when the water finally recedes. A pool of water has formed in the fissure where I stand. It's up to my ankles, but I'm not at risk of drowning. Yet.

From the water, something emerges. Something massive. A scaled forelimb with fins, tapered along its length, pushes against the rocks below me, the size of an old oak tree. My

Aether flares, pulsing my skin light blue. Its head rises from the water, grotesque, rounded with an infinite number of teeth like an anglerfish.

Horror crawls up my spine; it wasn't an asteroid that hit the ocean. It was this thing.

A tail fluke slaps against the ocean, sending another tidal wave for me. I gasp for air, closing my eyes as I wait for the water to recede. When it does, a booming voice echoes from the alien's mouth in the Universal Language.

"Daughter of Mēdeia, I've long awaited your arrival."

I whimper, warmth trailing down my legs with my incontinence. Somehow, the fact that it can talk makes it exponentially more terrifying. Unlike the other monstrous aliens I have faced, he's intelligent enough to know my family's origin. He knows my name just as I know his.

Ketos.

The Queen said that when the Andromeda Galaxy collapsed, it created the brightest light anyone had ever seen. The Harpyiai has been fumbling around Galaxia searching for the brightest light. I know she's been hunting me, and I finally know why.

I need to get out of here.

Now.

I visualize the cliffside, but the cortisol coursing through my veins distracts me. My fight-or-flight response is stuck in freeze mode. I'm panting. Desperate to open a wormhole on either side. Instead, a pain shoots from the top of my spine and makes my legs collapse beneath me. My arms tremble in protest as the chains hold them back.

"I've coveted to taste your power," Ketos booms, "The last of your blood."

Another forelimb emerges from the water. It drags itself up onto the shoreline. Aether sparks along the bronze chains shackling me to the rocks.

The foolish Harpyiai used metal chains. Metal I can use to channel. I let my fear, my anger, my intense desire to survive, build my Aether reserves. I can taste the pure electric pulse in the salt on my tongue.

I focus the Aether, a zap to either end of the chain. With a loud crack, they both pop free from the rocks, the heavy metal falling to the ground. I grit my teeth against the weight on my left shoulder. I taste blood. A warm stream drips down my nose, falling to my white-clad body.

Ketos pauses his advance, inhaling deeply as his nostrils flare, sniffing the air.

"My pawns have delivered a fruitful sacrifice. You smell like the cosmos themselves."

Sacrifice.

I hate that I was right. This is what the Harpyiai wanted me for. It wasn't to use me as a political pawn with the Commodore. It's to be Ketos' food. The Persei royals unknowingly delivered me right into her trap. I've never been so disappointed to be right.

My Aether bubbles to the surface, and the water at my feet hums. The mini tidepool begins to simmer, crackle, and then boils. My thermal energy uses water as a medium.

The round head juts forward. I leap to the side, tumbling down the rocks. The shoreline shakes with the impact of his head. He's been playing with me. Moving slowly to toy with me. Ketos rears back, shaking off the rocks he had freed from my previous position. I need to move. I don't know where I am, or where I need to go. I look up to the cliffs above me. A platform juts out from the cliffside. Maybe that will be high enough. I steady my shaking breath as much as I can, imagining the platform. I cannot fail now.

I Aether Cross.

I don't give myself time to adjust to the flash of light. My feet hit the platform roughly, both twisting in unnatural positions—my bruised knee throbs with the rapid beat of my heart. My muscles are struggling to support my weight with the tears in my flesh. I tumble to the ground, tripping over the uneven surface. The weight of the chains holds me down.

Ketos roars beneath me, the cliffside shaking from the baritone vibrations. His forelimbs dig into the cliffside on either side of the platform, raising himself until his head is at the base of the platform where I stand. My fear keeps my Aether alive, pulsing along my skin and down the bronze chains.

"Daughter of Mēdeia, you were never supposed to live. I will balance the cosmos with your death."

His fluke splashes against the water again. A spray of water comes high enough to keep his back wet, though he's dragged himself halfway out of the water. The chains spark like live wires as I drag them along the rocks.

If Ketos wants balance—if he wants a sacrifice this badly—I will make sure we both die today.

Ketos' open jaw launches again, and I have no time to reconsider my plan. In a flash of light, I Aether Cross.

My landing is more like a slide. I skid down the scales along his neck as he roars, rearing back vertically. I grab onto a bulbous piece of flesh along his neck, a dorsal spine. I grit through the pain of my dislocated shoulder and broken hand as I haul myself up, sitting upon the bump like a saddle. I have to grip the scaly neck as it thrashes back and forth. The chains along my wrists swing with the motion of the alien, making it harder to hold on.

The muscles of Ketos' back flex. He's backing himself into the water. He only has forelimbs; the rest of the body tapers into its fluked tail. The ground shakes as he recedes deeper into the water. His lower body is submerged; his head will soon follow suit.

I focus my Aether on my arms. I force the metal chains to move, to lift into the air. Sparks fly between the two ends, like two wires. The fluke rises out of the water, flexing, ready to send another tidal wave up his back. The fluke smacks into the water.

A dangerous combination: metal, water, electricity.

I send the end of the chains into his mouth, snagging on some of his thousands of sharp teeth. I hold my breath as the wave submerges me. The second cold water hits my skin, I release my charge. Fire erupts down the length of the chains. Electrons zapping as the electricity and water mix, boiling around us. Flames rip up my vambraces, dancing across my blood-covered flesh until I release them.

The water recedes, but Ketos howls—brown blood spewing from his lacerated mandible. There is still charge in the chains, in me. I surge all my Aether forward, visualizing the chains dragging back simultaneously. As I pull on the chains, I feel my Aether pulling back towards me. Except it doesn't feel like mine, it feels like when I took the flames from the Ignos and turned it into Aether. I'm drawing out Ketos' Aether.

My body is filled with Aether, a push and pull of mine and Ketos' back and forth. It feels wrong. Yet, I feel powerful, alive.

I'm a blue lighthouse illuminating the coast. The howling turns to a gurgle as a ripping sound builds, like Velcro being pulled apart. I mentally pull the chains closer until they snag.

Panting, I try to yank the chains again. The draw of his Aether doesn't meet mine anymore, only my energy pulling through a void in the universe. The chains refuse to budge, caught. Yet it's unnecessary since the gurgle of blood and splashing water has ceased. Gravity rushes around me as I hold onto my makeshift saddle for the beast. Ketos' head lolls sideways before hurling to the ground. I grit my teeth, readying for impact. His head makes a liquid splat before the rest of his body shakes the rocks with its collision. A flood of brown blood flows like a tidal wave of its own, covering the boulders around me. The lack of movement and sound from him confirms his death.

I want to lie down, I want to cry. In relief, and anger, and every overwhelming emotion still coursing through my body. I need to move, get away while the adrenaline is still pumping through my veins.

I send another jolt of focused Aether to my shackles, and the chains break at the top link. Only the bronze shackles on top of the golden vambraces remain. I have to crawl my way down the massive ridges of fish bones and flesh. The dead fish squishes beneath my bare feet with the squelch of mud. Finally, at the edge of his back, I can slide down his forelimb to the jagged rocks.

Izar and I have reflected in depth on the difference between aliens and monsters. Yet I believe even he would agree, Ketos is a monster. He wanted to consume me, for my Aether. The Harpyiai wanted to sacrifice me for her own gain of power. The sacrifice of others is monstrous.

I find a smoother surface on the cliff face farther up the coastline, where the water is clear, before kneeling. I use the ocean water to wash away the blood, both brown and red, that trails down my wet blue skin. I sway my hands underneath the surface of the water. They look like bioluminescent jellyfish.

I inspect the back of my hands, up my arms, my chest, my legs. My skin is blue, but those tiny white freckles I noticed stand out in contrast, a white glow of their own. They shine like stars. My body is covered in stars, like a map of a clear night sky. Yet those are the only imperfections visible on my skin. It is as if the Aether erased all evidence of the lacerations or broken bones, yet the pain isn't absent.

My silk dress is drenched and heavy, stained so severely in filth it will never be white again. I feel tears prickle in my eyes; my panting breath turns to a gasp. I look out to the water, the waves, their regular rise and fall returned as if Ketos was never there. Mirfak casts a rainbow of colors across the sky as it slips towards the horizon. Orange and fuchsia bleeding into a violet blue sky. A smear of sherbet ice cream blanketing Mycenae. The beauty fills me with rage.

Mycenae doesn't deserve this beauty. The Persei don't deserve this beauty. The prophecy book said Ketos repays sacrifice with an equal measure of energy. Repays it to the Persei. This is why the King brought me here.

The Harpyiai and Persei are both monsters.

Ketos is no bedtime story. The Persei should fear me as they sleep tonight.

The sound of wind rustling through wings makes me pause.

I don't have time to cry.

The Harpyiai soars overhead.

I won't let her get close to me again. I flip her off as a flash of white encompasses me.

CHAPTER 31

I stumble, my battered knee refusing to hold my weight as I land in the palace gardens. I'm once again amongst the cypress trees. I can see a staircase back to the palace just beyond the entrance of the pathway. I move as quickly as I can without running or drawing attention to my injuries. I move like a broken fawn, but I'm a wounded lion and far more dangerous. I don't want anyone asking me questions or slowing me down. I will be leaving this planet today.

My entire body is shaking by the time I make it to my room and scan my biometrics.

"Roa!"

I cringe at the sound of his voice—the heir to this corrupt Constellation. I slip through the door, but his hand catches it before I can slam it closed.

"There you are! What happened to you? Are you alright?" Andrin demands.

I turn to him, ire illuminating my skin while my Aether is too drained to make an appearance. "Do I look alright to you? No. First, the Harpyiai took me, then she tried to feed me to Ketos." I sweep my arms across my appearance for extra effect.

His eyes widen as his face twists in confusion. "Do you mean—"

I spin and wrap my right hand around his neck. I slam him against the door. My barley mended hand remains limp at my side. I wish I still had my dagger to slit his throat.

"Drop your act. I know your father allowed the Harpyiai to take me. You're all conspiring to keep the Persei rule strong," I spat in his face. "I should kill you for your deceit. For making me believe I was safe with you."

Andrin's face is crestfallen, his voice comes out shattered, "Roa–I promise, I didn't know. I didn't believe in Ketos until you cornered me this morning. I would never put you in harm's way."

I snarl in his face, but nothing breaks his mask of genuine concern. "You really didn't know?" I ask skeptically.

He tries to shake his head, but my hand still grips his throat. His hand wraps around my wrist gently. I'm weak enough that he could easily push me away if he wanted to.

"What can I do to prove to you that I am on your side?"

I glower at him and release his throat. "If you believe you ever really loved me, you would keep your promise, fire up the Orbital Station, and take me home now."

A ring of rose gold stretches across his neck from where my fingers held him, but he doesn't show any signs of discomfort. Instead, his eyes continue to scour my disastrous state.

"Okay, yes, I'll help you, of course." His mouth gapes like a fish, "Roa, have you seen your skin?"

I roll my eyes at the vain golden Persei. I'm lucky all my limbs are still attached. With a huff, I turn and stalk through my room. Pacing like a caged animal as I try to settle my never-ending ire enough to think.

"I'm sorry, I didn't think the Astrobleme would affect you so much. I wouldn't have given it to you when I first brought you to the Orbital Station—"

I ignore the rest of his words. My fingertips are white. The color drained from my hands in an ombre that disappears up my vambraces. I can't move them. They're stiff—like stone.

When he first brought me to the Orbital Station? As in, he gave it to me when I was abducted?

That was weeks ago. Months at this point.

I spin back towards Andrin. There's a hollow space in my chest where anger should be burning. My blood runs hot and cold at once. Andrin pauses, as if realizing his slip. I can feel Aether spark across my skin at the newest flash of rage; it's been weeks. My first time taking Astrobleme was supposed to be in Seriphus, right before we slept together for the first time. That's when I had agreed to take it.

Andrin seems almost as frozen as I feel, realizing his mistake. "It was only once when you passed out when you first started trying Aether manipulation. Then just once more on Argos, after you got injured. I was only trying to help you!" He argues defensively.

His alleged good intentions don't pacify my anger in the slightest. Andrin has been giving me Astrobleme since he abducted me. He's been injecting me without my permission, without my consent. No wonder I was suddenly able to manipulate Aether so much better after Argos. I barely survived the Scilla, but I unexpectedly had glowing eyes and levitated that stupid orb.

Hurt, betrayal, and deep rage swell within my body again.

"Get out!" I snarl as I charge Andrin. "Get away from me, or I will kill you!"

With genuine fear on his face, he turns and leaves. The door slams closed before I can reach him. I hold my hands out in front of me. My eyes fly towards the pile of books on the coffee table. An overdose of Astrobleme can cause Geaefication.

Geae.

Like Gaea or *Gaîa* from Greek mythology. The primordial Earth Goddess. Based on my hands, Geaefication really must mean turning into the earth.

I want to scream. First, the Harpyiai; then, Ketos; and now, I'm turning into a statue. The door rattles as if someone is trying to open it. My anger flares hot in my blood. I'm in no mood to see, let alone speak to Andrin again.

I need time to think. I need time to plan. I'm done waiting and delaying my transit home. I just need a second without Andrin in my face to figure out how I can get off a planet full of murderous Persei.

I stalk towards the door, but it swings open before I reach it.

"Andrin! What part of get out of my sight doesn't translate—" My words dry in my throat.

It's not Andrin at the door.

Izar stands in my doorway, his features emotionless. I open my mouth to speak, but the Persei Guards push past him into my room.

CHAPTER 32

"Hey! What are you doing?" I yell in protest.

The last two guards who enter grab my arms and pull me away from the door. Panic rises in my throat, choking any further protests. I don't know what is going on, but my body is screaming to fight. I beg my Aether to comply, but it only fizzles. I'm burnt out.

I whip my head around, trying to see what the other guards in my room are doing. The only bright side of my limbs turning to stone is that I can't feel the pain of my broken bones being squeezed beneath their grip.

I want to cry out for help, but I doubt anyone will help me. Not here. Not after everything I've learned. Somehow, Izar's betrayal stings worse than Andrin's. Andrin at least thought he was helping me. Izar won't even look at me.

Had trusted.

Every segment of his mosaic skin is still. Emotionless. Cold.

"What's going on?" I demand, despite the involuntary quiver in my voice.

Another guard approaches with a large gold breastplate. It looks like a metal corset. I'm in danger. I don't know what that thing will lead to, but I know I need to leave. Now.

I struggle to think of anywhere safe I can go. I already came from the cliffside to the gardens. There is nowhere else on the planet I know, and I still haven't thought of a way to get off the planet either. Even if I could, my Aether refuses to rise. Panic causes my limbs to tremble uncontrollably. Until I remember, this traitor also taught me how to fight.

I drop to my knees, my dislocated shoulder protesting. It distracts the guards on my arms just enough to loosen their grip. I slip my wet limbs from their grasp and dive forward. Short-term pain means nothing to my renewed adrenaline that thunders through my veins.

Survive. Survive. Survive.

In my desperation, I feel the ghost of a spark inside my chest. If I don't leave now, there is a very real possibility I will be killed. I close my eyes, preparing for the flash, but it doesn't come. Instead, a metaphysical wall slams against my brain and body. I crumble to the floor instead of Aether Crossing to safety. When I open my eyes, I'm still in the same spot in the room. The space in my chest is utterly empty.

"The barriers keep everything in and out," Izar sounds disappointed in me, "I told you that."

I glance behind me at the window barriers with their high-tech screens. I've been a prisoner this entire time. Since I entered the Spanish gardens, I've been trapped.

A guard lunges for me, but I kick his shin with one foot and launch my other foot into his groin. The guard grunts and doubles over. At least my encounter with Andrin taught me they share that vulnerability with human men.

Two other guards latch onto my biceps. I flail, kicking and pulling at my arms to try to get away. I have to keep that corset away from me. Another guard holds my ankles down. The one I had kicked picks up the discarded metal breast plate and approaches me with a sick grin. With his full strength, he presses the plate to my chest and compresses my lungs. I gasp, desperate for air, but he only pushes harder until I hear a metal click. The metal is cold where the too-tight corset clamps around my nearly bare body. My ribs bend inward beneath the metal jail, unable to expand enough to get a full breath.

As the guard leers over me, I spit in his face. His grin warps to fury. Standing, he reels his boot back, ready to kick me where I lie.

"That is enough." Izar's voice halts the guards' strike. "Get her to the Astrogen Chamber."

In a dizzying jerk, they haul me to my feet and drag me towards the door, my arms still spread like a scarecrow. I let my feet dangle. I will not make this easy on them.

As they drag me past Izar, I spit on him. "I hate you."

Why is he doing any of this? His warning, 'don't trust anyone,' repeats in my head. I had been so naïve that I hadn't considered that he had meant to include himself. After all those alien encounters, the hours spent training, the phony warnings he had given me. Even if he hadn't brought the guards to grab me, he is clearly in charge of the golden goons.

They drag me down the hall. Then we go down flights of stairs until we reach the main level. They continue their tug of war with my limbs down the North wing until we reach a set of double doors. The same doors I snuck through last night. Izar knocks before turning back to me.

He leans in to whisper, but I hiss. "I will never forgive you."

He flinches slightly but closes the distance between us anyway. His voice is so quiet that he is nearly inaudible. Yet the force behind his words promises to haunt me. Not a warning. Not a plea. A demand.

"You are not a Super Nova; you were born of one. Never forget who you are. Never forget what you are capable of."

He pulls back and opens the door. It is the chamber I had discovered last night, filled with Astrobleme and the giant crystal. The room is bright. Mirfak has long passed below the horizon, stars speckling the sky through the oculus. The crystal below it glows, throbbing in blue light. It pulses in time with my heartbeat, calling to me.

The knife of betrayal in my back twists further when I see the Harpyiai standing next to the crystal, her wings tucked behind her long body. She motions for the guards to bring me forward.

I hope she will be punished for her failure to deliver me to Ketos. I hope she feels the damage that I caused while chained to that cliffside, left for dead. I hope, despite my current circumstances, that I can be the one to inflict more pain upon her.

The guards push me towards the pearlescent pillars that stand in front of the giant crystal. With a shove, they release my arms, and I fall face-first to the stone floor. My face slams against the smooth, cold ground. My skin instantly swells at my cheekbones and brow bones. A bruise is surely forming since my stiff hands couldn't catch my fall.

I crane my neck towards the Harpyiai, ready to spew curses her way. As soon as her beady eyes meet mine, she throws a switch on the wall, and a shot of electricity shoots through my body. My head hangs limp as the electric pull hoists my arms and chest up. My body rises from the ground, my feet dangling below me. I roll my head to the side and see a thick rope of electricity suspending my body from my vambraces and corset.

Footsteps sound from behind us. The guards block my view of whoever approaches. Finally, the footsteps' source emerges and enters the room. I identify the male easily. Dread seeps through every fiber of my being.

Desperation grips my soul. A small jolt of adrenaline pumps through my veins, begging me to fight. I swing my legs up and wrap them around the guard in front of me. In surprise, he stumbles and clumsily raises his spear. I sink my teeth into his hand until he releases the spear, and I desperately clamp my legs together trying to catch it. I catch the spear between my thighs, but the other guards react faster. A barrage of spears smacks against my thighs, forcing my own legs to open as they shake in pain. It was a disaster of a plan, one with no thought and the same odds of success. I am severely out of options.

"Cease!"

The booming voice commands, and the beatings instantly comply. The guards smoothly part as the King approaches. His lip is curled in disgust as he takes in my dangling form.

"Tell me, how did you manage to defeat Ketos?" His words drip with enough venom. I wonder if it is a rhetorical question.

After a beat of silence passes, I answer. "His price is the brightest light in Persei."

The confusion and anger that settles on his face fuels me. I lick my front teeth, knowing I must be a gruesome sight with the guard's blood dripping down my chin, my hair and eyes surely wild. Before I could manipulate Aether, my favorite weapon was my words. Sometimes, words can strike more fear than any weapon.

"Perhaps the brightest light he always sought was his destruction in the end. As it will be yours." I echo the Queen's words, unsure now if they were meant as a warning, a threat, or both.

The King snarls. "You are nothing. You should have been consumed by Ketos and deposited in his leave of asteroids like all the others before you. You should have been a waste. No better than star dust, just like your parents."

A primal scream rips from my throat, and I launch my head forward. It slams against the Kings; he stumbles back, stunned. The guards launch forward, but he holds up a hand. Blood drips over my right eye, making it harder to see as he closes the distance between us again. His hands dart for my neck, and I gasp. He doesn't choke me; instead, a different golden choker encircles my neck. It's like the one Andrin always wears, but instead of a necklace of title, it marks my ownership—a true golden collar.

He holds his hand out behind him, and the Harpyiai delivers a familiar syringe of Astrobleme. I struggle between the disdain I feel and the pleasure Astrobleme pumps through me.

"You should know, it was my order to make my son administer this since he first got you from Earth. I wanted you to be a powerful sacrifice for Ketos. The more powerful the sacrifice, the more power he gives back to us."

He stabs the needle into my skin and presses the plunger. Burning heat spreads through my veins as the Astrobleme follows its regular path.

"Why do you do it? Why make sacrifices to Ketos?" I know it is a selfish thought, but I ask the questions anyway, "Why choose me as a sacrifice?"

"It was easy to convince my son to fetch you from Earth when the Imperial Commodore sent out his summons. The prophecy had revealed your location long ago. Yet the heir of an entire galaxy, as powerful as a star? I knew your sacrifice would be the last we would ever require. Of course, my weak-hearted son could not be trusted with the truth; he only wanted to save you because you are Andromeda's Heir. So, I had to send the Harpyiai to ensure you were detained."

The King rolls the empty vial of Astrobleme between his fingers lazily as he pontificates. He watches it move beneath my skin with shrouded interest.

"You see, to remain powerful, Constellations need a vast amount of energy. We have already exceeded the energy provided by all of our own stars. That is why we need to colonize other planets. Seriphus is an example of what all the useless planets will become. The power plant on Sarpedon will supply the energy we need to colonize Argos. I never did thank you for helping to sterilize the Scilla; it is so much easier to colonize without pesky native populations."

I squirm the best I can as I'm suspended in the air. The euphoria of Astrobleme is gone; only pain remains. The horror grows as the Harpyiai hands him another vial of Astrobleme. My body fights between desire and revulsion of the liquid.

"You already have a Constellation? What more could you want?" I gasp as my lungs constrict; it quickly becomes difficult to breathe.

The rulers of Galaxia have been in control for too long. Too long we have followed their orders, bowed to their power." The King's voice dips as he sends another injection into my bloodstream. "But the galaxy is changing. The Gigas are returning. You may have killed Ketos, but more are coming."

The room illuminates as my skin glows blue again; the Astrogen crystal below me amplifies the light. The world grows bright, as mine turns to darkness.

CHAPTER 33

I wake to the smell of smoke and metal. My tattered dress has dried, except for the area below my hips. My bladder gave out while I hung unconscious. I cannot find an ounce of shame to summon at my soiled state. As my head throbs and my skin burns, my dress is the least of my concerns.

I blink my heavy eyes open. I struggle to open my right eye; crusted blood has clotted my eyelashes together. Without being able to rub them clean, I rely on my tearing eyes to dilute the dried blood. I remember my blood dripping down my brow bone from head-butting the King, but my wound no longer aches. None of my wounds aches. I twist my face, testing to see if anything is broken or bruised. I lift my heels to my butt, one at a time. My knee no longer aches, but my joints do crack.

My only ache comes from my hands and arms. I can feel the torn flesh at my inner elbows from where numerous needles have forced Astrobleme into my system. My hands ache as if they've been soaking in snow. The bone-deep, throbbing pain I feel as I try to twitch my fingers makes me gasp.

Finally, my right eye pops open, and I can peer down at my hands. They are chalky white and impossibly stiff. Not just my fingertips, but up to my wrists.

A chair screeches across the floor, and I lift my head to the source of the noise. It's dark, but the glow of a Busen burner illuminates the vibrant red of the Harpyiai's feathers as she stalks forward.

"Really? You again?" My voice comes out scratchy, my sass dissolving under the strain.

She shoves her beak into my face, pressing against my own nose as we stare each other down. "You think you are so clever. You are nothing more than a glorified power source."

I force my fake bravado to the surface. "I don't think Ketos would agree with that."

She jabs her sharp claws into my bare shoulder, twisting as she sneers. The flesh tears, but as she moves, my own skin stitches back together. Great, the Astrobleme is healing my injuries just for her to torture me over and over again. Pleased with herself, she removes her claws and prowls back to the laboratory-style table. She returns with two syringes: one filled with Astrobleme, the other empty.

With gasping breath, I sputter, "What is that for?"

Without answering, she stabs the fleshy section of my arm and injects the blue liquid. My internal Aether pulses, greedily sucking it into my pumping heart beneath the metal corset. As my skin glows blue, the Astrogen crystal beneath me pulses in time. The chalkiness from my hands spreads, reaching up towards my elbows. The tips of my toes are pale. I try to curl them, but they refuse my demands. The Harpyiai waits at my side until my skin returns to its usual pale, and only the Astrogen crystal pulses. Then she sticks the needle of the empty syringe into my arm and pulls on the plunger. In a slow, viscous draw, my blood fills the syringe. She holds it in front of my face, sneering as my eyes follow the liquid.

My blood, it is not red anymore. Or at least not entirely, it is almost silver in parts, and moves within the vial on its own. Before I can inspect it further, the Harpyiai turns and heads back to her table.

"This is what we are looking for. This is calcium-aluminum. It is what comes from Astrogen and how we create Astrobleme. Normally, this can only be found in asteroids that are remnants of the beginning of the Galaxia."

Asteroids. Ketos had looked like a falling asteroid.

She pours the blood into a test tube and places it above the burner. It bubbles until the red portion evaporates, leaving only the silver liquid. Her eyes pierce through mine again with anger.

She continues as if talking to herself. "Yet, for some reason, the more Astrobleme your blood comes in contact with, the more calcium-aluminum it produces."

She pours the silver liquid into a large beaker, measures out a clear solution, and stirs.

"We thought you were meant to be a powerful sacrifice to Ketos, but instead of a one-time source of Astrogen asteroids, you can be our eternal on-demand producer."

The prophecy.

The stars will weep in silent decay.

It was about Ketos. About his consumption of a sacrifice and the Astrogen debris that would be left in his wake. I was supposed to be sacrificed to be turned into this poisonous blue liquid. Since I killed Ketos, a Gigas as old as the stars themselves, the Persei need a replacement.

"I won't be your Aether factory," I growl.

A shrill cackle leaves her beak. "Look at you, such a primitive ground dweller. You think you have a choice."

Anger pulses inside my blood. When they captured me, I lacked the Aether to stop them. Despite its best efforts to siphon my very soul, the Astrogen crystal has not stolen all my Aether yet. The flame from the burner beside the Harpyiai flickers in response to my Aether draw. On Sarpedon, I took energy from the Ignos' flaming breath. I wonder if I can feed a flame with my Aether. A sinister smile creeps across my face.

With nothing more than my intentions, I push Aether towards the flame. It roars to a blaze and lashes against the Harpyiai. Her feathers instantly ignite, and she howls in pain. She frantically flutters her wings to put out the fire, but it only gives the flame more oxygen.

She's distracted; this is my chance to escape. I send a volt of Aether back up the thick tendrils of electricity that hold my body up. The converging energies intertwine in an angry battle. My Aether doesn't win. Both energies shoot back, dancing across my vambraces and jumping to the corset. I'm covered in pain, the Aether that has provided me strength and power now revolts against me. A sharp pain jolts within my rib cage, and my lungs seize. My vision of the flaming Harpyiai blurs, and the world fades to black.

CHAPTER 34

I feel cold. Then hot. Then cold.

Every new injection sends fire through my veins. The metal adornments covering my body are not for my protection. Gold is a conduit for harnessing my energy. They are harnessing my Aether to steal it away from me now.

My body aches as I fight to breathe despite the constant tension in my rib cage. It might be my own Aether that holds me in place, suspended between the pillars in the air. It seeps from my very being and pools in silky tendrils into the sharp crystal below me. Every new injection makes it harder to control my body. I can see the Geaefication process spreading from my hands with every dose. My Aether leaks from me. The life in my body is leaving with it. I try to hold onto it, but it's so hard. When the Astrobleme is not floating through my blood, my pale skin looks almost translucent. I feel empty. It feels like my soul is being syphoned from my body. I suppose in a way, it is.

The Harpyiai strides through the double doors. I try to move my arms, my legs, anything. Yet my body refuses to cooperate. As if kidnapping me and dropping me like bird food to Ketos had not been enough, she has been the one administering most of the Astrobleme.

I took joy only in seeing her burnt figure the first time. She has made me pay for the damage I caused her with every injection she inflicts upon me. If we are counting wounds, she already got her cut of flesh from me when she brought me to Ketos. With every shot, she claws into the same wounds. A reminder that I am defenseless, helpless, to anything she deems to do to me.

The Harpyiai may have been my first threat, but she is only the harbinger of death. The Persei are to blame for all of this, along with anyone who has helped them.

The Harpyiai stabs another shot of Astrobleme into my flesh and digs her claws in deeper. I welcome the darkness as pain brings me under.

CHAPTER 35

The double doors creak open, causing me to flinch. I already know what is coming. I can't bear to watch another shot of blue liquid poison my blood. It's painful, but I also crave it. The few places where my skin has not yet crusted white pulse blue in conjunction with the Astrogen stone.

Every day that I grow weaker, its pull grows stronger. I take its source to recharge, so it steals my lifeforce in turn.

A warm, smooth hand gently squeezes my shoulder. The tenderness startles me. I swing my head towards the owner of the hand.

"Get away from me!" My voice screeches from my dry throat.

Izar holds a cup with clear liquid up to my mouth. "It's water, you need to drink, or you will die of dehydration."

"How do I know it's not poisoned?" I spit back.

Yet my body betrays me, begging for just a drop on my cracked lips.

"Stop being a brat and drink it. You are only punishing yourself."

A raspy snarl rips from my throat, but I lean my head forward. Izar tips the cup gently so the water slowly pours into my mouth. The precious moisture spills past my lips and across my sandpaper tongue. My body sings in sweet reprieve, desperate to live. If I had any liquid in my body to spare, I would cry in relief.

"I hope you don't expect me to thank you for basic decency even Humans can manage." I punctuate each syllable with as much venom as I can manage. With each word, I let my disgust for all aliens fly like poisoned thorns towards Izar.

"Please—" Izar steps in front of my face, pleading in earnest, "Roa, listen to me!"

"Why should I listen to you? Andrin might have been a naive fool, but you were my friend!"

Izar refuses to lower his gaze, his topaz eye blazing into mine. "I thought I had to. I didn't think I had a choice."

"How could you say that to me? You brought the guards to me, you let them bring me here! How long have you been lying to me?"

"I'm a servant to the Persei," he protests. "I have not lied to you. Through my blood, I can't disobey them. It was by the King's order."

My lips bleed as the cracked flesh parts, exposing my teeth. "You disgust me! I never would have let this happen to you!"

"My parents made a mistake swearing their loyalty to the Persei with a blood oath. That oath swore my obedience to them with my birth."

"That only makes your parents complicit. Complacency to monstrous actions makes you a monster."

He cringes. "I told you, we aren't monsters. Despite my parents' flaws, I love them. They have done what they thought was best for us, however misguided. Isn't that what parents do? Make the best choices for their children that they can with what they have? How can one see the evils of future choices while the present is shrouded in death?"

I refuse to budge. "We are not the products of our parents. We must choose to be better. To make the best choices with what we have. For the sake of the future."

"You're right." His face finally falls. "I've been taking the easy way out and calling myself virtuous simply because I questioned if it was the right path. I'm done following their footsteps. I will set things right."

"You have betrayed me beyond saving. They are killing me. They're going to take everything from me. You are as guilty as they are."

Izar takes a blade from his waist, causing me to flinch. My instincts to survive continue to fight despite my lost spirit. My body still fears death. It fears Izar using his blade against me in anger. A small voice in my head begs me to remember Izar wouldn't do that to me.

I force the thought from my brain. I thought he wouldn't do that to me. I never thought he could lead me into captivity. I have no reason to trust him at all now.

To my surprise, he doesn't use the blade against me. Instead, he makes a quick slash against the palm of his hand and holds it over the Astrogen crystal. He squeezes his fist until a stream of blue blood leaks across the gem, fizzing like water over hot stones.

"I will make it right. I swear to it, on my blood Roa. My parents may have made their blood oath to the Persei, but I make mine to you." His head flies up, topaz eyes flaring as bright as the Astrogen stone. "When the lights go out, remember, you are born of a Super Nova."

Izar storms out of the chamber, but I shout after him, "This doesn't change anything, Syntag Izar! I will never forgive you!"

Izar pauses just beyond the open door. "I don't need your forgiveness, Princess. Galaxia needs your safety." The doors slam shut.

CHAPTER 36

I'm halfway convinced I was imprisoned beneath the oculus in the ceiling as a form of mental torture. It allows me to see Mirfak rise and fall each day. I've counted at least six days. Yet I can't account for the time I've been unconscious. Perhaps it's been longer.

The Astrogen crystal beneath me shines every day at Apparent Noon. It's how I know it is time for another dose. The Harpyiai stabs my arm with a needle, and it throws me from my dissociative state. Her beaked face is always in a haughty sneer despite her burnt flesh. I want to break it right off her face. She will pay for this. They all will.

My time in captivity and poisoning via Astrobleme almost succeeded in breaking my spirit, until I remembered Aikido. Suspended above the Astrogen crystal, I forced myself to go within myself, to find my center. I needed to ground myself. To find the quiet amongst the chaos.

I have been desperately grasping for control. Yet now, I have none. Everything has been out of my control since I was first abducted. I've been trying to control where I'm going, desperate to get back to Earth. I've tried to control Andrin, manipulating him to take me back home. Foolishly, I tried to control my Aether. An energy source so powerful that it has created and destroyed galaxies.

I burned myself time and time again with Aether. Now, the Aether draws on my life source, taking as I take from the Astrobleme.

Aether manipulation isn't about control. Just like Aikido isn't really about control. It's about harmony. It's about balance.

I can't begin to pretend to understand how the balance works. Or how I will be able to find that harmony between myself and Aether. Although I do know that it won't be while I am imprisoned. It won't be while I am siphoned like a battery to be used against my will. I will get to decide my own fate in Galaxia. That will start with my escape.

I will get free of this Astrogen prison. I will make sure the Persei pay for what they have done, for what they have taken.

The King for his twisted scheme and stealing my Aether.

The Queen for being a complacent bystander.

The generations of Persei who have sacrificed innocents just for power.

Izar for his faux trust and allegiance.

Andrin for bringing me into all of this. For giving me Astrobleme in the first place. For stealing my Aether. For bringing me to Mycenae. For telling me he loved me when he is the reason I will probably never get the chance to make these aliens pay for what they have done.

No.

No, I will survive this.

Roa Mēdeia

I am Roa Mēdeia.

I am the heir of the Andromeda Galaxy.

I was born of a Super Nova.

They may take my Aether, but they cannot take my name from me.

They cannot take away who I am.

I will show them who I am. I will show them what I am capable of.

I will show them what happens when I dare to do the difficult. I will show them the stars.

R. A. SANDS

CHAPTER 37

I don't have the energy to tense when the door opens this time. Mirfak is high in the sky, about to crest over the oculus in the roof. I don't bother opening my eyes; I don't need to see the Harpyiai's beaked sneer. The footsteps are hurried, very unlike the clipped steps of the bird woman's clawed feet. Sluggishly, I peer my eyes open; instead of the Harpyiai, it's Andrin. A hiss escapes my lips. His frown deepens as he approaches. If I could move or use my Aether, I would fry his heart until his eyes bled.

"Roa—"

"What are you doing here?" My voice is scratchy from dehydration and disuse.

There is water in his pale green eyes. Pathetic.

"I am so sorry. I didn't know—"

"I don't want to hear any more of your lies. You lied right to my face when you told me you didn't bring me here to be slaughtered."

"I didn't know! I swear on my life, I didn't know. My father tricked me. After I left you, I went to get a spacecraft to get you out of here. I didn't know he sent Izar to do his dirty work."

He closes the space between us, stopping to kneel beside the crystal. I turn my head from him. The only rebellion the suspended energy field and my empty body will allow.

"So what? Have you come to gloat? Another generation of power secured?"

Andrin grips my fingers. Involuntarily, he pulls back slightly at the feel of my stone fingers. His Adam's apple bobs before he firms his grasp.

"No, Roa. We've come to save you."

I bristle in indignation, "We?"

Suddenly, the lights flicker. Then the beams of electricity suspending me by my vambraces, corset, and collar, spark. Darkness fills the room almost as heavy as the sudden silence. My body remains vertical for only a moment before I fall.

Andrin catches my limp body as I crumple to the ground like a rag doll. He sweeps me away from the crystal, so I don't hit it on the way down. My body won't move on its own, still weak from my Aether being stolen from me. I want to ask what is happening, but I can't. I open my mouth to speak when Izar bursts through the door.

"Are you ready yet?"

Andrin sighs. "No, I was – I was trying to explain."

I glare between Izar and Andrin. Both of their betrayals burn deeply inside of me.

Izar flashes me a mischievous smirk. "Did you hear we're going on another adventure, Princess?"

"Don't call me that. Especially after everything you two did."

Izar shoots me a look like he is scolding a child. "Andrin, we don't have time. I already cut the power."

I see the mental fight between the two of them. Izar grabs both of my vambraces, holding them together, and nods to

Andrin. I turn my head back to see the Andrin slide to the ground beside me again, a new vial of Astrobleme in hand. I whimper as he brings the syringe to my arm. I can't do it again. The fire that rips through my blood turns so cold as it seeps into the metal prison encasing me.

"No," I beg, "Please."

A tear slips down his gilded cheek.

"Just one last time, I promise," Andrin murmurs.

I can't fight back. My stony arms are stiff and immobile in Izar's hold.

"You need it. The Astrogen stole all your Aether. You need some back if you want to survive," Izar scolds.

I'm squealing, crying out.

Scared.

I'm so frightened that this will be the last shot it will take to turn me fully to stone. Andrin pushes the needle into my skin; he cringes as he has to force it through the thickened membrane.

Andrin's eyes meet mine. Pained.

His voice wobbles as he speaks, "I am so sorry, Roa. For everything."

He presses the plunger down, and I scream. Fire rips through my veins as I glow blue. Andrin holds the plungers down, forcing every drop of Astrobleme into my system.

Without the electricity field holding me in place, I'm unleashed.

A scream rips through my body, a pulse of Aether reverberating out, knocking Izar and Andrin both back and away from me. My metal encasements vibrate, shaking on my form as my lungs continue my world-shattering scream. The collar clatters off first, followed by the corset, and finally my vambraces.

Silence.

The Universe is silent.

Andrin returns to my side first, pulling the syringe from my arm. Izar helps me sit up next to the Astrogen crystal. I hiss at the touch. Most of my skin is hard and stiff, but beneath the metal, it's still alive. Alive as it had burned and healed over from the repetitive Astrobleme dosages.

A high-pitched scream, not of my own making, sounds from outside the room. A scream from a voice I recognize. It belongs to–

The double doors burst open.

The King storms in with a group of guards. I can't count them all. My eyes burn. My vision is clouded with white and blue speckles. Izar drops two shiny obsidian daggers onto my lap before jumping into action.

They fight spear to spear. Light flashes with every collision. Andrin joins the battle, stepping directly into his father's path. They both struggle, almost equal in power.

With the Astrobleme in my blood, I can feel the energy in the room. How it pulses and shifts—each transfer of raw energy into physical force, heat, and light. I am half Astrogen stone. I am Aether itself. The Astrobleme is incarnate in my system.

Yet my physical body still binds me. My limbs refuse to cooperate, struggling against the effects of Geaefication. My bones grate beneath my skin as I force my joints to move and demand my Aether fuel me—my head pounds. A splitting migraine threatens to unleash my stomach contents and pull me unconscious. The pulsing of life forces around me is overwhelming. Every move they make makes it harder for me to move my own.

A cold emptiness freezes my nervous system. Only the sound of rapid pumping of blood fills my ears.

Just beyond the door. I feel a void. A void of wispy Aether that should flow from a placid form on the ground, now lifeless. Her delicate form trampled, and foliage appendages broken. Flowers that were once pretty pink are wilted and brown.

Philomena.

That scream. It was her. She must have been guarding the door. The King—she had screamed right before he barged in.

He killed her.

A new rage surfaces inside of me. She was on my side from the first moment I met her. She gave me food, helped clothe me, revealed essential truths, held my secrets, and supported my discoveries. She had been assigned as my doera. As a slave. She was more than that; she was my friend, the only true friend I had here. She trusted me to create a better future. Until her very end, she was loyal to me.

She won't get to see a world where flora and fauna can coexist as she dreamed. She will never be united with Oki in inosculation at her final resting place, because she was loyal to me. I let her down. I wallowed in my prison, helpless, useless, a shell of what I once was.

My heart burns. Aether pulsing from the remains of my life force. Angry. Vengeful.

I watch as Izar fights two guards at a time. His feline grace is no match for the bulky brute force of the two Persei Guards. He is quickly losing his footing. Andrin doesn't appear to be faring well either. While he had taken extra doses of Astrobleme with me, which made him stronger, his father's years of consumption have left him superior in battle.

There are too many guards. They will win. They will trap me between the pillars again and use me as an eternal battery.

"Roa!" Izar calls as he pushes off guard in front of him. "The Astrogen crystal! It's been taking your Aether, take it back!"

I refuse to let them win.

I look to the jagged edges of the crystal beside me, large enough that it reaches my chest. Its original white crystals have a near-permanent blue glow since I was connected to it, charged with my Aether. Mine.

The crystal feels like a magnet, drawing Aether from me even as I seek the Aether it holds. My stiff white fingers desperately grasp the hilt of my dagger. My skin cracks like an aged stone. A stream of Aether pours from my chest to the bare obsidian metal, illuminating into a glorious rainbow sheen. I have no evidence that this will work, but my instincts make me move. I glance towards Andrin and the King, Izar, who grapples with two guards, then Philomena's lifeless form. The Harpyiai charges into the room, her singed feathers flare in an imperfect snowflake pattern as her wings spread. She doesn't even pause as she steps on Philomena in her stampede into the room, snapping Philomena's delicate foliage limbs further with a sickening crack.

I will make them all see stars.

I stab a dagger into the Astrogen crystal. Light, brighter than a thousand stars, erupts into the room.

Firey pain shoots from the crystal up my arm. I grit my teeth at the excruciating pain. My heart stops. Frozen. One beat. Two. Then I pull.

I pull the Aether, the Aether that the crystal took from me. I pull all the Aether that has ever been held in the crystal. The Aether from Ketos and every other sacrifice. I take it all, take Aether that has been stolen from so many to power the Persei and their corrupt power scheme of the Perseus Constellation.

The bright light dims, only enough to begin pulsing blue as my skin echoes its pattern. Starting at my hand, that shakily grips the dagger, the white of my skin comes back to life. I grip the hilt harder and reap the Aether from the crystal. My drained body pulses with life force. The crystal's Aether seeps into my body. I absorb it all.

I shine like a star, streaking through the night sky. My skin freckles with its own star map, a reflection of the galaxy beyond this cursed Constellation. The life I'm destined for.

I close my eyes for just a moment, letting the ethereal force encapsulate me. I accept its power within my body. I let the harmony of all the energy that has existed before me flow through my veins, and for once, stop fighting it for control.

The Harpyiai launches herself at my crouched form, but I grab my other dagger and stab between her ribs as she reaches for me. The line of Aether flows through my body, and she instantly seizes—another second and her form crisps to white dust before crumbling to the ground.

Every cell of my body is on fire, but I don't let go of either of my daggers. I don't let it slip from the crystal. I pull more and more. The guards stop trying to fight Izar and rush for me. Izar attacks them from behind, but they reach me anyway. With just a thought, Aether springs from my fingers, bolts of electricity surging for their chests. A single spasm from each guard and the first five drop. The second wave of guards hit the floor more easily.

Izar pants beyond the bodies that now lay on the floor, no more guards between him and I. His mouth is open in awe. I could end him. Kill him for his betrayal. My Aether halts, sensing my own hesitance. A clatter sounds to my right. Drawing my attention to Andrin and his father.

The King has proved more powerful—more years of Astrobleme. More stolen Aether reaped for his own taking. Andrin's on the floor, scrambling backwards as his father stalks towards him. Andrin's spear is broken, powerless, on the ground a few feet behind the King. He's going to kill him. His own son.

"You are weak. Unworthy to lead this kingdom," The King spits.

I should let Andrin die. This is his fault. He brought me here. My Aether surges inside of me. It knows my intentions better than I will admit. The spear in the King's hand is charged, aimed at his son's heart.

I let my Aether take over. A blast of light bursts forth from my hand. It spears the King through his center. Light, and fire, and the worst smell I've ever inhaled spread throughout the room. From the center of his chest outwards, my Aether burns him, ripping through his form. It is not a quick death like that of the Harpyiai or the guards. My Aether pulls his from the core of his being. I make it slow and painful. A flash of light fills the room.

Then there is nothing.

No sound. No smell. No indication that the King of the Perseus Constellation had ever existed.

We are all frozen. Izar moves first, his arm latches around mine.

"You need to go."

I can't move. Not from the Geaefication, or lack thereof, but from shock at what I'm now capable of. I stare at the absence in the room.

"Philomena got one last message back from the Commodore: his spacecraft is waiting above the airspace of the docking station." Izar kisses both of my cheeks. "By the stars, you will do great things."

Andrin turns, his distraught face stuck on mine. Profound betrayal slips down his face like the golden blood that drips down every slope of his body as he looks between Izar and me. I killed his father. I killed his King. I saved his life. Maybe I shouldn't have. I don't have time to dissect what thoughts may float through his pretty golden head.

I grab Izar's collar, and his eyes flare in surprise. "You're coming with me. You still owe me some answers."

The flash of light blinds me before I close my eyes.

R. A. SANDS

CHAPTER 38

I vomit on the ground where we land. Only bile rises; there is nothing else inside my stomach to heave. Izar does his best to hold my weak torso up with his arms looped under my armpits. I can't stand on my own. I'm too weak. It has been days since I ate. They pumped me full of Astrobleme as my only subsistence.

The scuff of boots on metal approaches. I lift my head, wiping my mouth with the back of my hand. A tall figure stops before us. Male, by the stature. Dressed in all black with a sleek helmet that covers his face. I can't see through the onyx visor to tell what kind of alien he might be. There is an energy field around him. It pulses through the air. I can still feel Aether around me.

"Commodore?" My voice was raspy from screaming and dehydration.

Izar straightens momentarily, salutes with his right hand, and supports my weight with his left arm. The figure in black only nods in response; no salute is returned. Fear sizzles through my body. I wonder if I delivered myself to another power-hungry alien.

While I've been assessing him, I've gotten the distinct feeling that he's been assessing me. Despite my shaking limbs,

I straighten. I stand on my own, as much as I can, but Izar still supports most of my weight. I keep my chin tilted up. Arrogant, or entitled, however it may be seen, I will not be seen as weak.

I have killed a Gigas. I have killed the King of an entire Constellation. I have absorbed the Aether of the stars themselves. I am the fusion of all those who have gone before me. I will cower before no one.

"I want you to take me home," I declare with as much force as I can muster.

The Commodore doesn't respond—a wave of unease floods over me. I must hold onto hope; I haven't made a mistake by coming here.

Finally, the Commodore speaks, "Welcome aboard the Void Runner. We have much to discuss." The mask makes his voice sound almost robotic.

The Commodore turns and walks away. Izar begins to move forward, but I dig my feet in. He stops and assesses me with concern. Blue and gold blood drips from his own face. Neither of us came out of that skirmish unharmed. At the airlock of the short hallway, the Commodore pauses. He turns and holds out his hand.

"Come on, Roa. Are you ready to save the rest of Galaxia?"

The rest of Galaxia?

He expects me to save it? Unlikely, but Andromeda is gone. I cannot let Galaxia fall; Earth is part of this galaxy. It is still my home. The Perseus King said power is shifting within Galaxia, and the Gigas are returning. Perhaps Earth will have to wait just a little longer for my return.

I am Roa Mēdeia.

I will dare to do the difficult. I will reach the stars.

ACKNOWLEDGMENTS

I cannot thank all my family and friends enough for their love and support on my journey as an independent author. A special thank you to Brian, your support and encouragement gave me the push I needed to start working on something that has been a dream of mine for decades.

My dear friends who served as Beta Readers: Katelyn, Kennedy, Brenna, Christina, Dom, and Michael, your criticism, encouragement, and support went a long way in developing my story into the finished product it is today. Katelyn, I honestly cannot thank you enough for the overtime you put in as a Beta Reader, unpaid editor, and personal cheerleader.

Cae Hawkmoor, hiring you as a developmental editor was the best decision I made in my writing process. You taught me so much about story structure and character development that I hope to continue refining them in future writing projects.

Thank you to all of my ARC readers who responded to my queries and took the time to read a debut independent author's work. While writing is a complex process and the literary industry is cutthroat, reader reviews and feedback are what make it worth it and fuel us to be better.

To you, my readers, thank you for taking a chance on an independent author. I'm excited to show you what else awaits beyond the stars in Galaxia.

Dare to do the Difficult.
Reach the Stars.

ABOUT THE AUTHOR

R. A. Sands is an indie author and active duty Surface Warfare Officer in the U.S. Navy with a background in technology, navigation, geographic politics, and global travel.

She is a Michigan native who earned a BS in Economics at the University of Wisconsin-Madison and now lives in sunny San Diego, CA. Outside of literature, she has a deep passion for travel, weightlifting, and baking. She'll never turn down a sweet treat and has an international collection of artistic fans that has grown out of control in recent years.

When she isn't navigating real-world oceans, she writes character-driven science fiction that blends epic adventure, mythic inspiration, and romance among the stars.

www.ingramcontent.com/pod-product-compliance
Lightning Source LLC
LaVergne TN
LVHW091708070526
838199LV00050B/2313